Ali and Nino

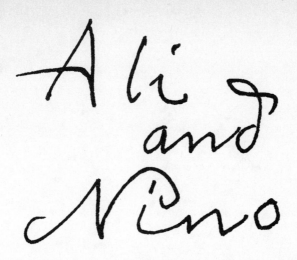

KURBAN SAID

Translated by Jenia Graman

Chatto & Windus
LONDON

Published by Chatto & Windus 2000

2 4 6 8 10 9 7 5 3 1

Copyright © Leela Ehrenfels
Translation copyright © Jenia Graman 1970

Originally published in 1937 in German by Tal Verlag, Vienna
First published in Great Britain in 1970 by Hutchinson

Published in this edition by arrangement with The Overlook Press, Peter Mayer
Publishers, Inc., 386 West Broadway, New York, NY 10012, USA

This edition published in Great Britain in 2000 by
Chatto & Windus
Random House, 20 Vauxhall Bridge Road, London SW1V 2SA

Random House Australia (Pty) Limited
20 Alfred Street, Milsons Point, Sydney,
New South Wales 2061, Australia

Random House New Zealand Limited
18 Poland Road, Glenfield,
Auckland 10, New Zealand

Random House (Pty) Limited
Endulini, 5A Jubilee Road, Parktown 2193, South Africa

The Random House Group Limited Reg. No. 954009
www.randomhouse.co.uk

A CIP catalogue record for this book is available from the British Library

ISBN 0 7011 6959 1

Papers used by Random House UK Limited are natural,
recyclable products made from wood grown in sustainable forests.
The manufacturing processes conform to the environmental
regulations of the country of origin

Printed and bound in Great Britain
by Creative Print and Design (Wales), Ebbw Vale

Ali and Nino

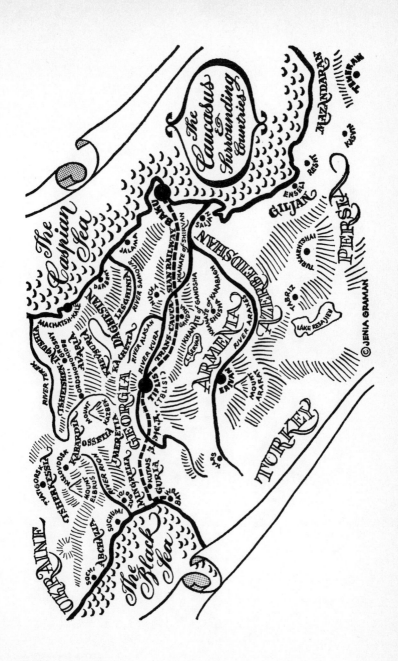

1

We were a very mixed lot, we forty schoolboys who were having a Geography lesson one hot afternoon in the Imperial Russian Humanistic High School of Baku, Transcaucasia: thirty Mohammedans, four Armenians, two Poles, three Sectarians, and one Russian.

So far we had not given much thought to the extraordinary geographical position of our town, but now Professor Sanin was telling us in his flat and uninspired way: 'The natural borders of Europe consist in the north of the North Polar Sea, in the west of the Atlantic Ocean, and in the south of the Mediterranean. The eastern border of Europe goes through the Russian Empire, along the Ural mountains, through the Caspian Sea, and through Transcaucasia. Some scholars look on the area south of the Caucasian mountains as belonging to Asia, while others, in view of Transcaucasia's cultural evolution, believe that this country should be considered part of Europe. It can therefore be said, my children, that it is partly your responsibility as to whether our town should belong to progressive Europe or to reactionary Asia.'

The professor had a self-satisfied smile on his lips.

We sat silent for a little while, overwhelmed by such mountains of wisdom, and the load of responsibility so suddenly laid upon our shoulders.

Then Mehmed Haidar, who sat on the back bench, raised his hand and said: 'Please, sir, we should rather stay in Asia.'

A burst of laughter. This was Mehmed Haidar's second year in the third form. And it looked as if he might stay there for another year, if Baku kept belonging to Asia. For a ministerial decree allows the natives of Asiatic Russia to stay in any form as long as they like.

Professor Sanin, who was wearing the gold-embroidered uniform of a Russian High School teacher, frowned: 'So, Mehmed Haidar, you want to remain an Asiatic? Can you give any reason for this decision?'

Mehmed Haidar stepped forward, blushed, but said nothing. His mouth was open, his brow furrowed, his eyes vacant. And while four Armenians, two Poles, three Sectarians and one Russian were highly delighted by his stupidity, I raised my hand and said: 'Sir, I too would rather stay in Asia.'

'Ali Khan Shirvanshir! You too! All right, step forward.'

Professor Sanin pushed his lower lip out and silently cursed the fate that had banished him to the shores of the Caspian Sea. Then he cleared his throat and said pompously: 'You at least can give us a reason?'

'Yes. I rather like Asia.'

'Oh you do, do you? Well, have you ever been in really backward countries, in Teheran, for instance?'

'Oh yes, last summer.'

'There you are. And have you found there any of the great aquisitions of European culture, for instance motor-cars?'

'Oh yes, very great ones indeed. Holding thirty and more people. They don't go through the town, only from one place in the country to the other.'

'These are called autobuses, and they are in use because there are no railways. This is reactionary. Sit down, Shirvanshir.'

I knew the thirty Asiatics were jubilant, they showed it by

the way they looked at me. Professor Sanin kept angrily silent. He was supposed to make his pupils into good Europeans. Suddenly he asked: 'Well—have any of you been to Berlin for instance?' It was not his day—the Sectarian Maikov raised his hand and said he had been to Berlin when he was a small boy. He remembered vividly a musty spooky Underground, a noisy railway and a ham sandwich his mother had prepared for him. We thirty Mohammedans were deeply indignant. Seyd Mustafa even asked to be allowed to leave the room, as the word 'ham' made him sick. And that was the end of our discussion about Baku and its geographical situation.

The bell rang. Relieved, Professor Sanin left the room. Forty pupils rushed out. It was the big break, and there were three things one could do: run into the courtyard and start a fight with the pupils of the adjoining school, because they wore gold cockades and buttons on their school uniforms, while we had to be content with silver ones, or talk amongst ourselves in a loud voice in Tartar, because the Russians could not understand it and it was therefore strictly forbidden—or cross the street quickly and slip into the Girls' Lyceum of the Holy Queen Tamar. This I decided to do. The girls strolled about in the garden, wearing chaste blue dress-uniforms and white aprons. My cousin Aishe waved to me. She was walking hand in hand with Nino Kipiani, and Nino Kipiani was the most beautiful girl in the world. When I told the girls of my geographical battle the most beautiful girl in the world looked down the most beautiful nose in the world and said: 'Ali Khan, you are stupid. Thank God we are in Europe. If we were in Asia they would have made me wear the veil ages ago, and you couldn't see me.' I gave in. Baku's undecided geographical situation allowed me to go on looking into the most beautiful eyes in the world. I left the girls and dejectedly played truant for the rest of the day. I looked at the camels, at the sea, thought of Europe and Asia, of Nino's lovely eyes and was sad. A beggar approached me, his face and hands rotten with disease. I gave him money, he made to kiss my hand, but I was frightened and snatched it away. Ten minutes later it occurred to me that this had been an insult, and for two hours I ran around looking for him, so I could put it right. But I could not find him, and went home with a bad conscience. All this had been five years ago.

During these years many things had happened. A new headmaster had arrived, who liked to grab our collars and shake us, because it was strictly forbidden to box the pupils' ears. Our religious instructor explained at great length how merciful Allah had been to let us be born into the Mohammedan faith. Two Armenians and one Russian joined, and two Mohammedans were not with us any more: one because he, in his sixteenth year, had married, the other because during the holidays he had been killed in a blood-feud. I, Ali Khan Shirvanshir, had been three times to Daghestan, twice to Tiflis, once in Kislovodsk, once in Persia to stay with my uncle, and I was nearly kept down for another year because I did not know the difference between the Gerundium and the Gerundivium. My father went for advice to the Mullah at the mosque, who declared that all this Latin was just vain delusion. So my father put on all his Turkish, Persian and Russian decorations, went to see the headmaster, donated some chemical equipment or other and I passed. A notice had been put up in the school stating that pupils were strictly forbidden to enter school premises with loaded revolvers, telephones were installed in town, and Nino Kipiani was still the most beautiful girl in the world.

Now all this was coming to an end, the final exam was only one week away, and I sat at home and pondered on the futility of Latin tuition on the coast of the Caspian Sea. I loved my room on the second floor of our house. Dark carpets from Buchara, Ispahan and Koshan covered the walls. The patterns represented gardens and lakes, woods and rivers, as the carpet weaver had seen them with his inner eye, unrecognisable to the layman, breathtakingly beautiful to the connoisseur. Nomad women in far away deserts collected the herbs for these colours from wild thorny bushes, Long slender fingers squeezed out the juice. The secret of blending these delicate colours is hundreds of years old. Often it takes more than a decade for the weaver to finish his work of art. Then it hangs on the wall, full of secret symbols, allusions, hunting scenes, knights fighting, with one of Firdausi's verses, or a quotation from the works of Sa'adi in ornamental script running at the sides. Because of these many rugs and carpets the room looks dark. There is a low divan, two small stools, inlaid with mother-of-pearl, many soft cushions, and among all this, very disturbing and very unnecessary, books of Western knowledge: chemistry, physics, trigonometry—foolish stuff, invented by barbarians, to create the impression that they are civilised. I closed the books and went up to the flat roof of the house. From there I could see my world, the massive wall of the town's fortress and the ruins of the palace, Arab inscriptions at the gate. Through the labyrinth of streets camels were walking, their ankles so delicate that I wanted to caress them. In front of me rose the squat Maiden's Tower, surrounded by legends and tourist guides. And behind the tower the sea began, utterly faceless, leaden, unfathomable Caspian Sea, and beyond, the desert— jagged rocks and scrub: still, mute, unconquerable, the most beautiful landscape in the world. I sat quietly on the roof. What was it to me that there were other towns, other roofs and other landscapes. I loved the flat sea, the flat desert and the old town between them. The noisy crowd who come looking for oil, find it, get rich and leave again are not the real people of Baku. They don't love the desert.

The servant brought tea. I drank it and thought of the exam. It did not worry me. Surely I would pass. But even if not, it would not really matter. The farmers of our estates would say that I could not tear myself away from the House of Wisdom. And indeed it would be a pity to leave school. The grey uniform with its silver buttons, epaulettes and cockade was very smart. I would feel degraded in civilian clothes. Not that I should wear them for long. Only for one summer and then—

then I would go to Moscow to the Lazarev Institute for Oriental Languages. I had decided this myself, for there I will be miles ahead of the Russians. It will be very difficult indeed for them to learn all the things that are second nature to me. And the uniform of the Lazarev Institute is the best of all: red coat, gold collar, a slender gilt sword, and kid gloves even on weekdays. A man has to wear uniform, or the Russians despise him. And if the Russians despise me Nino will not take me for her husband. But I must marry Nino, even though she is a Christian. Georgian women are the most beautiful in the world. And if she refuses? Well, then I'll get some gallant men, throw her across my saddle, and off we go over the Persian border to Teheran. There she will give in, what else can she do? Life was beautiful and simple, seen from the roof of our house in Baku.

Kerim, the servant, touched my shoulder. 'It is time,' he said. I rose. On the horizon, beyond the Island of Nargin, a steamboat appeared. If one could trust a printed slip of paper, delivered by the Christian telegraph messenger, then my uncle was on that boat with his three wives and two eunuchs. I was to meet him. I ran down the stairs to the waiting carriage. Quickly we drove to the noisy port.

My uncle was a person of distinction. Shah Nasr-ed-Din had graciously bestowed upon him the title Assad-ed-Dawleh— 'Lion of the Empire', and now no one was allowed to address him in any other form. He had three wives, many servants, a palace in Teheran and big estates in Mazendaran. He came to Baku because one of his wives, little Zeinab, was ill. She was only eighteen, and my uncle loved her more than his other wives. But she could not have any children, and just from her my uncle wanted an heir. Neither the amulets given to her by the dervishes of Kerbela, nor the magic words of the wise men of Meshed, nor the old women of Teheran, experienced as they might be in the arts of love had helped her. She had even made the journey to Hamadan. There stands, hewn from the red stone, the giant statue of a lion, staring forever across the vast desert with strange, mysterious eyes. It was erected by old, half-forgotten kings. For many centuries women have made the pilgrimage to this lion, kissed his mighty member and hoped for motherhood and the blessing of children. Poor Zeinab had not been helped by the lion.

Now she was coming to Baku, seeking the skill of Western doctors. Poor uncle! He had to take along the two other wives, old and unloved as they were. For thus custom decrees: 'You may have one, two, three or four wives, if you treat them equally.' Treating them equally means giving the same to all, for instance a journey to Baku.

But really all this had nothing to do with me. The women's place is in the anderun, in the inner part of the house. A well brought up man does not talk of them, nor does he enquire after them or ask to give them his regards. They are a man's shadow, even if the man only feels happy in the shadow. This is good and wise. We have a proverb in our country: 'A woman has no more sense than an egg has hairs'. Creatures without sense must be watched, lest they bring disaster on themselves and others. I think this is a wise rule.

The little steamboat came to the landing stage. Hairy-chested broadly-built sailors put up the accommodation ladder. Passengers hurried out: Russians, Armenians, Jews, quickly, hastily, as if it were important not to lose a single minute. My uncle did not show himself. 'Haste comes from the devil,' he would say. Only after all other travellers had left did the neat figure of the 'Lion of the Empire' appear on deck. He wore a coat with silk lapels, a small black fur cap, and slippers. His broad beard and his nails were tinted with henna, in memory of the Martyr Hussein's blood shed a thousand years ago for the true faith. His eyes were small and tired and his movements slow. Behind him, visibly agitated, walked three figures, sheathed in black veils: the wives. Then came the eunuchs: one with a face like a wise dried-up lizard, the other small, bloated and proud because he was the guardian of His Excellency's honour. Slowly my uncle descended. I embraced him, reverently kissing his left shoulder, though strictly speaking this was not necessary in a public place. I did not waste a glance on the wives. We stepped into the carriage. Wives and eunuchs followed in covered equipages. Our entourage was such an impressive sight, that I ordered the driver to make a detour along the Esplanade, so the town might admire my uncle's splendour.

Nino stood on the Esplanade and looked at me with laughing eyes. My uncle stroked his patrician beard and asked for news in town. 'There is nothing much,' I said, for I knew my duty was to start off with unimportant things, and only later to pass on to what really mattered. 'Dadash Beg has stabbed Achund Sadé to death last week, because Achund Sadé came back to town although he knew the danger, having kidnapped Dadash Beg's wife eight years ago. He was stabbed on the day he came. Now the police are looking for Dadash Beg. But they won't find him, although everybody knows that he is in the village of Mardakjany. Wise men say Dadash Beg has done well.' Uncle nodded, he agreed. Was there any other news? 'Yes. The Russians have found much new oil in Bibi-Eibat. The great firm of Nobel has brought a big German machine into the country, to fill up part of the sea, and drill for oil.' Uncle was very surprised. 'Allah, Allah', he said, and pursed his lips in a worried frown. '. . . at home everything is all right, and God willing I shall leave the House of Learning in a week's time.'

I went on talking, and the old man listened attentively. Only when the carriage drew near our house I looked to the side and said indifferently: 'A famous doctor from Russia has arrived in town. People say his knowledge is great, that he sees past and present in people's faces, and that from this he can predict the future.' Uncle's eyes were closed in noble boredom. Quite detachedly he asked for the wise man's name, and I saw that he was very satisfied with me. For all this was what we called Good Manners and Aristocratic Upbringing.

2

On the flat roof, soft, many-coloured, grotesquely barbarian patterned rugs were spread out, and we sat on them cross-legged, sheltered from the wind: my father, my uncle and I. Servants stood behind us, holding lanterns. Before us on the carpet a whole collection of oriental delicacies tempted us: honey cakes, candied fruit, shish kebab, and rice with chicken and currants. I admired my father's and my uncle's elegance, as I often had before. Without moving their left hands at all they tore off large pieces of black bread, formed them into cones and lifted them to the mouth. With exemplary grace my uncle put two fingers and the thumb of his right hand into the greasy steaming rice, took some of it, squeezed it into a ball and put this into his mouth without losing a single grain. Why are the Russians so conceited about their art of eating with knife and fork? Even the most stupid person can learn this within a month. I eat quite easily with knife and fork and know how to behave at a European table. But even though I am already eighteen, I cannot eat the many courses of oriental dishes with complete aristocratic grace, as my father and my uncle do, using only two fingers and the thumb of the right hand, and not drop a morsel, not even into the palms of their hands. Nino says our way of eating is barbaric. In the Kipiani's house they always eat at table, the European way. In my home we do this only when we have Russian guests, and Nino is horrified at the thought of my sitting on the floor, eating with my hand. She forgets that her own father was already twenty years old when he took his first fork into his hand.

The meal was finished. We washed our hands, and uncle said a short prayer. Then the food was taken away. Tiny cups of strong, dark tea were served, and my uncle started to talk as old people do after a good meal—circumloquacious and a little garrulous. My father did not say much, and I said nothing at all, because that is the custom. As always when he came to Baku, my uncle talked of the times the great Nasr-ed-Din Shah had reigned, when he himself had played a very important, if to me not quite clearly defined, role at the court. 'For thirty years,' my uncle said, 'I sat on the King of King's carpet of favour. Three times His Majesty took me with him on his travels abroad. During these travels I came to know the world of the unbelievers better than anyone else. We visited the palaces of Kings and Kaisers and met the most renowned Christians of that time. It is a strange world, and the strangest thing of all is the way they treat their women. Women, even the Kaisers' and Kings' women, walk about the palaces naked, and nobody is disgusted. Perhaps this is because Christians are not real men, perhaps for some other reason, God only knows. But in contradiction to this the unbelievers are disgusted by quite harmless things. One day His Majesty was invited to a banquet at the Czar's palace. The Czarina sat next to him. On His Majesty's plate was a very nice piece of chicken. To show his courtesy His Majesty took this nice fat piece very elegantly with two fingers and thumb and put it on the Czarina's plate. The Czarina went quite white, and began to cough, she was so frightened. Later we heard that many courtiers and princes at the Czar's palace were quite appalled by the Shah's amiability. So low is the European's estimate of their women!

They show their nakedness to the whole world, but do not bother to be courteous to them. After the meal the French

Ambassador was even allowed to embrace the Czar's wife and circle round the hall to the sounds of horrible music. The Czar himself and the officers of his guard looked on, but nobody defended the Czar's honour. In Berlin we saw something even more strange. We were taken to an opera, called 'L'Africaine'. On the stage stood a very fat woman and sang dreadfully. We disliked the woman's voice very much. Kaiser Wilhelm noticed this and punished the woman on the spot. In the last act many negroes came and erected a big pyre. The woman was bound hand and foot and slowly burnt to death. We were very pleased about that. Later somebody told us that the fire had been only symbolical. But we did not believe this, for the woman shrieked just as terribly as the heretic Hürriet ül Ain, whom the Shah had had burnt to death in Teheran just before we set out on our journey.'

For some time uncle sat, silently lost in his thoughts and memories. Then he sighed deeply and continued: 'There is one thing I cannot understand about the Christians. They have the best weapons, the best soldiers and the best factories, in which they produce everything they need to conquer their enemies. Every man who invents something to kill other people easily, quickly and in as great numbers as possible is highly praised, he makes much money and a decoration is bestowed on him. That is good and right. War must be. But on the other hand the Europeans build many hospitals, and a man who during a war cures and feeds enemy soldiers is also praised and decorated. The Shah, my illustrious master, was always puzzled to see that men who do the opposite of each other are equally highly rewarded. Once he had a talk about this with the Emperor in Vienna, but it was impossible to get an explanation for this absurd behaviour. And yet the Europeans despise us, because we are allowed to have four wives, even though they have often more than four themselves, and because we live and reign the way God ordered us to.'

Uncle fell silent. The night was dark. His shadow looked like an old thin bird. He straightened his back, coughed, as old men do, and said fervently: 'But even so, though we do everything our God commands us and the Europeans do nothing of what their God commands, their might and force grows continuously, whereas ours diminishes. Who can tell me why this should be so?' We could not tell him. He rose, a tired old man, and stumbled downstairs to his room. My father followed him. The servants took the teacups away. I was left on the roof, alone, but I did not feel like going to sleep.

Darkness enfolded our town, and it seemed to be an animal in ambush, ready to pounce or to play. There were really two towns, one inside the other, like a kernel in a nut. Outside the Old Wall was the Outer Town, with wide streets, high houses, its people noisy and greedy for money. This Outer Town was built because of the oil that comes from our desert and brings riches. There were theatres, schools, hospitals, libraries, policemen and beautiful women with naked shoulders. If there was shooting in the Outer Town, it was always about money. Europe's geographical border began in the Outer Town, and that is where Nino lived. Inside the Old Wall the houses were narrow and curved like oriental daggers. Minarets pierced the mild moon, so different from the oil derricks the House of Nobel had erected. The Maiden's Tower rose on the Eastern Wall of the Old Town. Mehmed Jussuf Khan, Ruler of Baku, had it built in honour of his daughter, whom he wanted to marry. This incestuous marriage was never consummated. The daughter threw herself from the tower while her love-crazed father was hurrying to her room. The stone on which the maiden fell to her death is called the Virgin's Stone. Sometimes this stone is covered with flowers, the offering of a bride on the day before her wedding.

Much blood has flowed through the centuries in the alleys of our town. And this blood makes us strong and brave. Zizianashvili's Gate rises up opposite our house, and here too noble human blood has been shed, becoming part of my family's history. That was many years ago, when our country Azerbeidshan still belonged to Persia, and Hassan Kuli Khan ruled over Baku, its capital. Prince Zizianashvili, a Georgian, and a General in the Czar's army, besieged our town. Hassan Kuli Khan declared he would surrender to the Great White Czar, opened the gate, and let Prince Zizianashvili enter. The Prince rode into the town, accompanied by only a few officers. A banquet was held on the square behind the gate. Pyres were burning, whole oxen roasted. Prince Zizianashvili had had too much to drink, he leaned his tired head on Hassan Kuli Khan's breast. Then my forefather, Ibrahim Khan Shirvanshir, drew a big crooked dagger and gave it to Lord Hassan Kuli Khan. Hassan Kuli Khan took the dagger and slowly cut Prince Zizianashvili's throat. Blood spurted on his robe, but he went on cutting, till the Prince's head was in his hand. The head was put into a sack full of salt, and my forefather took it to Teheran to the King of Kings. But the Czar decided to avenge the murder. He sent an army against Baku. Hassan Kuli Khan locked himself in the palace, prayed and thought of the coming day. When the Czar's soldiers climbed over the wall he fled through an underground passage to the sea, and from there to Persia. Before he entered the underground passage he wrote on the door a single, but very wise sentence: 'He who thinks of tomorrow can never be brave'.

On my way home from school I often strolled through the ruined palace. The Hall of Justice with its immense moorish colonnades is empty and desolate. Citizens seeking justice are supposed to go to the Russian judge outside the wall. But hardly anybody goes to the Russian judge, and if he does, wise men despise him, and the children on the street put their tongues out at him. Not because the Russian judges are bad or unjust. On the contrary, they are mild and just, but in a manner that our people dislike. A thief is put in jail. There he sits in his clean cell, is given tea, even with sugar in it. But nobody gets anything out of this, least of all the man he stole from. People shrug their shoulders and do justice in their own way. In the afternoon the plaintiffs come to the mosque where wise old men sit in a circle and pass sentence according to the laws of

Sharia, the law of Allah: 'An eye for an eye, a tooth for a tooth'. Sometimes at night shrouded figures slip through the alleys. A dagger strikes like lightning, a little cry, and justice is done. Blood-feuds are running from house to house. Sometimes a sack is carried through the alleys when the night is darkest. A muffled groaning, a soft splash in the sea, and the sack disappears. The next day a man sits on the floor of his room, his robe torn, his eyes full of tears. He has fulfilled the law of Allah: death to the adulteress. Our old town is full of secrets and mysteries, hidden nooks and little alleys. I love these soft night murmurs, the moon over the flat roofs, and the hot quiet afternoons in the mosque's courtyard with its atmosphere of silent meditation. God let me be born here, as a Muslim of the Shiite Faith, in the religion of Imam Dshafar. May he be merciful and let me die here, in the same street, in the same house where I was born. Me and Nino, a Christian, who eats with knife and fork, has laughing eyes and wears filmy silk stockings.

3

The school-leaver's gala uniform had a collar laced with silver. Silver belt buckles and silver buttons shone. The stiff grey material had been ironed and was still warm. Hatless and quiet we stood in the big school hall. The solemn part of the exam began, in which we all implored the God of the Orthodox Church to help us, the forty of us, of whom only two belonged to the State Church.

The Orthodox priest, clad in the heavy gold of the ceremonial vestments, his long hair scented, the big gold cross in his hand, began the prayer. The air was heavy with incense, the teachers and the two State Church followers knelt down. The priest's words, spoken in the sing-song modulation of the Orthodox Church, sounded hollow in our ears. How often had we heard this, unresponsive and bored, during these eight years: 'For the Most Devout, Most Mighty, Most Christian Ruler and Czar Nikolaus Alexandrovich God's Blessing . . . and for all Mariners and Travellers, for all Learners and Sufferers, and for all Fighters who have lost their lives on the field of Honour for the True Religion, for Czar and Homeland, and for all Orthodox Christians God's Blessing . . .' I stared at the wall, bored. There in a wide golden frame hung the picture of the Most Devout and Most Mighty Ruler and Czar, life-sized, looking like a Byzantine ikon under the big double eagle. The Czar's face was longish, his hair yellow, he looked straight ahead with light cool eyes. The number of medals on his chest was overwhelming. For eight years I had tried to count them, but always lost count in the wealth of decorations. In former times the Czarina's picture had hung next to the Czar's. But it had been removed. The Mohammedans of the country resented her low-cut dress, and had stopped sending their children to school.

While the priest was praying we began to feel solemn. It was after all, a most exciting day. I had started early in the morning to do my utmost to try and pass it in a way suitable to the grand occasion. First I resolved to be nice to everybody in the house. But most of them were still asleep. Then, on the way to school, I gave money to every single beggar I passed—just to be on the safe side. I was so excited I even gave a whole ruble to one of them, instead of five kopeks. When he thanked me profusely I said full of dignity: 'Do not thank me, but thank Allah, who used my hand to distribute charity.' Surely I could not fail after quoting such a pious saying.

The prayer came to an end. We formed a queue and proceded to the desk of the examiners. Sitting in a row behind the long desk they looked like a prehistoric monster, composed of black beards, sombre glances and golden gala uniforms. Everything was very solemn and frightening, even though the Russians hate to fail a Mohammedan. For we all have a lot of friends, and our friends are hefty lads who carry daggers and pistols. The teachers know this and are as afraid of the wild bandits who are their pupils as the pupils are afraid of the teachers. Most professors look on a posting to Baku as one of God's punishments. Instances of teachers' being assaulted and beaten up in dark alleys are not rare. The culprits are never found, and the teacher is posted to some other place. That is why they look the other way when the pupil Ali Khan Shirvanshir rather cheekily copies the maths solution from his neighbour Metalnikov. Only once while I was doing this the teacher came close to me and hissed desperately: 'Not so openly, Shirvanshir, we are not alone!'

So the written maths were all right. Happily we strolled along Nikolai Street, already feeling a breath of freedom. The next day's programme was written Russian. The themes came, as always, in a sealed packet from Tiflis. The headmaster broke the seal and read out solemnly: 'Turgeniev's Female Characters as the Embodiment of Russian Womanhood.' This was easy. As long as I praised Russian women the day was won. Written Physics was more difficult. But where knowledge forsook me the useful art of cribbing helped. So Physics were all right too, and the commission granted a day's rest to the delinquents. Then came the Oral. And there you were on your own. You had to give complicated answers to simple questions. The first was Religion. Our religious teacher, the Mullah, normally kept quietly in the background, but today he suddenly sat in front, in a long flowing robe, wearing the Prophet's descendant's green sash. His heart was mild towards his pupils. He asked me only for the Article of the Creed, and gave me full marks after I had repeated like a good boy the Shiitic Declaration of Faith: 'There is no God but Allah, Mohammed is his Prophet and Ali Allah's Vice-Regent.' This last bit was especially important, as it is the one thing that separates the pious Shiites from the lost brethren of the Sunnite Faith, but even from them Allah had not wholly withdrawn his mercy. Thus we were taught by the Mullah, for he was a man of liberal opinions.

To make up for that the History master was not liberal at all. I drew the paper with the theme, and it was not so good. It read: 'Madatov's Victory at Gandsha.' The teacher did not feel so comfortable either. In the battle of Gandsha the Russians treacherously killed the famous Ibrahim Khan Shirvanshir, my forefather, who had once helped Hassan Kuli Khan to cut off Prince Zizianashvili's head. 'Shirvanshir, you have the right to ask for another question.' The teacher's words were mild. I looked suspiciously at the glass bowl which contained sheets of paper with the questions written on them, for all the world like a lottery. Each pupil had the right to change his lot once. He only lost his chance of the highest mark. But I did not want to tempt providence. At least I knew all about my forefather's death. And there in the glass were absolutely mystifying questions about the Friedrich Wilhelms in Prussia, or about the causes of the American Civil War. Who could possibly know these things? I shook my head. Then I told, as well and as politely as I could, of the Prince Abbas Mirza of Persia, who set out from Tabriz with an army of forty thousand men to chase the Russians from Azerbeidshan. How the Czar's Armenian General Madatov met him with five thousand men at Gandsha, and fired guns at the Persians, who had never heard of guns before, how Prince Abbas Mirza fell off his horse and crawled into a ditch, the whole army ran, and Ibrahim Khan Shirvanshir was captured and shot when he tried to flee across the river, and a host of knights with him. 'The victory was due, not so much to the bravery of the Russian troops, as to the technical superiority of Madatov's guns. The outcome of the victory was the peace treaty of Turkmentshai, at which the Persians had to agree to pay a tribute, the exaction of which devastated five provinces.' With this I threw away my 'passed with honours'. I should have said: 'The victory was due to the Russian's great courage, with which they forced the enemy, though eight times their strength, to flee. The result of the victory was the peace treaty of Turkmentshai, on the strength of which it became possible for Persia to make contact with Western culture and the Western markets.' But I did not mind —my forefather's honour meant just as much to me as the difference between 'passed with honours' and 'passed'.

That was the end. The headmaster made another speech. Full of dignity and moral solemnity he declared us to have matriculated, and then we ran down the staircase like prisoners set free. The sun was dazzling. Fine yellow desert sand covered the streets. The policeman on the corner, who had watched over us for eight years, congratulated us, and we each gave him five kopeks. Then we exploded into town like a gang of bandits, shouting and screaming. I hastened home and was received like Alexander after his victory over the Persians. The servants looked at me with awe. My father covered me with kisses and gave me three wishes—anything I wanted. My uncle felt that such a wise man ought to be at Teheran, where he was bound to go far.

When the first excitement was over I sneaked to the telephone. I had not spoken to Nino for two weeks. A wise rule demands that a man should keep away from women when he stands at life's crossroads. Now I lifted the grip of the unwieldy apparatus, turned the bell and shouted into the mouthpiece: '3381!' Nino's voice replied: 'Passed, Ali?'

'Yes, Nino.'

'Congratulations, Ali!'

'When and where, Nino?'

'Five o'clock at the lake in the Governor's Garden, Ali.' I could not go on talking. Behind my back lurked the curious ears of my relations, servants and eunuchs. Behind Nino's— her aristocratic mother. Better to stop. Anyway, a bodiless voice is so strange that one cannot really enjoy it.

I went upstairs into my father's big room. He sat on the divan, my uncle beside him, they were drinking tea. Servants stood along the wall, staring at me. The exam was not finished yet, not by a long way. For now, when I was about to begin my adult life, father had to instruct son in the wisdom of life, formally and in public. It was touching and a bit old fashioned. 'My son, now that life begins for you I have to remind you once more of a Muslim's duties. We are living here in the country of the unbelievers. If we are not to perish we must keep the old customs, and our way of life. Pray often, my son, do not drink alcohol, do not kiss strange women, be good to the poor and the frail, and always be prepared to draw your sword for our faith. If you die on the battlefield, I, the old man, will mourn you, but if you live dishonourably, I, the old man, will be ashamed. Do not forgive your enemies, we are not Christians.

Do not think of tomorrow, for that would make you a coward. And never forget the Faith of Mohammed, in the Shiitic interpretation of Iman Dshafar.' My uncle and the servants seemed to be in a solemn trance. They listened to my father's words as if they were revelations. Then my father rose, took my hand and said, his voice suddenly forced and shaking: 'And one thing I beg of you—do not enter politics! Do anything you want, but not politics!' I could swear that with a very easy conscience. Politics were far from my way of thinking. Nino was no political problem. My father embraced me once more. Now I was really grown up.

At half past four I strolled along Fortress Alley towards the Esplanade, still resplendent in my gala uniform. Then I turned to the right, past the Governor's palace to the Garden which had been laid out with such tremendous efforts in the desert earth of Baku. It was a strange feeling. The Governor of the town passed me in his carriage, and I did not have to spring to attention with a military salute, as I had had to for the past eight years. I had taken off my cap the silver cockade of Baku High School. This proclaimed me to be one of the graduates. So now I promenaded as a private citizen, and for one wild moment I toyed with the idea of lighting a cigarette, for everybody to see. But my dislike of tobacco was stronger than the temptation of freedom. I gave up the idea of smoking and turned into the park.

It was a big dusty garden with spare sad-looking trees and asphalt paths. On the right was the old fortress wall. In the centre stood the white marble columns of the City Club. Between the trees were innumerable benches. Three flamingoes were standing amongst dusty palm trees, looking fixedly at the red ball of the setting sun. Near the Club was the lake, that is to say, an enormous round and deep reservoir, built of stone slabs. The Town Council's idea had been that it should be filled with water and have swans swimming about. But that was as far as it went. Water was expensive, and there was not a single swan in the country. The reservoir stared up at the sky eternally, like the empty eyesocket of a dead cyclop.

I sat down on a bench. The sun glared behind the tangled pell-mell of the square grey houses and their flat roofs. The shadows of the trees behind me lengthened. A woman passed by, wearing a blue striped veil and clip-clopping slippers. Over the veil a long curved nose protruded. The nose sniffed at me. I looked away. A strange lassitude began to creep over me. It was good that Nino did not wear the veil and did not have a long curved nose. No, I would not make Nino wear the veil. Or would I? I did not quite remember any more. I saw Nino's face in the glow of the setting sun. Nino Kipiani—a beautiful Georgian name, respectable parents with European tastes. What did it matter? Nino had a fair skin, big laughing dark Caucasian eyes under long delicate lashes. Only Georgian girls have such sweet and gay eyes. No other girls, European or Asiatic. Delicate half-moon eyebrows, and a Madonna's profile. I was sad. The comparison made me feel melancholy. There are so many comparisons for a man in the Orient. But these women can only be likened to the Christian Mirjam, symbol of a strange uncomprehensible world.

I looked down on the asphalt path of the Governor's Garden, covered with dazzling sand from the great deserts. I closed my eyes. Then I heard carefree laughter at my side: 'Holy St. George! Look at Romeo, falling asleep waiting for his Juliet!' I jumped up. Nino stood beside me, still wearing the chaste blue uniform of the Holy Tamar. She was very slim, far too slim for the taste of the Orient. But just this fault made me feel tenderly protective. She was seventeen years old, and I had known her since the day she went along Nikolai Street on her first day of school. Nino sat down. Her eyes shone. 'So you passed after all? I was a bit afraid for you.'

I put my arm around her shoulder.

'It was quite exciting. But you see, God helps the God-fearing.'

Nino smiled. 'In a year's time you'll have to play God for me. I can't do without you sitting under my bench at our exam and whispering the maths answers to me.'

That had been settled many years ago, ever since Nino, twelve years old and bathed in tears, had come running across the road during break and had dragged me into her classroom, where, throughout the whole lesson, I had to sit under her bench and whisper the solutions of the maths problems to her. Since that day I have been a hero in Nino's eyes.

'How is your uncle and his harem?' asked Nino. My face became stern. Strictly speaking the harem's affairs are kept secret. But before Nino's harmless curiosity all rules of Eastern decency melted away. My hand lost itself in her dark hair: 'My uncle's harem is about to return home. Surprisingly enough Western medicine seems to have helped, though it has not really been proved yet. So far it is my uncle who is expecting, and not aunt Zeinab.'

Nino's childish brow became furrowed. 'All that is not really nice. My father and mother are very much against it. The harem is a disgraceful thing.' She spoke like a schoolgirl reciting her lesson. My lips touched her ear: 'I will not have a harem, Nino, never.'

'But I suppose you will make your wife wear a veil!'

'Maybe, it depends. A veil is useful. It protects from the sun, dust and strangers' looks.'

Nino blushed. 'You will always be an Asiatic, Ali. What is wrong with strangers' looks? A woman wants to please.'

'Only to please her husband. An open face, a naked back, a bosom half uncovered, transparent stockings on slender legs— all these are promises which a woman must keep. A man who sees as much as that wants to see more. To save the man from such desires, that is why women wear the veil.'

Nino looked at me in astonishment. 'Do you think seventeen-year-old girls and nineteen-year-old boys talk about such things in Europe?'

'I shouldn't think so.'

'Then we won't talk about them either,' said Nino severely and pressed her lips together. My hand glided over her hair. She lifted her head. The last ray of the setting sun was in her eyes. I bent towards her . . . her lips opened tenderly and submissively. I kissed her for a very long time, and very improperly. She breathed heavily. Then she tore herself away. We were silent and stared into the twilight. After a while we got up, a little shamefacedly. Hand in hand we left the gardens. 'I really should wear a veil,' she said as we went out. 'Or fulfil your promise.' She smiled shyly. All was good and simple again. I saw her home.

'I'm coming to your ball, of course,' she said.

'What will you be doing in summer, Nino?'

'In summer? We are going to Shusha in Karabagh. But you needn't be conceited. That doesn't mean that you should come to Shusha too.'

'All right, I'll see you in Shusha in summer.'

'You're terrible. I don't know why I like you.' The door closed after her.

I went home. My uncle's eunuch, the one with the face of a wise dried-up lizard, grinned at me: 'Georgian women are beautiful, Khan. But they should not be kissed so openly, in the public gardens, where many people walk past.' I pinched his pale ear. A eunuch can be as cheeky as he likes. He is a neuter, neither man nor woman. I went to see my father. 'You gave me three wishes. I know the first one now: I want to spend this summer in Karabagh, alone.' My father gave me a long look, then he nodded, smiling.

4

Seinal Aga was a simple peasant from the village of Binijady near Baku. He owned a plot of dusty dry desert land, which he farmed until a little, everyday earthquake tore a cleft in his poor farm, and from this cleft rivers of oil gushed forth. From then on Seinal Aga had no need to be crafty or clever. He simply could not run away from his money. He spent it, generously and lavishly, but more and more money accumulated, and was a burden to him till it crushed him. He felt that sooner or later punishment was bound to follow all this good luck, and he lived his life waiting for this punishment like a convict waiting for his execution. He built mosques, hospitals, jails. He made a pilgrimage to Mecca, and founded children's asylums. But fate takes no bribes. His eighteen-year-old wife, whom he had married at the age of seventy, dishonoured him. He avenged his honour as he should, cruelly and severely, and became a tired man. His family fell apart, one son left him, another brought unspeakable dishonour on him by committing the sin of suicide. Now he lived in the forty rooms of his palace in Baku, grey, sad and stooped. Iljas Beg, the only son left to him, was one of our classmates, and so the ball was at Seinal Aga's house, in the big hall with the ceiling made of rock crystal.

At eight o'clock I came up the wide marble staircase. Iljas

Beg stood there, greeting the guests. He, like myself, was wearing the Tsherkess costume with an elegant slender dagger in his belt. From now on we, too, were entitled to this privilege. 'Seljam-Alejkum, Iljas Beg!' I cried, and touched my cap with my right hand. We shook hands the old native way: my right hand pressed his right, and his left my left. 'Tonight we'll close the Leprosarium,' Iljas Beg whispered to me. I nodded gaily.

The Leprosarium was the invention and the secret of our form. The Russian teachers had no idea of what was going on in our town and the surrounding countryside, even if they had been living and working here for years. To them we were just wild natives, who might do anything. So we had told them that there was a Leprosarium near Baku. If any of us wanted to play truant, the form's spokesman went to the form's teacher, and, teeth chattering, told him that some of the sick had broken out and were in our town. The police were looking for them. They were supposed to be hiding in the part of the town where the pupils lived, who wanted a bit of time off. The teacher blanched and gave his pupils permission to stay away till the sick were arrested. This might be a week, or even more, it depended. No teacher ever dreamt of enquiring at the Bureau of Sanitation whether there really was a Leprosarium near. But tonight the Leprosarium would be closed.

I went into the already crowded hall. In a corner sat, surrounded by his teachers, our headmaster, wearing a solemn and grandiose look for the occasion. I went to him and bowed respectfully. When it came to dealing with the headmaster I was the spokesman for the Mohammedan pupils, because I had a monkey's instinct for languages and dialects. While most of us betrayed their non-Russian descent in their first Russian sentence, I could even imitate the separate dialects. Our headmaster came from Petersburg, and therefore one had to speak 'Petersburgian' to him, i.e. lisp the consonants and swallow the vowels. This does not sound very beautiful, but very, very high class. The headmaster never dreamt I was pulling his leg, and was pleased about the progressive russification of this far borderland.

'Good evening, sir,' I said modestly.

'Good evening, Shirvanshir, have you recovered from your exam fright?'

'Oh yes, sir. But since then I have had an awful shock.'

'What was that?'

'Well, this thing about the Leprosarium. My cousin Suleiman was there. You know he is a Lieutenant in the Saljan Regiment. It made him quite sick, and I had to nurse him.'

'But what is the matter with the Leprosarium?'

'Oh? Sir, you don't know? Yesterday all the sick broke out, and marched towards the town. Two companies of the Saljan Regiment had to be turned out to deal with them. The sick had occupied two villages. The soldiers surrounded these villages and shot down everybody, sick or not sick. Just now all houses are being set on fire. Isn't it dreadful, sir, the Leprosarium has ceased to exist. The sick, rotting pieces of flesh falling off them, rattling in their throats, lie outside the town gates, they are being slowly drenched with oil and burnt to death.' Pearls of sweat appeared on the headmaster's forehead. He was probably thinking that really it was time to ask the Minister for a transfer to a more civilised place.

'Terrible country, terrible people,' he said huskily. 'But there you see, children, how important it is to have an efficient government and magistrates who can act quickly.' The form surrounded the headmaster and listened grinning to the lecture about the Blessings of Order. The Leprosarium was finished. Our successors would have to think up some new idea of their own.

'Does Sir know that Mehmed Haidar's son is already in his second year in our school?' I asked innocently.

'Whaaat?' Sir's eyes bulged. Mehmed Haidar was the school's bane. He was kept for at least three years in each form. At the age of sixteen he had married, but kept on going to school. His son was nine years old, and had entered the same institute. At first the happy father had tried to keep this a secret. But one day a small tubby child came up to him during the big break and said in the Tartar language, looking at him with big innocent eyes: 'Papa, if you don't give me five kopeks for chocolate I'll tell Mummy that you copied your maths homework from somebody else.' Mehmed Haidar was terribly ashamed, boxed the cheeky brat's ears, and asked us to tell the headmaster at a suitable moment of his parenthood.

'Do you mean, that the pupil of the sixth form, Mehmed Haidar, has a son who is already in the second form?' asked the headmaster.

'That is so. He asks your forgiveness. He wants his son to be a scholar like himself. It is really quite touching how the urge for Western knowledge is expanding.' The headmaster blushed. Silently he wondered whether father and son going to the same school was not against any of the school's rules and regulations. But he could come to no decision. And so daddy and son were allowed to lay siege to the fortress of western wisdom.

A small door opened. A ten-year-old boy pushed the heavy curtains aside, and led in four dark-skinned blind musicians from Persia. Holding hands they went to a corner of the hall and sat down on the carpet. Their strange instruments had been made in Persia centuries ago. A plaintive note sounded. One of the musicians put his hand to his ear—the classical pose of the oriental singer. The hall became quiet. Now another beat the tambourine, full of enthusiasm. The singer began in high falsetto:

'Like a Persian dagger is your form.
Your mouth like a glowing ruby.
If I were the Turkish Sultan I would take you for my
    wife,
I would string pearls into your plaits,
And kiss your heels.
I would bring you in a golden bowl
My own heart.'

The singer was silent. Then his neighbour's voice arose loud and brutal. Full of hate he cried:

'And each night
Like a rat you scuttle
Across the courtyard to the neighbour's house.'

The tambourine sounded wildly. The one-stringed violin
sobbed. The third singer cried passionately:

'He is a jackal, an unbeliever.
O woe, o misfortune, o dishonour!'

For a moment there was silence. Then after three or four short
bars of music the fourth singer started softly, romantically,
even tenderly:

'For three days I sharpened my dagger,
On the fourth I stab my enemy to death.
I cut him into small pieces.
I throw you, my beloved, over the saddle,
I cover my face with the cloth of war
And ride with you into the mountains.'

Next to me stood the headmaster and the Geography
teacher. 'What horrible music,' said the headmaster softly.
'Like a Caucasian donkey howling in the night. I wonder what
the words mean?'

'Nothing probably, just like the music.'

I was about to tiptoe away, when I noticed that the heavy
damask curtain behind me was moving. I looked round cautiously. An old man with snow-white hair and strange light
eyes was standing behind the curtain, listening to the music and
crying: His Excellency Seinal Aga, Iljas Beg's father. His soft
hands with the thick blue veins trembled. These hands could
hardly write their owner's name, but they ruled over seventy
million rubles. I looked away. He was a simple peasant, this
Seinal Aga, but he understood more of the singers' art than the
teachers who had declared us mature. The song was ended. The
musicians started a Caucasian dance. I walked about the hall.
The pupils stood together in groups. They were drinking wine,

even the Mohammedans. I did not drink. Girls, sisters and friends of our classmates, were chattering in the corners. There were many Russian girls, their plaits were yellow, their eyes grey or blue, and their hearts dusted with powder. They only talked to Russians, even to Armenians and Georgians. But if a Mohammedan approached them they were embarrassed, giggled, said a few words and turned away. Somebody opened the piano and began to play a waltz. The headmaster danced with the Governor's daughter.

At last! Her voice from the staircase. 'Good evening, Iljas Beg. I am a little late, but it is not my fault.' I dashed out. Nino was not wearing evening dress nor the uniform of the Lyceum of the Holy Tamar. From her shoulders hung a short velvet waistcoat with gold buttons. Her waist was firmly laced and so slim that I thought I could span it with one hand. A long black velvet skirt reached down to her feet, showing the gilt points of her kid slippers. Perched on her hair was a small round cap and from it two rows of heavy gold coins hung over her forehead. It was the ancient ceremonial robe of a Georgian princess, and hers was the face of a Byzantine Madonna. The Madonna laughed. 'No, Ali Khan, you must not be angry. It takes hours to lace this skirt. I have squeezed myself into it only in your honour.'

'The first dance with me!' cried Iljas Beg.

Nino looked at me, I nodded. I dance badly, and do not even like it. And I can trust Iljas Beg with Nino. He knows how to behave. 'Shamil's Prayer!' called Iljas Beg to the musicians. Immediately a wild melody arose. Iljas Beg jumped into the middle of the hall. He drew his dagger. His feet moved in the fiery rhythm of the Caucasian Mountain Dance. The blade glittered in his hand. Nino danced up to him. Her feet looked like small strange toys. Shamil's Mystery began. We clapped to the rhythm of the music. Nino was the bride to be abducted. . . . Iljas put the dagger between his teeth. Like a bird of prey his arms outstretched, he circled round the girl. Nino's feet flew whirling round the hall, her supple arms depicting all stages of fear, despair and submission. In her left hand she held a handkerchief. Her whole body trembled. Only the coins on her cap lay quietly on her forehead, and that was the correct way—this is the most difficult part of the dance. No one but a Georgian girl can do such fantastically quick turns and not let even one coin on her cap tinkle. Iljas raced after her. Without stopping he chased her round and round. The wide gestures of his arms became more and more dominating Nino's defensive movements more and more tender. At last she stopped, like a deer overtaken by the hunter. Closer and closer Iljas Beg circled. Nino's eyes were soft and humble. Her hands trembled. A wild short howl from the music, and she opened her left hand. The handkerchief fluttered to the floor. And suddenly Iljas Beg's dagger flew on to the little piece of silk and nailed it to the floor. The symbolic dance was finished.

By the way, did I mention that before the dance I gave Iljas Beg my dagger and took his? It was my blade that pierced Nino's handkerchief. It is best to be on the safe side, for a wise rule teaches: 'Before you trust your camel to Allah's protection, tie it fast on to your fence.'

5

'When our illustrious forefathers, O Khan, first set foot into this country, where they were to make a great and much feared name for themselves, they cried: "Kara Back!"—"Behold—there lies snow!" But when they came to the mountains and saw the jungle they cried: "Karabagh!"—"Black Garden!" Since then this country has been called Karabagh. Before that it was called Sünik, and before that Agwar. For you must know, Khan, we are a very old and famous country.' My host, old Mustafa, with whom I had taken rooms in Shusha, fell into a dignified silence. Then he drank a small glass of Karabagh fruit liquor and cut a piece of the strange cheese that is fashioned from innumerable strands and looks like a girl's plait, then he carried on: 'The Karaulik, the dark ghosts, live in our mountains and guard enormous treasures, as everybody knows. There are sacred stones in the woods, and holy wells flow there. We have everything. Walk through the town and look around—does anybody work? Hardly anybody! Is anybody sad? Nobody! Is anybody sober? Nobody! You'll be amazed, sir!'

It really was amazing, what wonderful liars these people were. There is no story they would not invent to glorify their country. Only yesterday a fat Armenian tried to tell me that the Christian Maras Church in Shusha was five thousand years old. 'Don't tell such tall stories,' I told him. 'The Christian Faith is not yet two thousand years old. They can't have built a Christian church before Christianity was even thought of.' The fat man was very hurt and said reproachfully: 'You are, of course, an educated man. But let an old man tell you: The Christian Faith may be only two thousand years old in other countries. But to us, the people of Karabagh, the Saviour showed the light three thousand years before the others. That's how it is.' Five minutes later the same man went on to tell me without batting an eyelid that the French General Murat had been an Armenian from Shusha. He had gone to France as a child to make Karabagh's name famous there as well. Even when I was just on the way to Shusha the driver of my coach pointed at the little stone bridge we were about to cross and said proudly: 'This bridge was built by Alexander the Great when he went forth to immortal victories in Persia!' '1897' was chiselled in big figures on the parapet. I pointed this out to the coachman, but he only waved his hand: 'Och, sir, the Russians put that in later, because they were jealous of our glory!'

Shusha is a strange town. It stands five thousand metres high up in the mountains, surrounded by woods and rivers. Armenians and Mohammedans live there together in peace. For centuries this had been the bridge between the Caucasian countries, Persia and Turkey. The native nobles—the Armenian Nacharars and Meliks, and the Mohammedan Begs and Agalars—had their houses in the hills and valleys around the town. Often, in rather endearing childlike presumption, their little mud huts were called palaces. These people never tired of sitting on the steps that led up to their doors, smoking their pipes and telling each other how many times the Russian Empire and the Czar himself had been saved by Karabagh generals, and what horrible fate would have overtaken them if their defence had been left to anyone else. It had taken my Kotshi and myself seven hours on the shaking path to drive up to Shusha. Kotshis are armed servants by profession, and brigands by inclination. They have the faces of warriors, are festooned with daggers, swords, pistols and ammunition, and generally immersed in dark brooding silence. Maybe they are meditating on some past heroic banditry and plunder, maybe it is just their way and does not mean a thing. My father had insisted on the Kotshi, either to safeguard me from strangers or strangers from me. But it was all right with me, he was a good man, in some way or other related to the House of Shirvanshir, and dependable as only such oriental servants can be.

It was now five days since I had arrived in Shusha, waiting for Nino and listening to everyone I met telling me all day long that all rich, brave, or in any way outstanding people in the world came from Shusha. I had looked at the civic gardens and counted church steeples and minarets. Obviously Shusha was a very religious town: seventeen churches and ten mosques were more than enough for sixty thousand inhabitants. Then there were innumerable holy places near the town, but the most important ones were of course the famous grave, the chapel and the two trees of St. Sary Beg. I was dragged there by my bragging new friends on my first day. The saint's grave is an hour's journey from Shusha. Every year the whole town makes a pilgrimage there, and banquets are held in the Holy Grove. The outstandingly devout make the whole journey on their knees. This is rather uncomfortable, but it heightens considerably the esteem in which the pious pilgrims are held. Two sacred trees grow near the saint's grave. To touch them is sacrilege. Touch as much as a leaf and you will be paralysed immediately, so immense is the saint's power—though whether this had ever actually happened, or what other miracles the saint had worked nobody could tell me. But to make up for that I was told in great detail how once, when chased by enemies, he rode up the mountains, to the summit, to where even today Shusha stands. His enemies were quite near. Then his horse took a terrific leap, over the mountains, over the rocks, over the whole town of Shusha. On the spot where the horse landed, the devout can see even today, impressed deep into the stone, the trace of the noble animal's hooves. So they told me. When I dared to utter a few doubts about the possibility of such a leap they said indignantly: 'But sir, it was a horse from Karabagh.'

Then they told me the story of the Horse of Karabagh: 'Everything in the country was beautiful,' they said. 'But the most beautiful thing in it was the Horse of Karabagh, this famous Horse, for which Aga Mohammed, Shah of Persia, offered to give his entire harem'—(did my friends know that Aga Mohammed was a eunuch?)—'This Horse,' they said, 'was almost holy. For centuries wise men had pondered and matched, until this miracle of breeding was born: the best horse in the world, the famous red-gold Noble Animal of Karabagh.' Having listened to so much praise I became curious, and asked them to show me one of these wonderful horses. My companions looked at me pityingly. 'It is easier to force one's way into the Sultan's harem, than to get into the stable of the Karabagh horses. There are only twelve genuine red-gold animals in the whole town. To see them is to become a horse-thief. Only when war breaks out the owner mounts his red-gold miracle.' So I had to be content with the tales they told me of the legendary horse.

Now I sat on the verandah in Shusha, listened to old Mustafa's chatter, waited for Nino, and liked this fairytale country. 'Oh Khan,' said Mustafa, 'your forefathers have waged war, but you have sat in the House of Wisdom and are a learned man. So you have heard of the fine arts. The Persians are proud of Sa'adi, Hafis and Firdausi, the Russians of Pushkin, and far away in the West there was a poet called Goethe, who wrote a poem about the devil.'

'Were all these poets from Karabagh too?' I interrupted.

'No, noble sir, but our poets are better, even if they refuse to imprison their words in dead letters. They are too proud to write down their poems—they just recite them.'

'Who are these poets? The Ashouks?'

'Yes, the Ashouks,' said the old man weightily. 'They live in the villages around Shusha, and tomorrow they hold a competition. Will you go and marvel at them?' Native poets live in almost every village of Karabagh. They compose poems throughout the winter, and in spring they come out into the world to recite their songs in huts and palaces. But there are three villages which are populated by poets only, and to show the high esteem in which the Orient holds poetry, these villages are freed from all taxes and tributes. One of these villages is Tash-Kenda.

It needed but one glance to show that the men of this village were no ordinary farmers. The men wore their hair long, their robes were of silk, and they looked at each other suspiciously. Their women walked behind them, looking depressed, carrying their musical instruments. The village was full of rich Armenians and Mohammedans, who had come from all over the country to admire the Ashouks. An eager crowd had gathered in the little main square. In the centre stood two valiant lords of song, who were here to fight a hard duel. They looked at each other with scorn. Their long hair fluttered in the breeze. One of them cried: 'Your clothes stink of dung, your face is that of a pig, your talent is as thin as the hair on a virgin's stomach, and for a little money you would compose a poem on your own shame.'

The other answered, barking grimly: 'You wear the robe of a pimp, you have the voice of a eunuch. You cannot sell your talent, because you never had any. You live off the crumbs that fall from the festive table of my genius.'

So they went on slanging each other fervently and not a little monotonously. The public clapped. Then an old grey-haired man with the face of an apostle arrived and announced the two themes for the competition: 'The moon over the river Araxes' and 'The death of Aga Mohammed Shah!' The poets looked up to the sky. Then they sang. They sang of the grim eunuch Aga Mohammed Shah, who travelled to Tiflis, there to regain his lost virility at the sulphur springs. When the springs failed to help him, the eunuch destroyed the town and had all men and women in it cruelly executed. But fate overtook him on his way back in Karabagh. During the night, when he was asleep in his tent, he was stabbed to death. The great Shah had not enjoyed life. On his campaigns he had suffered hunger, had eaten black bread and drunk sour milk. He conquered innumerable countries and was poorer than a beggar in the desert. The eunuch Aga Mohammed Shah. All this they recited in classic verses. One of them described at great length the sufferings of the eunuch in the land of the most beautiful women in the world, while the other described at equally great length the execution of these women. The public was satisfied. Sweat fell in heavy drops from the poets' foreheads. Then the more soft-spoken one cried out: 'What is like the moon over the Araxes?'

'The face of thy beloved', interrupted the grim one.

'Mild is the moon's gold!' cried the soft-spoken one.

'No, it is like a fallen warrior's shield,' replied the grim one. In time they exhausted their similes. Then each of them sang a song about the beauty of the moon, of the river Araxes, that winds like a maiden's plait through the plain, and of lovers who come to the banks at night to look at the moon reflected in the waters of the Araxes. . . . The grim one was declared to be the winner, and with an evil smile he took his opponent's lute. I went to him. He looked glum, while his bowl was being filled with coins. 'Are you happy to have won?' I asked him.

He spat disgustedly. 'This is no victory, sir. In former times there were victories. A hundred years ago the victor was allowed to cut the vanquished one's head off. In those days art was held in high esteem. Now we have become soft. No one gives his blood for a poem any more.'

'You are now the best poet in the country.'

'No,' he repeated. 'I am just a craftsman. I am no real Ashouk.'

'What is a real Ashouk?'

'In the month of Ramadan,' said the grim one, 'there is a mysterious night, the night called Kadir. During this night all

48

nature sleeps for an hour. Rivers cease to flow, the evil spirits do not guard their treasures. Grass can be heard growing and trees talking. Nymphs arise from the rivers, and those men who are fathered during this night become wise men and poets. On this night the poet must call the Prophet Elias, the patron saint of all poets. At the right hour the Prophet appears, lets the poet drink from his bowl and says to him: 'From now on you are a real Ashouk, and you will see everything in the world with my eyes.' He who is thus blessed, rules over the elements: animals and men, winds and seas obey his voice, for in his word is the Power of the Prophet.' The grim one sat down on the ground and rested his face in his hands. Then he wept, quickly and bitterly. He said, 'But nobody knows which night is the Night Kadir, nor which hour of the Night is the Hour of Sleep. And there are no real Ashouks any more.' He got up and went away. Lonely, dark and sullen, a wolf of the Steppes in the green paradise of Karabagh.

6

The well of Pechapür murmured in its stony, narrow bed. Around it the trees looked up to heaven like tired saints. The view was glorious: in the south, Armenia's meadows spread out like biblical pastures, sweet and full of promises for a full harvest. Shusha was hidden behind the hills. In the east, the fields of Karabagh disappeared into the dusty deserts of Azerbeidshan. The glowing breath of Zarathustra's fire swept across the plain on the wings of the desert wind. But no leaf in the grove around us stirred, it was as if the gods of the classical ages had departed just a moment ago and the enchantment still lingered on. Our smoking fire might have been the descendant of the many fires consecrated to this holy place. Sitting and lying around the flames on many-coloured rugs was a party of Georgians, and I was with them. Cups of wine, heaped platters of fruit, vegetables and cheese were arranged around the fire, where meat was rotating on the spit. Near the well sat the Sasandari, the wandering minstrels. Even the names of the instruments in their hands sounded like music: dairah, tshianouri, thara, diplipito. They began to sing one of the Bayats, a love song in Persian rhythm. The urban Georgians had asked for this to enhance the exotic charm of the scene. 'Dionysic mood', that is what our Latin teachers would have called this wanton way of becoming part of the country's customs. It was the Kipiani family, who had finally arrived, and had invited all the gay holiday-makers to this nocturnal feast in the grove of Shusha.

In front of me sat Nino's father, tonight 'the Tamada', who, according to the strict rules, directed the feast. His eyes were gleaming, he had a bushy black moustache on his reddish face. He held a cup in his hand and drank to me. I sipped at my glass, even though normally I do not drink. But the Tamada was Nino's father, and it would have been impolite not to drink when invited by him. Servants brought water from the well. This is one of the innumerable marvels of Karabagh: drink of it, and you can eat as much as you like, without feeling any of the unpleasant effects of overeating. As we drank of the waters the mountains of food became smaller. Nino's mother was sitting next to her husband at the flickering fire. Her profile was severe, but her eyes were laughing. Those eyes came from Mingrelia, from the plain of Rion, where once Medea the Sorceress had met the Argonaut Jason. The Tamada raised his glass: 'A cup in honour of His Highness Dadiani'. An old man with the eyes of a child thanked him, and the third round began. All emptied their glasses. No one was drunk, for at a banquet the Georgians feel the uplifting happiness in their hearts, and their heads stay clear like the Pechapür waters, which, amongst their other fabulous qualities, have the power to keep one sober.

Ours was not the only party. The grove was bright with the light of many fires. Every week the whole of Shusha makes the pilgrimage to the wells. The feasts go on until dawn. Christians and Mohammedans together celebrate in the heathen shades of the holy grove.

I looked at Nino sitting beside me, and she returned my look. She was talking to the grey-haired Dadiani. That was good and proper. Reverence for the old, love for the young. 'You must come and stay with me sometime at my castle Zugdidi,' said the old man, 'on the river Rion, where long ago Medea's slaves used to catch the gold in fleeces. And you too, Ali Khan. You will see the ancient trees in the tropical jungle of Mingrelia.'

'With pleasure, your Highness, but for your sake only, not for the trees.'

'What have you against trees? To me they are the embodiment of life fulfilled.'

'Ali Khan is afraid of trees the way a child is afraid of ghosts,' said Nino.

'It's not as bad as that. But what you feel for the trees I feel for the desert,' I replied.

Dadiani's childish eyes blinked. 'The desert,' he said, 'fallow bushes and hot sand.'

'The world of the trees perplexes me, your Highness. It is full of fright and mystery, of ghosts and demons. You cannot look ahead. You are surrounded. It is dark. The sun's rays are lost in the twilight of the trees. In this twilight everything is unreal. No, I do not love the trees. The shadows of the woods oppress me, and it makes me sad to hear the rustling of the branches. I love simple things: wind, sand and stones. The desert is simple like the thrust of a sword. The wood is complicated like the Gordian knot. I lose my way in the woods, your Highness.'

Dadiani looked at me thoughtfully: 'You have the soul of a desert man,' he said. 'Maybe that is the one real division between men: wood men and desert men. The Orient's dry intoxication comes from the desert, where hot wind and hot sand make men drunk, where the world is simple and without problems. The woods are full of questions. Only the desert does not ask, does not give, and does not promise anything. But the fire of the soul comes from the wood. The desert man —I can see him—has but one face, and knows but one truth, and that truth fulfills him. The woodman has many faces. The fanatic comes from the desert, the creator from the woods. Maybe that is the main difference between East and West.'

'That is why we Armenians and Georgians love the wood,'

Melik Nachararyan interrupted, a fat man from one of the noblest Armenian families. He had protruding eyes, bushy eyebrows, and was inclined to philosophy and drinking. We got on well together. He drank to me and cried: 'Ali Khan! Eagles come from the mountains, tigers from the jungle. What comes from the desert?'

'Lions and warriors,' I answered, and Nino clapped her hands happily.

Roast mutton was handed round on spits. Again and again the cups were filled. Georgian happiness filled the wood. Dadiani was deep in a discussion with Nachararyan, and Nino looked at me with a sly question in her eyes. I nodded. Darkness had fallen. By the light of the fires people looked like ghosts or like bandits. No one paid any attention to us. I got up and walked slowly to the well. I bent over the water and drank from my hand. That was good. For a long time I stared at the reflection of the stars in the water. Then I heard steps behind me. A dry branch cracked under a small foot . . . I stretched out my hand and Nino took it. We went into the wood. It was not quite right that we had left the fire, that Nino sat down on the edge of a little meadow and drew me down to her. The customs are strict in happy Karabagh. Old Mustafa had told me, full of horror, that eighteen years ago there had been a case of adultery in the country. Since then the fruit harvest had never been the same. We looked at each other, and Nino's face was pale and mysterious in the moonlight. 'Princess,' I said, and Nino looked at me sideways. She was a Princess of twenty-four hours standing, and it had taken her father twenty-four years to get his claim for the title agreed to in Petersburg. This morning he had received a telegram stating his request had been granted. This had made the old man feel as happy as a child who has found his lost mother, and tonight we celebrated. 'Princess,' I repeated, and took her face into my hands. She did not resist. Perhaps she had drunk too much of the Kachetian wine. Perhaps the wood and the moon had intoxicated her. I kissed her. The palms of her hands were soft and warm, her body yielding. Dry branches crackled. We were lying on the soft moss, Nino looking into my face. I touched the small roundness of her firm breasts. A new strange feeling reached out from Nino to me, and overwhelmed both of us. She had become one with the mysterious urges of the earth, living only in her senses. Her face became small and very serious. I opened her dress. Her skin shone like an opal in the moonlight. Her heart was beating and she spoke broken words of tenderness and longing. I buried my face between her small breasts, her skin was fragrant and had a faint salty taste. Her knees trembled. Tears were running down her face, I kissed them away and dried her wet cheeks. She got up and was now silent, unsure in her own mysteries and feelings. She was only seventeen years old, my Nino, and went to the Lyceum of the Holy Queen Tamar. She said:

'I think I really love you, Ali Khan, even though I am now a Princess.'

'Maybe you won't be one for very long,' I said, and Nino looked at me, puzzled.

'What do you mean? Will the Czar take the title away again?'

'You will lose it when you marry. But never mind, Khan is a very nice title too.'

Nino crossed her hands behind her neck, threw her head back and laughed: 'Khan maybe, but Khaness? There is no such thing. And anyway, you have a funny way of proposing— that is, if this is meant to be a proposal?'

'Yes, it is meant to be one.'

Nino's fingers stroked my face and came to rest in my hair. 'And if I say yes, will you always be grateful to the wood of Shusha and make your peace with the trees?'

'I think I will.'

'But for our honeymoon you will go to your uncle in Teheran, and I may, for a special treat, visit the Imperial Harem, drink tea and make conversation with the fat women in it.'

54

'Well?'

'And then I will be allowed to look at the desert, because there isn't anybody around who could look at me.'

'No, Nino, you needn't look at the desert. You wouldn't like it.'

Nino put her arms round my neck and pressed her nose against my forehead. 'Maybe I will marry you, Ali Khan. But have you ever thought of all the things we will have to overcome, quite apart from woods and deserts?'

'What things?'

'First of all my father and mother will die of sorrow because I marry a Mohammedan. Then your father will put a curse on you and demand that I become a Mohammedan. And if I do that, little father Czar will send me to Siberia because I have betrayed the Christian Faith. And you too, because you made me do it.'

'And then we sit in the middle of the Arctic sea on an iceberg and the big white bears eat us,' I laughed. 'No, Nino, it won't be as bad as all that. You needn't become a Mohammedan, your parents will not die of sorrow, and for our honeymoon we will go to Paris and Berlin, and you can look at the trees in the Bois de Boulogne and the Tiergarten. What do you say to that?'

'You are good to me,' she said, astonished, 'and I don't say No, but there is still lots of time to say Yes. I won't run away, don't worry. Let's talk to our parents when I have finished school. But don't kidnap me. Whatever you do, don't do that. I know your ways: across the saddle, into the mountains, and from then on a long drawn out blood-feud with the house of Kipiani.' Suddenly she was full of irrepressible gaiety. All of her seemed to laugh: her face, her hands, her feet, her skin. She was leaning against a tree, her head bent, and she looked up at me as I stood in front of her. In the shade of the tree she looked like an exotic animal, hiding in the woods, afraid of the hunter. 'Let's go,' said Nino, and we walked through the wood to the big fire. On the way she suddenly had a thought. She stopped and looked up to the moon. 'But our children, what religion will they have?' she asked anxiously.

'Oh, a very nice and agreeable one, I'm sure,' I said evasively. She looked at me suspiciously and for a while she was silent, thinking. Then she said sadly: 'And anyway, am I not too old for you? I'll soon be seventeen, and your future wife should be now about twelve.' I put her mind at rest. No, she was certainly not too old. Too clever, perhaps, for is it really a good thing to be too clever? Sometimes it seems to me that all we Orientals become mature, old and clever far too soon. And yet, sometimes it seems to me that we are all just stupid and simple. I did not really know what to think: I was bewildered by the trees, by Nino, by the far-away glow of the fires, and most of all by myself, for maybe I, too, had sipped too much of the Kachetian wine, and roved like a desert bandit in the quiet garden of love. Not that Nino seemed to feel like a desert bandit's victim. She looked calm and serene. All traces of tears, laughter and enchanted longing had disappeared. It took me much longer to appear normal again.

We came back to the well of Pechapür, but no one seemed to have noticed our absence. I filled my glass with water and drank greedily—my lips were burning. When I put the glass down I met Melik Nachararyan's eye, who stared at me understandingly: friendly and a little patronising.

7

I was lying on the divan on the terrace, dreaming of love. My love was so very different from that of my father, my uncles and my grandfathers, so different from the way it should have been. Instead of meeting Nino at the well, when she was filling her pitcher, I met her on Nicolai Street, on her way to school. It is at the well the Oriental's love begins, at the small murmuring village well or at the big singing fountains in the towns rich with water. Every evening the girls go to the well, carrying big clay pitchers on their shoulders. Near the well the young men sit in a circle, chattering of war and robberies, not taking any notice of the girls. Slowly the girls fill the pitchers, slowly they walk back. The pitchers are heavy, filled to the brim. The girls might stumble, so they push back their veils and look down chastely. Every evening the girls go to the well, every evening the young men sit at one end of the square, and that is how love begins in the Orient. Quite, quite by chance one of the girls raises her eyes and glances at the young men. They do not pay any attention. But when the girl comes back again one of them turns and looks up to the sky. Sometimes his glance and the girl's cross, sometimes they do not. Then somebody else sits in his place the next day. But when two people's glances have crossed a few times at the well everyone knows love has begun.

The rest follows naturally: the lovelorn boy wanders about the countryside around the town singing ballads, his relatives negotiate the bride-price, and wise men calculate how many warriors the young couple will raise. Everything is simple, every step decided and laid down beforehand.

But what about me? Where is my well? Where is the veil on Nino's face? It is strange: you cannot see the woman behind the veil, but you know her: her habits, her thoughts, her desires. The veil hides her eyes, her nose, her mouth. But not her soul. There are no problems in the Oriental woman's soul. Unveiled women are quite different. You see their eyes, their noses, their mouths, even more, much more. But you will never know what is hiding behind those eyes, even when you think you know her well. I love Nino, yet she perplexes me. She is pleased when other men look at her in the street. A good Oriental girl would be disgusted. She kisses me. I may touch her bosom and caress her thighs, yet we are not even engaged. When she reads love stories her eyes become soft and dreaming, as if she is longing for something. But when I ask her what she is longing for she just shakes her head, astonished—she does not know. When she is with me I don't wish for anything more. I think she has been to Russia too often. Her father used to take her to Petersburg, and everybody knows that all Russian women are mad. Their eyes are too full of yearning, they often betray their husbands, and yet they seldom have more than two children. That is how God punishes them! But I love Nino. Her eyes, her voice, her way of talking and thinking. I will marry her, and she will become a good wife like all Georgian women, even if they are gay, carefree or dreamy. *Inshallah*.

I turned over. All this thinking made me tired: it was much more agreeable to close my eyes and dream of the future, and that meant Nino. For the future begins on the day Nino becomes my wife. It will be an exciting day. I will not be allowed to see her. Bride and bridegroom must not see each other on their wedding day, nothing could be more fatal for the wedding night. My friends, armed and on horseback, fetch

Nino. She is heavily veiled. On this day she must wear the Oriental robe. The Mullah asks the questions, my friends stand in the four corners of the hall, whispering incantations against impotence. Thus custom decrees, for every man has enemies, who on the wedding day draw their daggers out of the sheath, turn their faces towards the west and whisper: '*Anisani, banisani, mamawerli, kaniani*—he can't do it, he can't do it, he can't do it.' But, thank God, I have good friends, and Iljas Beg knows all the protecting incantations by heart. Immediately after the wedding we separate. Nino goes to her friends and I to mine. We celebrate goodbye to our youth. And then? Then?

For a moment I open my eyes and see the wooden terrace and the trees in the garden, but then I close them again, so I can see better what comes then. For the wedding day is the most important, perhaps the only important day in one's life. But it is also a very difficult day. It is not easy to get to the bridal chamber on the wedding night. At each door of the long passage masked figures are standing, and the bridegroom is allowed to pass only after he has put coins into their hands. In the bridal chamber itself well-meaning friends have hidden a cock, a cat or other unexpected things. I must have a good look round. Sometimes an old hag is giggling in the bed, and she also will want money before she leaves. At last I am alone. The door opens and Nino comes in. Now the most difficult part of the wedding begins. Nino smiles and looks at me expectantly. Her body is pressed into a kid leather corset. It is held together by cords, fastened in front with highly complicated knots. Expert hands have laced them together to baffle the bridegroom. And I must undo them all by myself. Nino is not allowed to help me. But maybe she will. For these knots are really terribly complicated, and it would bring shame and dishonour on me if I just cut them. A man must demonstrate self-control, for on the next morning his friends will come to see the untied knots. Woe to the wretch who cannot show them. The whole town will laugh at him. During the wedding night the house is like an ant-heap. Friends, friends' relatives, and friends of the friends' relatives stand about in the passages, on the roof, even on the street, waiting and getting impatient if it takes too long. They knock at the door, miaou and bark, until at last the eagerly awaited pistol shot goes off. Then they immediately start shooting into the air, full of enthusiasm. They run out of the house and form themselves into a sort of Guard of Honour, and they will not let Nino and me out of the house until they consider it right. Yes, it will be a wonderful wedding, in the grand old way, as our fathers' customs decreed.

I must have fallen asleep on the divan. For when I opened my eyes my Kotshi was squatting on the floor, cleaning his nails with his long dagger. I had not heard him coming. 'What's the news, little brother?' I asked lazily and yawned.

'Nothing special, little master,' he answered in a bored voice. 'The neighbour's women have quarrelled, a donkey has bolted, it ran into the well, and there it still is.' The Kotshi put his dagger back into the sheath and continued indifferently: 'The Czar has deigned to declare war on several European monarchs.'

'What? What war?' I jumped up and looked at him, puzzled.

'Oh, just an ordinary war.'

'What do you mean? Against whom?'

'Several European monarchs. I couldn't remember their names. There were too many of them. But Mustafa wrote them down.'

'Call him at once.'

The Kotshi shook his head disapprovingly—such unseemly curiosity!—then he disappeared through the door and came back, accompanied by my host. Mustafa grinned, because he felt superior, and he was radiant, because he knew all. Of course the Czar had declared war. The whole town knew it. Only I was asleep on the terrace. Mind you, exactly why the Czar had declared war nobody really knew. He had just decided in his wisdom to do so.

'But against whom has the Czar declared war?' I cried,

exasperated. Mustafa dived into his pocket and brought out a bit of paper on which he had scribbled his notes. He cleared his throat and read out, full of dignity, but with difficulty: 'On the German Kaiser and the Austrian Emperor, the King of Bavaria, the King of Prussia, the King of Saxony, the King of Württemberg, the King of Hungary and many other Lords and Princes.'

'As I told you, little master, I couldn't remember all that.' said the Kotshi humbly. Mustafa folded his bit of paper and said: 'On the other hand, His Imperial Majesty the Khalif and Sultan of the High Ottoman Empire, Mehmed Rashid, as well as His Imperial Majesty the King of Kings of Iran, Sultan Achmed Shah, have declared that until further notice they will not participate in this war. It is therefore a war of the unbelievers amongst themselves and has not much to do with us. The Mullah in the Mehmed-Ali Mosque thinks the Germans will win.' Mustafa could not finish. From the town, drowning every other sound, the bells of the seventeen churches began to ring. I ran out. The glowing August sky hung over the town, threatening and motionless. Far away the blue mountains looked on like indifferent witnesses. The sound of the bells broke against their grey rocks. The streets were full of people. Hot excited faces looked up to the cupolas of the churches and mosques. Dust was whirling in the air. People's voices were hoarse. Mute and weatherbeaten the walls of the many churches looked at us like the stony eyes of eternity. Their towers rose above us like silent threats. The bells stopped ringing. A fat Mullah, in a flowing, many-coloured robe, climbed up the minaret of the mosque near us. He brought his hands to his mouth like a funnel and called out, proud and melancholy: 'Rise for prayer, rise for prayer, prayer is better than sleep!' I ran into the stable. The Kotshi saddled my horse. I mounted and galloped through the streets, the crowds making way for me with frightened glances. The horse's ears stood up in happy expectation as I rode from the town. Before me lay the wide ribbon of the serpentine path. I galloped past the houses of the Karabagh nobility, and the simple farm-lords waved to me: 'Are you rushing into battle, Ali Khan?' I looked down into the valley. There was the little flat-roofed house, in the middle of the garden. When I saw this house I forgot all rules of horsemanship and rode down the steep hill in a wild gallop. The house became bigger, and behind it the mountains disappeared, the sky, the town, the Czar and all the world. I turned the corner into the garden. A servant came from the house and looked at me with dead eyes: 'The noble family has left the house three hours ago.' My hand went mechanically to the dagger. The servant stepped aside. 'Princess Nino left a letter for His Highness Ali Khan.' His hand went to his breast pocket. I dismounted and sat down on the steps of the terrace. The envelope was soft, white and scented. Impatiently I opened it. She wrote in big childish letters:

'Dearest Ali Khan! Suddenly it's war, and we have to go back to Baku. No time to send you a message. Don't be angry. I cry and I love you. This was a short summer. Follow us quickly. I wait for you and I long for you. I will think only of you on our journey. Father thinks the war will soon be over, and our side will win. I feel quite stupid in all this confusion. Please go to the market in Shusha and buy me a carpet. I did not have the time. I want one with a pattern of little horses' heads in many colours. I kiss you. It will be terribly hot in Baku!'

I folded the letter. Everything was all right, really. Just that I, Ali Khan Shirvanshir, had jumped into the saddle like a silly boy, instead of doing the right and proper thing: congratulating the town's Governor on the war, or at least praying in one of the mosques for the victory of the Czar's armies. I sat on the stairs that led to the terrace and stared ahead unseeingly. I was a fool! What else could Nino have done except go home with her father and mother, and ask me to follow as soon as possible. To be sure: when there is war in the country the beloved should come to the lover, not write scented letters. But there was no war in our country, the war was in Russia, and that did not really matter to Nino and me. Even so, I was mad with rage—with the war, with old Kipiani, who was in such a hurry to get home, with the Lyceum of the Holy Tamar, where they did not teach girls how to behave, and most of all with Nino, who just went away, while I, forgetting duty and dignity, could not hurry to her quickly enough. I read and re-read her letter. Suddenly I drew my dagger, I raised my hand—a short flash, and with a sobbing sound the blade flew into the bark of the tree in front of me. The servant took the dagger from the tree, looked at it with the eyes of a connoisseur and gave it back: 'Genuine Kubatshine steel, and your hand is strong,' he said diffidently.

I got on my horse. Slowly I rode home. Far away the town's cupolas rose up. I was not angry any more. I had left my anger in the tree's bark. Nino was quite right. She was a good daughter and would become a good wife. I was ashamed and rode on, my head bent. The street was dusty. The red sun was sinking in the West. Suddenly I heard the neighing of a horse. I raised my head and stopped, petrified. For a minute I forgot Nino and the whole world. Before me stood a horse with a small, narrow head, haughty eyes, a slender rump and the legs of a ballerina. His skin glistened red-golden on the slanting rays of the sun. An old man with a drooping moustache and a crooked nose was in the saddle: Count Melikov, the lord of a manor nearby. What was it they had told of the famous horses of St. Sary Beg when I first came to Shusha? 'It is red-golden, and there are only twelve of them in the whole of Karabagh. They are guarded like the ladies of the Sultan's harem.' Now the red-golden miracle stood before my eyes.

'Where are you going, Count?'

'To the war, my son.'

'What a horse, Count!'

'Yes, you are surprised, aren't you? Only a very few men have seen the red-golden . . .' The Count's eyes became soft. 'His heart weighs exactly six pounds. When you pour water over his body it glows like a golden ring. He had never seen the sunlight. When I took him out today, and the rays of the sun shone into his eyes, they sparkled like a well just broken from the rocks. So must the eyes of the man who invented fire have shone when he saw the first flame. He is a descendant of Sary Beg's horse. I have never shown him to any one. Only when the Czar calls to war does Count Melikov mount the red-golden miracle.' Proudly he saluted and rode on, his sabre clinking softly. War had come to the country indeed.

It was dark when I came home. The whole town was wild with war lust. Native noblemen ran about noisily drunk, firing their guns into the air. 'Blood will flow!' they cried. 'Blood will flow! O Karabagh, thy name will be great!'

A telegram was waiting for me. '*Come home immediately. Father*.' 'Pack our things,' I told the Kotshi, 'we leave to-morrow.' I went out into the street and watched the tumult. I was worried, but I did not know why. I looked up to the stars and thought long and deeply.

8

'Tell me, Ali Khan, who are our friends?' said my Kotshi. We were going down the steep serpentine from Shusha. The simple country lad never tired of asking the strangest questions about everything that had to do with war and politics. In our country the normal person has only three topics of conversation: religion, politics and business. A war touches on all three of them. You can talk of war when, where and as often as you like, and you will never exhaust the theme.

'Our friends, Kotshi, are the Emperor of Japan, the Emperor of India, the King of England, the King of Serbia, the King of the Belgians and the President of the French Republic.'

The Kotshi pursed his lips in disapproval. 'But the President of the French Republic is a civilian, how can he go to battle and wage war?'

'Maybe he'll send a general.'

'One must fight one's own war, not leave it to others, or it just won't be any good.' He looked worriedly at our coachman's back and then spoke like a craftsman: 'The Czar is a small and thin man. But Kaiser Giljom is hefty and strong. He will overcome the Czar even in the first battle.' The good fellow was convinced that to start a war the two enemy monarchs ride against each other on horseback. It was useless to try and tell him otherwise. 'When Giljom has struck the Czar down the Czarewitch has to go into battle. But he is young and sick. And Giljom has six strong healthy sons.'

I tried to reassure him. 'Giljom can only fight with his right hand, his left is lame.'

'Och, he only needs his left to hold his horse's bridle. The right hand is for fighting.' Deep thought made deep creases appear on his forehead. He asked suddenly: 'Is it true, that Emperor Franz Josef is a hundred years old?'

'I'm not quite sure. But he is a very old man.'

'Terrible,' said the Kotshi, 'that such an old man must mount his horse and draw his sword.'

'He hasn't got to.'

'Of course he has. There is blood between him and the Serbian Kralj. They are now blood-enemies, and the Emperor must revenge the blood of his crown prince. If he were a farmer from our village he might be able to pay the blood price, about a hundred cows and a house. But an Emperor cannot forgive bloodshed. If he did then everybody would do it, and there would not be any blood-feuds any more, and the country would be ruined.' The Kotshi was right. The blood-feud is the most important basis of state order and good conduct, no matter what the Europeans say. To be sure: it is good to forgive the shedding of blood if old and wise men beg for it—beg for it from their hearts. Then a high price may be asked, and forgiveness attained. But the principle of blood-feuds must be maintained. Otherwise, how would it all end? Humanity is divided into families, not into nations. And the families hold between them a certain balance, God-given, and founded on the virility of the men. If this balance is disturbed by a murderous force, then the family which has offended against God's will has to lose a member too. Thus the balance is restored. Of course the execution of a blood-feud can sometimes be a bit awkward, shots missed, or more people killed than necessary. Then the blood-feud would go on and on. But the principle is good and clear. My Kotshi understood this well, and nodded

66

satisfied: yes, the hundred-year-old Emperor who mounted his steed to avenge the blood of his son was a good and just man.

'Ali Khan, if Emperor and Kralj have to fight for blood, where do the other monarchs come in?'

That was a difficult question, and I did not myself know the answer. 'Look,' I said, 'our Czar has the same God as the Serbian Kralj, therefore he helps him. The Kaiser Giljom and the other enemy monarchs are related to the Emperor, I think. The King of England is related to the Czar, and so one thing leads to another.' The Kotshi was not at all satisfied with this answer. He was sure that the Emperor of Japan had quite a different God from the one our Czar worshipped, and this mysterious civilian, who ruled France, could not possibly be related to any monarch. Apart from that, as far as Kotshi knew, there was no God at all in France. That's why the country was called a republic. I was not very clear about all this myself. I answered him vaguely, and in the end started questioning him: would he go to war? He looked dreamily at his weapons. 'Yes,' he said, 'of course I will go to war.'

'You know that you needn't? We Mohammedans are excused from active service.'

'I know, but I do want to go.' The simple fellow became suddenly quite loquacious. 'War is good. I'll travel far in the great world. I'll hear the wind whistle in the west, and see tears in my enemies' eyes. I'll have a horse and a gun and ride with my friends through conquered villages. When I come back I'll have lots of money, and they will all praise me, because I'll be a hero. If I die it will be a real man's death. Then everybody will speak highly of me and honour my son or my father. No, war is a wonderful thing, it doesn't matter who it is against. Once in his life a man must go to war.' He went on and on. He counted the wounds he meant to inflict on his enemies, the loot he was already seeing before him, his eyes shone with the awakening lust for battle, and his brown face looked like that of an old warrior from the divine book of Shah Nahmeh. I envied him, because he was a simple man, who was sure of what he had to do, while I was looking ahead, thoughtfully and irresolutely. Too long had I been at the Russian Imperial school, and had become infected by the Russian's introspective ways.

We arrived at the station. Women, children, old men, farmers from Georgia, nomads from Sakataly besieged the buildings. Impossible to find out where to and wherefore they wanted to go. They did not even seem to know themselves. They were lying on the fields like lumps of mud, or storming the arriving trains, regardless of which way they were going. An old man in a torn sheepskin coat, his eyes full of pus, sat at the door of the waiting room, sobbing. He came from Lenkoranj, on the Persian border. He was convinced that his house was destroyed and his children dead. I told him that Persia was not at war with us. He was inconsolable. 'No, sir, Iran's sword has been rusty for a long time. Now they are sharpening it. Nomads will attack us, Shahsevans will destroy our houses, for we live in the country of the unbelievers. The Lion of Iran will devastate our country. Our daughters will become slaves and our sons joy boys.' His senseless lamentations went on and on. My Kotshi pushed the crowd back, and we managed at last to get on the platform. The engine looked like the mask of a prehistoric monster. It stood black and vicious against the background of the yellow desert. We got into the train, and the conductor, after receiving a generous tip, gave us a compartment all to ourselves. The Kotshi sat on the bench, which was covered with red velvet into which the letters SJD (Sakavkasnaja Jelesnaja Doroga—Transcaucasian Railway) were woven. The train started to move through the desert landscape. Yellow sand, stretching far into the distance, little bald hills, soft and round, weatherbeaten rocks, glowing red. From the sea, many miles away, came a cool breeze. Here and there dusty herbs trailed round low cliffs. Then a caravan came into view: a hundred camels or more, some with one hump, some with two, some big, some small, but all staring anxiously at the train. They moved along with wide flabby steps, their heads

68

nodding in time to the monotonous tinkling of the little bells they wore round their necks. If one of them stumbles, his bell goes wrong, and the rhythm of the caravan is disturbed. All the other animals feel this and become restive until unity is restored, and they move as one again. This is the symbol of the desert: this strange being, bastard of animal and bird, graceful and awkward, attractive and repulsive, born from and made for the hot dreams of the desert.

And for me this was the bell that went wrong: my first impulse to go to war as soon as possible. Now I had time to think. The caravan was wandering eastwards over the soft sand, lost in a dream. The train was pushing westwards along its iron rails, mindless and mechanical. Why did I not raise my hand to pull the communication cord? This was where I belonged, to the camels, to the men leading them, to the sand! What was it to me, this world behind the mountains? These Europeans with their wars, their cities, their Czars, Kaisers and Kings? Their sorrows, their happiness, their cleanliness and their dirt—we have a different way of being clean or dirty, good or bad, we have a different rhythm and different faces. Let the train rush to the West. My heart and soul belong to the East.

I opened the window wide and leaned out as far as I could. My eyes followed the caravan, now already far away. I was calm and serene, my mind was made up. There was no enemy in my country. No one threatened Transcaucasia's steppes. Therefore this war was not my war. It was different for my Kotshi. He did not care whether he fought for the Czar or for the West. He was the bondsman of his own lust for adventure. Like all Asiatics he wants to shed blood and see his enemies weep. I too want to go to war, my whole soul yearns for the freedom of combat, for the smoke of a battlefield in the evening. War—a wonderful word, manly and strong, like the thrust of a lance. But I must wait. For this I feel dimly: whoever may win this war—danger is building up for us, drawing closer, a danger greater than all the Czar's conquests put together.

Therefore enough men must be left in our country, to fight this future enemy, when he invades our town, our country, our continent. An invisible hand is even now gripping the reins of the caravan, trying to force it to new pastures, new ways. And these ways can only be the ways of the West, the ways I do not want to follow.

This then is why I will stay at home. Only when the invisible one attacks my world—only then will I draw my sword. I leaned back in my seat. It was good to have thought this out to the very end. Other people will probably say I stay at home because I do not want to leave Nino's dark eyes. Maybe. Maybe these people will even be right. For to me those dark eyes are my native earth, the call of home to the son a stranger tries to lead astray. I will defend the dark eyes of my homeland from the invisible danger.

I looked at the Kotshi. He was fast asleep, snoring in martial enthusiasm.

9

The town stood lazy and listless in the glare of the Transcaucasian August sun. Its ancient lined face had not changed at all. Many Russians had disappeared, gone to war for Czar and Homeland. The police were searching the homes of the Germans and Austrians. Oil prices rose, and people inside and outside the great wall did well and were happy. Only the professional tea house regulars read the despatches. The war was far away, on another planet. . . . The names of towns taken or lost in battle sounded foreign and remote. Pictures of generals were on the front pages of all journals, looking friendly and full of confidence, certain of victory. I did not go to Moscow to the Institute, as I did not want to leave home during the war, and my studies would not run away. Many people despised me for this, and because I did not go to war. But when I looked down from the roof of our house on the many-coloured whirl of the old town, I knew that no Czar's order would ever tear me from the wall round my home.

My father was surprised and worried: 'You really do not want to go to war? You, Ali Khan Shirvanshir?'

'No, father, I do not want to go.'

'Most of our ancestors have fallen on the battlefield. It is the natural death of our family.'

'I know, father. I too will die on the battlefield, but not now, and not so far away. . . .'

'It is better to die than to live in dishonour.'

'I do not live dishonourably. This war does not concern me.' My father looked at me suspiciously. Was his son a coward? For the hundredth time he told me our family history: How under Nadir Shah five Shirvanshirs had fought for the Realm of the Silver Lion. Four fell in the campaign against India. One only returned from Delhi with rich loot. He bought estates, built palaces and survived the grim ruler. And when Shah Rukh fought against Hussein Khan this ancestor took the side of the wild Kadjar Prince Aga Mohammed. He and his eight sons followed him through Send, Khorassan and Georgia. Only three survived, and went on serving the great eunuch, even after he became Shah. Their tents stood in Aga Mohammed's camp in Shusha on the night of his murder. With the blood of nine members the Shirvanshirs had paid for the estates which Feth Ali, Aga Mohammed's gentle heir, gave them in Shirvan, in Mazendaran, in Giljan and Azerbeidshan. The three brothers became the King of King's hereditary vassals, and ruled over Shirvan. Then the Russians came. Ibrahim Khan Shirvanshir defended Baku, and his hero's death at Gandsha gave new honour to our name. Only after the Peace of Turkmenshai the Shirvanshirs separated. The Persian members of the family fought and died under Mohammed Shah and Nasreddin Shah, in the campaigns against the Turkmenians and the Afghans, and the Russian ones bled to death for the Czar in the Crimean War, in battles against the Turks, and in the Japanese war. This is how we earned our many decorations and medals, and the sons of our family pass their exams even if they can't tell the Gerundium from the Gerundivium.

'Now the country is at war again,' my father finished, 'but you, Ali Khan Shirvanshir, are sitting on the carpet of cowardice, hiding behind the Czar's mild edict. Words are no use, if our family's history is not in your blood. You should read our ancestors' heroic deeds not in dead dusty books, but in your heart and your veins.' Sadly my father fell silent. He despised me, because he did not understand me. Was his son a coward? The country was at war, and his son did not rush into battle, did not thirst for the blood of enemies, did not want to see tears in their eyes. This son must be a degenerate! I was sitting on the carpet, leaning against the soft cushions, and said jokingly: 'You have given me three wishes. The first one was a summer in Karabagh. Here is the second: I will draw my sword when I want to. I don't think it will ever be too late. For a long time, peace will be a thing of the past. Our country will need my sword later.'

'All right,' said my father. After that he did not talk of war any more, but looked at me sideways, searchingly. Maybe his son was not a degenerate after all. I talked to the Mullah of the Mosque Taza-Pir. He understood me immediately. He came to our house in his flowing robes, spreading the fragrance of ambergris, and was closeted with my father for a long time. He told him that according to the Koran this war was not a part of a Muslim's duty, and quoted many of the Prophet's adages in support of this. After that I had peace and quiet in my house. But in my house only. Lust for war was spreading amongst the young folks, and not every one had sense enough to hold back. Sometimes I went to see my friends. I passed Zizianashvili's Gate, turned right into Ashum Alley, crossed the Street of Holy Olga, and strolled towards Seinal Aga's house.

Iljas Beg was sitting at the table, bent over military treatises. Next to him crouched Mehmed Haidar, the school's dunce, his brow furrowed, looking frightened. The war had shaken him. He had immediately left the House of Wisdom, and, like Iljas Beg, had just one desire: to feel the golden officer's epaulettes on his shoulders. So they were both preparing for the Officer's Examination. When I came into the room I generally heard Mehmed Haidar's despairing murmur: 'The Duty of the Army and the Fleet is to defend Czar and Homeland against the Outer and the Inner Enemy.' I took the poor chap's book and examined him: 'Who, esteemed Mehmed Haidar, is the Outer Enemy?'

He drew his brows together, thought very hard, and suddenly exploded: 'The Germans and the Austrians.'

'Quite wrong, my dear chap,' I rejoiced, and read triumphantly: 'The term Outer Enemy describes any Military Formation which threatens to overstep our borders with warlike intent.' Then I turned to Iljas Beg: 'What is the definition of a shot?'

He answered like an automaton: 'The definition of a Shot is the expulsion of the bullet from the muzzle of the barrel with the help of powder.' This game of questions and answers went on for quite a while. We were all very surprised to see how difficult it was to kill an enemy according to all the rules and regulations. What a bunch of dilettantes we in our country had been in practising this art! Then Mehmed Haidar and Iljas Beg started to enthuse about the delights of their future campaigns. Foreign women, picked up safe and sound on the ruins of destroyed towns played the main part in these daydreams. Then they said that every soldier carried his Field-Marshal's baton in his knapsack, and looked at me condescendingly. 'When I am an officer,' said Mehmed Haidar, 'you will have to let me precede you on the street, and honour me. Because I defend your lazy bones with my brave blood.'

'When you are an officer the war will be over long ago, and the Germans will have conquered Moscow.' My two future heroes were not at all disgusted with this prophecy. They did not care who won the war, any more than I did. Between us and the front was a territory covering one sixth of the world. It was plainly impossible for the Germans to conquer all that. Instead of one Christian monarch another Christian monarch would reign over us. That was all there was to it. No, for Iljas Beg it was an adventure, and for Mehmed Haidar the welcome excuse to finish his studies in a dignified manner and dedicate himself to a natural and manly occupation. I was sure both of them would be good front officers. Our people were brave enough. But brave for what? Neither Iljas Beg nor Mehmed Haidar ever asked themselves this question, and all my warnings would have been in vain, for the blood lust of the Orient had awakened in them.

After they had despised me enough, I left Seinal Aga's house. Cutting through the tangle of little alleys in the Armenian quarter I came to the Esplanade. The Caspian Sea, salty and lead coloured, was licking the granite stones. A gunboat was lying in the harbour. I sat down and looked at the little native sailing boats, battling valiantly with the waves. In one of them I could easily and comfortably go to the port of Astara in Persia, to a tumble-down, peaceful nest in the Shah's big green country. There I would find melancholy sighs of love fashioned into beautiful verses by the classical poets, memories of Rustem the Hero's valiant deeds and the fragrant rose gardens in Teheran's palaces. A wonderful dreaming country.

Up and down the Esplanade I paced, gaining a little time, for it still felt strange to go and see Nino in her home. It was against all conceptions of correct behaviour. But as there was a war on, old Kipiani felt he might stretch a point. At last I drew a deep breath, and ran up the stairs of the house where she lived. It had four floors, and on the second floor was a brass plate with the words *Prince Kipiani*. A servant girl, wearing a white apron, opened the door and courtesied. I gave her my cap, though in the Orient the guest keeps his cap on. But I knew how to behave in European company. The illustrious family were in the drawing room, having tea.

It was a big room. The furniture was covered in red silk, palms and potted flowers were standing in the corners, and the walls were neither painted nor covered with carpets, but papered. The illustrious family were drinking English tea with milk from big beautifully decorated cups, the English way. There were biscuits and rusks, and as I kissed Nino's mother's hand, I smelt biscuits, rusks and lavender water. The Prince shook hands with me, and Nino gave me three fingers, looking sideways into her teacup. I sat down and was given tea. 'So you have decided not to go to war for the time being, Khan?' the Prince asked graciously.

'No, your Highness, not yet.'

The Princess put her cup down. 'But if I were you I would join some sort of committee helping the war effort. At least you would have some sort of uniform.'

'Maybe I will, Princess. It is a good idea.'

'I will do that too,' said the Prince. 'Even if I cannot be spared in my office, I will sacrifice my free time for the Fatherland.'

'Of course, Prince. But unfortunately I have so little free time, that I am afraid the Fatherland will not get much out of me.'

The Prince was genuinely astonished: 'But what do you do?'

'I am busy with the administration of my estates, Prince.' That did it. I had read this sentence in some English novel or other. If a noble Lord is not doing anything, he is busy with the administration of his estates. I could see that I went up considerably in the esteem of the illustrious parents. We exchanged a few more elegant phrases and then I was graciously permitted to take Nino to the opera that night. Again I kissed the Princess's hand, bowed from the waist, even pronounced the 'R' the Petersburg way, and promised to be back at half past seven.

Nino saw me to the door, and when I took my cap from the servant she blushed deeply, bent her head and said in her enchanting broken Tartar: 'I'm terribly glad, that you're staying here. Really, I'm glad. But tell me, Ali Khan, are you really afraid to go to war? Surely men must love battle. I would even love your wounds.' I did not blush, but took her hand and pressed it.

'No, I'm not afraid. The time will come when you will nurse my wounds. But until that time you can think me a coward if that makes you happy.' Nino looked at me without understanding. I went home and cut an old chemical textbook into a thousand pieces. Then I had a cup of real Persian tea and booked a box for the opera.

76

10

Close your eyes, cover your ears with your hands and open your soul. Remember that night in Teheran? An enormous blue stone hall, the noble signature of Shah Nasreddin over the entrance. In the middle of the hall is a square stage, and all around, sitting, standing, lying, dignified men, excited children, fanatic youths—the devout public at the Passion Play of Holy Hussein. The hall is dimly lit. On stage bearded angels comfort the young Hussein. Grim Khalif Jasid sends his riders into the desert, to bring him the youth's head. Mournful songs are interrupted by the clinking of swords. Ali, Fatima and Eve, the first woman, wander across the stage, singing many-versed rubaiyats. Someone hands the young Hussein's head on a gold plate to the Khalif. The spectators tremble and weep. A Mullah passes along the rows collecting tears in cotton wool. There are strong magic powers in those tears. The deeper the beholder's faith, the greater is the effect of the play on him. A plank of wood becomes the desert, a box the diamond-studded throne of the Khalif, a few wooden poles the Garden of Eden, and a bearded man the daughter of the Prophet.

Now open your eyes, drop your hands and look around: Dazzling light from innumerable electric bulbs. Walls and chairs are covered in red velvet, boxes are held aloft by gilt plaster-of-Paris gods. Bald heads in the stalls shine like stars on the night sky. The women's white backs and naked arms add to the excitement. A dark abyss separates the spectators from the stage. Down there, nameless, faceless musicians are sitting, tuning their instruments. The auditorium is filled with the sound of soft conversations, one flowing into the other, of rustling programmes, of flapping fans and lorgnettes: this is the Baku Opera a few minutes before the beginning of *Eugene Onegin*. Nino was sitting beside me. Her oval face was turned to me, her lips moist and her eyes dry. She did not say much. When the lights went out I put my arm round her shoulder. She bent her head to the side and seemed immersed in Tschaikovsky's music. Eugene Onegin wandered about on the stage in his Regency costume, and Tatyana sang an aria.

I prefer the opera to the theatre. The opera stories are comparatively simple, and most of them are well known anyway. I do not mind the music if it is not too loud. But in the theatre it is often a real effort for me to try and follow the strange goings-on on the stage. It is dark, and when I close my eyes my neighbours think my soul is sunk in an ocean of musical enchantment. This time I kept my eyes open. Nino was leaning forward and behind her delicate profile I saw the first row of the stalls. In the middle sat a fat man with sheep's eyes and a philosophical forehead—my old friend Melik Nachararyan. His head kept moving in time to the music between Nino's left eye and her nose.

'Look, there's Nachararyan,' I whispered.

'Look at the stage, barbarian,' she whispered back, but glanced quickly at the fat Armenian. He turned and nodded a friendly greeting.

During the interval, I met him at the buffet, where I was getting chocolates for Nino. He came to our box and sat there, fat, clever and a bit bald.

'How old are you, Nachararyan?' I asked.

'Thirty,' he answered.

Nino looked up. 'Thirty?' she said. 'Then we won't see you in our town much longer, I suppose.'

'Why's that, Princess?'

'Your age group has already been called up.'

He laughed aloud, his eyes protruding and his stomach wobbling: 'Unfortunately, Princess, cannot go to war. My doctor has found an incurable empyem ɔf the kidney atrabilarian, so I have to stay behind.' The name of the illness sounded exotic, and made me think of stomach ache. Nino's eyes opened wide.

'Is that a very dangerous illness?' she asked full of sympathy.

'It depends. With the help of a doctor who knows his business any illness can become dangerous.'

Nino was astonished and disgusted. Melik Nachararyan was a member of the noblest family in Karabagh. His father was a general, and he himself as strong as an ox, as healthy as anyone could possibly be, and unmarried. When he was leaving our box I asked him to dine with us. He thanked me politely and accepted. The curtain rose, and Nino put her head on my shoulder. During the famous Tschaikovsky waltz she raised her eyes to me and whispered: 'Compared to Nachararyan you are quite a hero. At least you have no kidney atrabilarians.'

'Armenians have more imagination than Mohammedans.' I tried to excuse Nachararyan.

Nino kept her head on my shoulder even when the heroic tenor Lensky stepped in front of Eugene Onegin's gun, and was killed, as per schedule. It was an easy, elegant and complete victory, and we felt we should celebrate. Nachararyan was waiting for us at the entrance. He had a motor car, which looked very elegant and European standing next to the two-horse carriage of the House of Shirvanshir. We drove through our town's dark alleys, passing our two schools. At night these buildings seemed to look a bit more friendly. We stopped at the City Club's marble staircase. That was rather dangerous. But if one of the escorts is called Shirvanshir and the other

Nachararyan, a Princess Kipiani need not worry about the Lyceum of the Holy Queen Tamar's rules and regulations.

The wide terrace was brightly lit by white lamps. We took a table that overlooked the governor's dark garden, the softly gleaming sea, and the lighthouse of the island of Nargin. The glasses clinked. Nino and Nachararyan were drinking champagne. But as nothing in the world, not even Nino's eyes, could make me drink in public, I sipped, as usual, an orange-ade. When the six-man dance band gave us a rest at last, Nachararyan said seriously and thoughtfully: 'Here we are, representatives of the three greatest Caucasian people: a Georgian, a Mohammedan, an Armenian. Born under the same sky, by the same earth, different and yet the same, like God's Trinity. European, and yet Asiatic, receiving from East and West, and giving to both.'

'I always thought,' said Nino, 'that fighting was the Caucasian's element. Yet here I am, sitting between two Caucasians, neither of whom wants to fight.'

Nachararyan looked at her indulgently: 'We both want to fight, Princess, but not against each other. There is a high wall between us and the Russians. That wall is the Caucasus. If the Russians win our country will become completely russified. We will lose our churches, our language, our identity. We will become European-Asiatic bastards, instead of forming the bridge between the two worlds. No, whoever fights for the Czar fights against Caucasia.'

Nino's lips spoke her school learning: 'Persians and Turks tore our country apart. The Shah destroyed the East, the Sultan the West. How many Georgian girls became slaves, dragged far away into the harems! The Russians did not even come of their own accord. We asked them to come. George XII abdicated voluntarily in the Czar's favour. "Not to enlarge the already illimitable territories of our empire do we take upon us the protection of the Kingdom of Georgia" . . . don't you know these words?' Of course we did. For eight years these words had been drummed into us at school, this manifesto that Alexander I had decreed for us a hundred years ago. They could be seen in the main street of Tiflis, engraved on a bronze plaque: 'Not to enlarge the already illimitable territories of our Empire do we take upon us . . .' Nino was not so far wrong. The harems of the Orient were at that time full of captive Christian women, the streets of Caucasian towns full of Christian corpses. I could of course have answered: 'I am a Mohammedan, you are a Christian, you were given to us by God as our legitimate prey.' But I kept silent and waited for Nacharáryan's answer.

'Well, you see, Princess,' he said, 'a person who thinks in terms of politics must have the courage sometimes to be unfair, even to be injust. I concede: the Russians brought peace to the country. But we, the people of Caucasia, can now keep that peace without them. They pretend that they must protect us, one against the other. Therefore Russian regiments are here, Russian civil servants and governors. But Princess, say for yourself: do you have to be protected from me? Must I be protected from Ali Khan? Were we not, all of us, sitting peacefully together near the well of Pechapür? Surely the time is past when the Caucasian peoples had to think of Persia as an enemy. The enemy is in the north, and this same enemy is trying to tell us that we are children, who have to be protected from each other. But we are not children any more, we have been grown up for quite some time.'

'And is that why you are not going to war?' asked Nino.

Nachararyan had drunk too much champagne. 'Not only because of that,' he said. 'I am lazy, and I like my comforts. I hold it against the Russians that they confiscated the Armenian Church Estates, and it is nicer here than in the trenches. My family has done enough for fame. I am a hedonist.'

'I think in a different way,' I said. 'I am no hedonist, and I love war.'

'You are young, my friend,' said Nachararyan, and lifted his glass again. He went on talking for a long time, and probably very cleverly. When we started for home Nino was nearly, but not quite convinced, that he was right. We went in Nachararyan's car. 'This wonderful town,' he said during the drive, 'the Gate of Europe. If Russia were not so reactionary we'd already be a European country.'

I thought of the happy days of my geography lesson and laughed aloud. It had been an enjoyable evening. When we said good night I kissed Nino's eyes and hands, while Nachararyan looked at the sea. Later he drove me to the Zizianashvili Gate ... further than that the car could not go. Behind the wall was Asia. 'Will you marry Nino?' was the last thing he asked.

'*Inshallah*, if it is God's will.'

'You will have to overcome a few difficulties, my friend. If you should need any help—I'm at your disposal. I'm all for intermarriage between the first families of our people. We must stand together.'

I pressed his hand warmly. It just showed: there really were decent Armenians. This was quite a disturbing thought. Tired, I went into the house. The servant was squatting on the floor, reading. I glanced at the book. The Koran's Arabic ornamental script meandered over the pages. The servant rose, saluting me. I took the divine book and read: 'Oh you, who you believe, behold that wine, gambling and pictures are an abomination and the work of Satan. Avoid them, and you may fare well. Satan is trying to turn you from the thought of Allah and from prayer.' A sweet fragrance drifted from the pages. The thin, yellowish paper rustled. God's word, enclosed between two leather covers, was severe and warning. I returned the book, and went up to my room. The divan was wide, low and soft. I closed my eyes, as I always do when I want to see with special clarity. I saw champagne, Eugene Onegin at the ball, Nachararyan's light sheep's eyes, Nino's soft lips, and the enemy's hordes flooding over the mountain wall to conquer our town.

Monotonous singing sounded from the street. It was Hashim the Lovelorn. He was very old, and no one knew the love he mourned for. People honoured him by giving him the Arabic name of Madjnun, the Love-Sick. At night he would slink through the empty alleys, sit down at some corner, weep, and sing of his sorrow till dawn. The monotonous melodies sent me to sleep. I turned to the wall and sank into darkness and dreams. Life was still wonderful.

11

A stick has two ends: an upper and a lower one. Turn the stick upside down, and the upper end is down, while the lower end is now up. But the stick itself has not changed at all. Thus it is with me. I am still the same as a month ago, a year ago. The same war goes on in the great world, and the same generals are victorious or defeated. But those who only a short while ago called me a coward now lower their eyes when they meet me: friends and relatives now praise my wisdom, and my father looks at me admiringly. But the stick itself has not changed at all. One day rumours were flying all round the town: His Imperial Majesty the Sultan of the High Ottoman Empire, Mehmed V. Rashid, had decided to declare war on the world of the unbelievers. His victorious armies were moving eastward and westward, to free the believers from Russia's and England's yoke. The Holy War had been declared, it was said, and the Prophet's green banner was fluttering over the Khalif's palace. So I became a hero. Friends came to see me, speaking highly of my foresight. I had been quite right in refusing to go to war. A Mohammedan should never fight against the Sultan. The Turks, our brothers, would come to Baku, and united with the Turks our people would become one big nation of believers.

I kept silent, and bowed, without answering their praises.

The wise man must not let himself be disturbed by either praise or blame. My friends spread out maps. They quarrelled violently about through which part of the town the Turks would come marching in. I stopped the quarrel by pointing out that, regardless of which direction they might come from, the Turks would most definitely come in through the Armenian quarter. My friends looked at me admiringly and again praised my wisdom.

Man's soul changes overnight. No Muslim rushed to take up arms any more. Iljas Beg had suddenly tired of war, and Seinal Aga had to pay an enormous amount of money to get him back to Baku garrison. The poor fellow had passed his Officers' Exam just before the Turkish declaration of war, and the miracle had happened: even Mehmed Haidar had managed to pass. Now they were both lieutenants, sitting in their barracks, envying me, who had not sworn alliance to the Czar. There was no way back for them. No one had forced them. They had pledged their oath voluntarily, and I would have been the first to turn from them if they had broken it.

I was very quiet in those days, for I could not think clearly. Only once in a while I went out in the evening and walked quickly to the little mosque near the fort. There, in an old house, lived an old school friend of mine, Seyd Mustafa. He was a descendant of the Prophet. His face was pockmarked, he had small slit eyes, and he wore the green sash of his rank. His father was the Imam of the little mosque, and his grandfather a famous sage at the grave of Imam Reza in the Holy Town of Meshed. He prayed five times a day. He wrote the name of the godless Khalif Jesid with chalk on the soles of his feet, so as to tread daily into the dust the name of him who hated the True Faith. On the tenth of Moharram, the Holy Day of Mourning, he tore the skin of his breast till the blood flowed. Nino thought him bigoted and despised him for it. I loved him for the clarity of his vision, for like no one else he could distinguish between good and bad, truth and untruth.

He greeted me with the gay smile of a wise man. 'Have you heard, Ali Khan? That rich Jakub Oghly has bought twelve crates of champagne to drink with the first Turkish officer who comes to this town. Champagne! Champagne in honour of the Mohammedan Holy War!'

I shrugged my shoulders. 'That surprises you, O Seyd? The world has gone mad.'

'Allah leads astray those against whom he has turned his wrath,' Seyd said grimly. He jumped up and his lips trembled. Yesterday eight men deserted to fight in the Sultan's army. Eight men! I ask you, Ali Khan, what do these eight think they're doing?'

'Their heads are as empty as the stomach of a hungry ass,' I replied cautiously.

Seyd's fury knew no bounds: 'Look!' he cried, 'Shiites are fighting for the Sunnite Khalif! Has not Jesid shed the blood of the Prophet's grandson? Has not Moawia murdered Ali, whose name be praised? Who is the Prophet's heir? The Khalif or the Unseen, the Imam of Eternity, in whose veins flows the Prophet's blood? For centuries the people of the Shiites have been mourning, blood has been flowing between us and the renegades, who are worse than the unbelievers. Shia here—Sunna there—there is no bridge between us. It is not so very long ago that Sultan Selim had forty thousand Shiites slaughtered. And now? Shiites are fighting for the Khalif, who has stolen the Prophet's heritage. Everything is forgotten: the blood of the devout, the mystery of the Imams. Here in our Shiite town, men are longing for the Sunnites to come and destroy our faith. What does the Turk want?! Enver has advanced even to Urmia. Iran will be cut in half. The True Faith is destroyed. O Ali, come with your sword of flame, pass sentence on the renegades! O Ali, Ali. . . !' His tears were flowing, he beat his breast with his fist.

I looked at him, shaken. What was right, what was wrong? True, the Turks were Sunnites. And yet my heart longed to see Enver coming to our town. What did that mean? Had our martyrs' blood really flowed in vain? 'Seyd,' I said, 'the Turks are of our blood. Their language is our language. Turan's blood flows in both our veins. Maybe that is why it is easier to die under the Half Moon of the Khalifs than under the Czar's Cross.'

Seyd Mustafa dried his eyes: 'In my veins flows Mohammed's blood', he said coolly and proudly. 'Turan's blood? You seem to have forgotten even the little you learned at school. Go to the mountains of the Altai, or yet further to the border of Siberia: who lives there? Turks, like us, of our language and our blood. God has led them astray, and they have remained pagans, they are praying to idols: the water-god Su-Tengri, the sky-god Teb-Tengri. If these Jakuts or Altai-men were to become powerful and fight us, should we Shiites be glad of the pagan victories, just because they are of the same blood as we?'

'What are we to do, Seyd?' I asked. 'Iran's sword is rusty. Whoever fights against the Turks is helping the Czar. Should we in Mohammed's name defend the Czar's Cross against the Khalif's Half Moon? What shall we do, Seyd?' Mustafa was shrouded in a terrible sadness. He looked at me, and it seemed that all the despair of a dying millennium was in his eyes.

'What shall we do, Ali Khan? I do not know.' He was in agony, yet even now he did not hide behind empty phrases.

I fell silent, perplexed. The little oil lamp was smoking. In the small circle of light the prayer rug's colours were gleaming, like flowers in a garden that can be folded up and taken on a journey. And Seyd Mustafa was only in this world as if on a journey, so it was easy for him to condemn other people's sins. In another ten or twenty years he would be an Imam at the grave of Reza in Meshed, one of those sages who guide Persia's fate, unseen and unperceived. Already he had the tired eyes of an old man, who knows of his old age and embraces it. He would not give away an inch of the True Faith, even though by doing so he could make Persia great and mighty again. Better to go under than find the will-o'-the-wisp of earthly splendour by passing through the morass of sin. And so he was silent and did not know what to do. And so I love him, the lonely guard on the threshold of our True Faith. 'Our fate is in Allah's hand, Seyd Mustafa,' I said, getting off the subject, 'may God lead us on the right way. But tonight I wanted to talk to you about something else.' Seyd Mustafa looked at his henna-stained nails. An amber rosary was gliding through his fingers. He looked up, and his pockmarked face became one broad grin.

'I know, Ali Khan, you want to get married.'

I jumped up, amazed. I had wanted to talk about the founding of a Mohammedan-Shiitic Boy Scout Organisation. But already he took upon himself the office and knowledge of an ecclesiastical minister.

'How do you know that I want to get married, and what's it got to do with you?'

'I see it in your eyes, and it's got to do with me because I am your friend. You want to marry Nino, who does not like me, and who is a Christian.'

'That is so. Well, what do you say?'

Seyd gave me a wise, searching look. 'I say yes, Ali Khan. A man must marry, preferably the woman he likes. She need not like him in return. A wise man does not court a woman. The woman is just the acre, on which the man sows. Must the field love the farmer? Enough that the farmer loves the field. Marry, but never forget: the woman is just an acre.'

'So you believe that a woman has neither soul nor intelligence?'

He looked at me pityingly: 'How can you ask, Ali Khan? Of course she hasn't. Why should a woman have either? It is enough for her to be chaste and have many children. The Law says: the evidence of one man is more than the evidence of three women. Never forget that, Ali Khan.' I had been quite prepared to hear the pious Seyd Mustafa curse me for wanting to marry a Christian, who did not like him, so I was really touched by his answer. It proved again that he was honest and wise. I said mildly: 'So you don't mind her being a Christian? Or should she become a Muslim?'

'Why should she?' he asked. 'A creature without soul and intelligence has no faith anyway. No Paradise or Hell is waiting for a woman. When she dies she just disintegrates into nothing. The sons must of course be Shiites.' I nodded. He rose and went to the bookcase. His long hands, the hands of a wise monkey, drew out a dusty book. I glanced at the cover. The Persian title read: *Dshainabi: Tewarichi Al-Y-Seldjuk* (*The story of the House of the Seldjuks*). He opened the book. 'Here we are,' he said, 'page 207.' Then he read aloud: 'In the Year of the Flight 637 Sultan Alaeddin Kaikobad died in the castle of Kabadia. Chajasseddin Keichosrov mounted the throne of the Seldjuks. And he took in marriage the daughter of a Georgian Prince, and so great was his love for this Christian Georgian, that he ordered her image to be stamped next to his own on the coins of his realm. Then the wise men and the pious men came to him and said: "It is not for the Sultan to go against the Laws of God. This scheme is a sin." The Mighty One became full of wrath and said: "God has placed me above you. Your fate is obedience." Then the wise men and the pious men went away and were sad, but God enlightened the Sultan. He called the wise men and the pious men back and spoke thus: "I will not go against the Holy Laws God has imposed upon me. Be it therefore thus: The Lion with a Long Mane and a Sword in his Right Paw—I am that. The Sun rising above my Head—that is the woman I love. Let that be the Law." Since that time the Lion and the Sun are the symbols of Persia. But wise men say: "there are no women more beautiful than the women of Georgia."' Mustafa closed the book and grinned. 'There you are— you're doing what Keichosrov did then. There's no law against it. Georgian women are part of the loot the Prophet has promised his devout followers: "Go and take them." Thus it is written in the book.' His gloomy face had suddenly become soft. The wicked little eyes shone. He was happy to disperse the small-minded scruples of the twentieth century with the words of the Holy Book. May the unbelievers see where real progress lies. I embraced and kissed him. Then I went home, and my steps were firm and strong in the dark alleys. The Holy Book, the old Sultan and wise Mustafa were on my side.

12

The desert is the gate to a mysterious and unfathomable world. Dust and stones are whirling under my horse's hooves. My Terek Cossack's saddle is soft, as if filled with down. In this saddle the Cossack can sleep, stand up and lie down. All his earthly goods are in his saddle bags: a loaf of bread, a bottle of vodka, and a bag of gold coins, his loot from a Kabardin village. My saddle bags are empty. I am charging along in the blustering desert wind, nothing in the endless grey sands. From my shoulder hangs the Burka, the black Kabardin felt cape, softly protecting me from heat or cold. Robbers and riders have invented this garment for robbing and riding. Neither the sun's rays nor the drops of rain can penetrate it. It can easily be made into a tent, and all the profit from a daring robbery can be hidden in the black folds of the Burka. Like parrots in a cage kidnapped girls crouch behind their captors, protected by the wide felt cape.

I ride to the Gate of the Grey Wolf. Prehistoric titans erected these two weatherbeaten grey rocks in an ocean of sand, in the middle of the desert near Baku. Sary Kurt, the Grey Wolf, the ancestor of the Turks, once led the tribe of the Osmans through this strong narrow gate to the green plains of Anatolia, so says an old legend. In the nights of the full moon the jackals and desert wolves gather at the rocks and howl, like dogs howling at a corpse. They have a cosmic sense for the smell of death, and they feel that the moon is a corpse. The dogs in his house begin to howl when a man is about to die. They can smell death even while the man is still alive. They are kin to the desert wolves, just as we, Russian subjects, are kin to the wolves Enver Bey is leading to Caucasia. I am riding through the emptiness of the big desert, my father next to me. When he is in the saddle he seems to be one with his horse, a centaur. 'Safar Khan,' my voice is hoarse, it is only seldom that I call my father by his name. 'Safar Khan, I must talk to you.'

'Talk while we're riding, my son. It is easier to talk when horse and rider are united.' Is my father laughing at me? My whip grazes my horse's flank. My father raises his eyebrows. One small movement of his thighs, and he has caught up with me.

'Well, my son?' his voice seems to mock me.

'I want to marry, Safar Khan.'

A long silence. The wind is whistling by. Stones are whirling under our horses' hooves. At last his answer: 'I'll build a villa for you. I know of a place on the Esplanade. I suppose there's a stable there. During the summer you can stay at Mardakjany. You'll have to call your first son Ibrahim, in honour of our ancestor. I'll give you a motor car, if you want one. But there's really no point in having one, we haven't got the roads for them. A stable full of horses is better.'

Silence again. The Gate of the Grey Wolf is behind us. We are riding towards the sea, towards the suburb of Bailov. My father's voice sounds far away: 'Shall I go and find a beautiful wife for you, or have you managed to find one yourself? Nowadays it seems to happen quite often that young people chose their women for themselves.'

'I want to marry Nino Kipiani.'

My father's face is immobile. His right hand caresses the

horse's mane. 'Nino Kipiani,' he says, 'Her hips are too narrow. But I believe all Georgians are built like that. Yet they bear healthy children.'

'Father!' I do not quite know why I feel disgusted, but I do. He looks at me sideways and smiles.

'You are still very young, Ali Khan. A woman's hips are much more important than her knowledge of languages.' He was deliberately casual: 'When do you want to marry?'

'In autumn, when Nino has finished school.'

'Very good. Then the child will be born next May. May is a lucky month.'

'Father!' Again I was overwhelmed by a fury that I did not understand myself. I feel my father is making a fool of me. I am not marrying Nino because of her hips or her knowledge of languages—I'm marrying her because I love her. My father smiles. Then he stops his horse and says: 'The desert is wide and empty. It does not matter which hill we breakfast on. I'm hungry. Let us rest here.' We get off our horses. From his saddle my father takes a loaf of bread and some sheep's cheese, and offers me half of it. But I am not hungry. We are lying in the sand, he is eating and looking into the far distance. Then his face becomes serious, he raises himself and sits straight like a ramrod, his legs crossed. He says: 'It is very good that you marry. I have been married three times. But the women died, like flies in autumn. And now, as you know, I am not married at all. But when you get married, I might marry too. Your Nino is a Christian. Do not let her bring the foreign faith into our home. A woman is a fragile vessel. That is important to know. Do not beat her when she is pregnant. But never forget: you are the master, and she lives in your shadow. You know that every Muslim is allowed four wives at a time. But it is better for you to be content with just one. Except if Nino does not have children. Do not be unfaithful. Your wife has the right to every drop of your sperm. Eternal damnation awaits the adulterer. Be patient with her. Women are like children, only much more sly and vicious. That, too, is important to know.

Cover her with presents if you want to, give her silks and jewels. But if you ever need advice, and she gives it to you, do the exact opposite. That is perhaps the most important thing to know.'

'But father, I love her.'

He shook his head. 'Generally speaking it is not a good thing to love a woman. One loves one's homeland, or war. Some men love beautiful carpets, or rare weapons. But—it does happen, that a man loves a women. You know all the songs about the love of Leila and Madjnoun, or Hafis' Ghasels of Love. All his life Hafis was singing about love. But some wise men say: "never in all his life has Hafis slept with a woman". And Madjnoun was just a crank. Believe me: the man must look after the woman, but it is for her to love him. That is God's will.' I was silent, and my father did not say another word either. Maybe he was right! Love is not the most important thing in the world for a man. It was just that I had not yet reached his high pinnacle of wisdom. Suddenly my father laughed and cried merrily: 'All right, tomorrow I'll go to Prince Kipiani and talk it over with him. Or do the young people of today propose on their own?'

'I'll talk to the Kipianis myself,' I said quickly.

We mounted our horses again and rode into Bailov. Soon we saw the oil derricks of Bibi-Eibat. The black scaffolding looked like an evil dark wood. The smell of oil filled the air. Workers, oil dripping from their hands stood near the drill holes, where the wide stream of oil gushed over the greasy earth. As we were passing Bailov prison we suddenly heard shots. 'Is that an execution?' I asked. No, this time it was not an execution. The shots came from the barracks of Bailov garrison. They were practising the art of warfare there. 'Do you want to see your friends?' asked my father. I nodded. We rode into the big parade ground, where Iljas Beg and Mehmed Haidar were exercising their companies. Sweat was running down their faces.

'Right—Left—Right—Left!'

Mehmed Haidar's face was very serious. Iljas Beg seemed to be a delicate puppet, directed by a mind other than his own. They came to us and saluted. 'How do you like the army?' I asked. Iljas Beg was silent. Mehmed Haidar looked black. 'Better than school, anyway,' he grunted.

'We're getting a new Commander. Count Melikov from Shusha!' said Iljas Beg.

'Melikov? I know him. Isn't he the one with the red-golden horse?'

'That's the one. The whole garrison is already full of tales about this horse.'

We were silent. Thick dust lay on the parade ground. Iljas Beg looked dreamily at the gate, jealousy and longing in his eyes. My father clapped a hand on his shoulder: 'Don't be jealous of Ali Khan's liberty. He is just about to give it away.' Iljas Beg laughed, embarrassed:

'Yes, but he's giving it to Nino.'

Mehmed Haidar raised his head inquisitively. 'Huhu,' he said, 'and about time too.'

He was a husband of long standing, his wife wore the veil. Neither Iljas Beg nor I knew as much as her name. He looked at me patronisingly, his low brow furrowed, and said: 'Now you'll see what life is really about.' That, coming from him, sounded very silly. What could Mehmed Haidar and his veiled wife possibly know of life? I shook hands with both my friends and we left.

When I came home I lay down on the divan. An Asiatic room is always cool. During the night coolness fills it like water running into a well. And during the day one comes into it out of the heat as if into a cool bath. Suddenly the telephone rang. Nino's voice complained: 'Ali Khan, I'm dying of heat and mathematics. Come and help me!'

Ten minutes later Nino stretches out her slender arms to me. Her delicate fingers are inkstained, and I kiss these stains. 'Nino, I have talked to my father. He agrees.' Nino trembles and laughs. Shyly she looks round the room and blushes. She stands quite close to me, and I looked into her widened pupils. She whispers: 'Ali Khan, I'm afraid, I'm so afraid.'

'Of the exam, Nino?'

'No.' She turns away and looks at the sea. Then she pushes her hand through her hair and says: 'Ali Khan, a train goes from the town X to the town Y, doing 50 miles an hour . . .' My sweet! I bend over her schoolbooks.

13

Thick fog rolled in from the sea, filling the town. On the street corners lanterns smoked darkly. I was running along the Esplanade, faces appearing before me and disappearing, indifferent or frightened. I stumbled over a wooden plank, thrown across the road, and fell against the squatting form of an ambal, a worker from the port. His eyes had a veiled look, gazing into the far distance. His thick mouth was moving, he was chewing hashish, having wild visions. I thumped my fist on his back and ran on. The windows of the little houses near the port winked at me. I stepped into some glass that was lying about, heard it breaking and saw a Persian face, distorted with terror. A stomach suddenly appeared before me. This vision of human obesity made me raving mad; I pushed my head into it with all my might. It was soft and fat. A voice said good naturedly: 'Good evening, Ali Khan.' I raised my head and saw Nachararyan looking down on me, a smile on his face. 'Damnation!' I cried, and was about to run on, but he got hold of me:

'You're upset, my friend. You'd better stay with me.' His voice sounded friendly. Suddenly I was very tired. I just stood there, exhausted and dripping with sweat. 'Let's go to Filli-pojanz,' he said. I nodded. It was all one to me. He took my hand and led me along Barjatinsky Street to the big coffee house. When we sank into the deep chairs he said understandingly: 'Amok, Caucasian amok. It's probably this oppressive heat. Or is there any special reason, Ali Khan, that makes you rush about raging like that?' I sat in the coffee house in the room with soft chairs and walls covered with red silk, sipped hot tea and told Nachararyan the whole story: how I had telephoned the old Kipianis, asking to be received today, how Nino had tiptoed out of the house, stealthily and afraid, how I had kissed the Princess's hand and shaken hands with the Prince, how I had spoken of our ancient family tree, and of my family's revenues, how I had asked for the Princess Nino's hand in marriage, and all that in such perfect Russian, that even the Czar might have envied me.

'And then, my friend?' Nachararyan seemed very interested indeed.

'And then? Just listen to this!' I copied the Prince's move-movements and his voice with its slight Georgian accent: 'My dear son, esteemed Khan. Please believe me, I could not imagine a better husband for my child. What happiness for a woman to be chosen by a man of your character. But there is Nino's age. After all, she is still a schoolgirl. What does a child like that know of love? Surely we are not going to have the Indian child marriage system here. And then: the differences in religion, upbringing, descent. I say this for your own sake as well as for hers. I'm sure your father thinks the same. And then: these times, this terrible war. God knows what will become of us all. I don't want to stand in her way. But let's just leave it like that for the moment, let's leave it till the end of the war. You'll both be older then. And if you then feel as strongly about it as you do today, we can have another talk.'

'And what will you do now, Khan?' asked Nachararyan.

'Kidnap Nino and take her to Persia. I can't take this lying down! To say No to a Shirvanshir! Who does he think he is? I feel dishonoured, Nachararyan. The House of Shirvanshir is older than the Kipianis. Under Aga Mohammed Shah we destroyed the whole of Georgia. Then any Kipiani would have been only too pleased to give his daughter to a Shirvanshir. What does he mean, difference in religion? Is Christianity better than Islam? And my honour? My own father will laugh at me. A Christian refuses me his daughter. We Mohammedans are wolves who have lost their teeth. A hundred years ago . . .' My fury choked me and stopped my outburst. Just as well—already I had said much that would better be left unsaid. Nachararyan was a Christian too. He had every right to feel insulted. But he was not:

'I understand your rage. But he has not refused you. Of course it is ridiculous to wait for the end of the war. He just cannot realise that his daughter has grown up. I'm not against kidnapping her. It is an old, well established way of settling things, quite in the tradition of our country. But surely it is a last resort. Somebody should explain to the Prince the cultural and political significance of this marriage, I'm sure he'd come round then.'

'But who would do that?'

Nachararyan clapped his broad palm on his breast and cried: 'I will. Depend on me, Khan!'

I looked at him, astonished. What did this Armenian have in mind? It was the second time he had interfered in my life. Maybe he was trying to make friends among the Mohammedans, seeing that the Turks were advancing. Or maybe he really planned to form an Alliance of the Caucasian People. I did not care. Obviously he was an ally. I gave him my hand. He kept it in his: 'Just leave it to me. I'll keep you informed. And no kidnapping. Only as a last resort.'

I got up. I had a strong feeling that I could trust this fat man. I embraced him and left the coffee house. When I came out into the street someone followed me. I turned and saw Suleiman Aga, an old friend of my father's. He had been sitting inside. His hand was heavy on my shoulder: 'For shame, a Shirvanshir embraces an Armenian.' I gasped. But already he had disappeared into the fog. I walked on. What a good thing it was, I thought, that I had not told my father why I went to the Kipianis today. I will just say that I have not spoken to them yet. When I put the key into the keyhole of our door I shook my head thoughtfully: 'Isn't it stupid—this hatred for the Armenians.'

All through the next few weeks my life revolved round the black box of the telephone. This ill-formed thing with the big crooked handle had suddenly become an instrument of overwhelming significance. I sat at home day after day and growled something incomprehensible when my father asked me why I was hesitating to put my proposal. From time to time the black ogre gave the alarm, I raised the earpiece, and Nino reported the dispatches from the battlefield: 'Is that you, Ali? Listen: Nachararyan is sitting with Mama, talking about the poems of her grandfather, the poet Iliko Tshavtshavadse.' And a bit later: 'Ali, can you hear me? Nachararyan says that Rustaveli and Tamar's epoch have been strongly influenced by Persian culture.' And later again:

'Ali Khan! Nachararyan is having tea with Papa. He just said: "The magic of this town lies in the mystical bond between its races and peoples".' Half an hour later: 'He oozes wisdom like a crocodile oozing tears. He says: "The race of a peaceful Caucasus is forged on the anvil of Baku".' I laughed and put the earpiece down.

And so, it went on, day after day. Nachararyan was eating and drinking and sitting with the Kipianis. He went on excursions with them, and gave them advice, some of it practical, some mythical. I followed this show of Armenian cunning with amazement: 'Nachararyan says the moon was the first money. Gold coins and their power over people are the result of the ancient moon cult of the Caucasians and the Iranians. Ali Khan, I can't stand this nonsense any more. Come to the garden.'

We met at the old fortress wall. Quickly and hastily she told me how her mother had entreated her not to trust her life to a wild Muslim. How her father, half jokingly, had warned her that I would certainly put her into the harem, how she, little Nino, had laughed, but at the same time warned her parents: 'You just wait—he might kidnap me. What will you do then?' I caressed her hair. I knew my Nino. She gets what she wants, even if she does not really know what it is. 'This war could go on for another twenty years,' she complained. 'Isn't it terrible that they want us to wait such a long time?'

'Do you love me so much Nino?'

Her lips trembled. 'We just belong together. My parents make it so difficult for me. But I'd have to be old and weather-beaten like this stone to give way. And moreover: I really do love you. But woe to you if you kidnap me.' Then she was silent, for you cannot kiss and talk at the same time. Then she crept home stealthily, and the telephone game began again: 'Ali Khan, Nachararyan says his cousin in Tiflis has written that the Governor is all for mixed marriages. He calls it the physical penetration of the Orient with Western Culture. Can you understand that?' No, I could not. I just hung about the house, saying as little as possible. My cousin Aishe, who was in the same form as Nino, came to tell me that Nino had been given the lowest marks five times in three days, and that everybody was saying it was all my fault. I should think more of Nino's homework than of her future. I was ashamed and played Nardy with my cousin. She won and promised to help Nino at school. Again the telephone rang: 'Is that you? They have been talking for hours of politics and business. Nachararyan says he envies the Mohammedans because they are free to invest money in Persian estates. Who knows what will become of Russia? Maybe everything will be smashed to pieces. Only Mohammedans can buy land in Persia. He knows for certain that already half of Giljan belongs to the Shirvanshir family. Surely the best insurance against any upheaval in Russia is to have estates in other countries. My parents are terribly impressed. Mother says there are some Mohammedans who have civilised souls.'

Another two days, and the Armenian battle of wits was won.

Nino was laughing and crying over the telephone. 'We have the parents' blessing, Amen.'

'But now your father must call me. He has insulted me.'

'Just leave it to me.'

And that's how it was. The Prince's voice was soft and mild: 'I have looked into my child's heart. Her feeling for you is genuine and holy. It would be a sin to stand in her way. Come, Ali Khan.'

I went. The Princess cried and kissed me. The Prince talked solemnly about marriage, but quite differently from the way my father had talked, who never thought that marriage consisted of mutual trust and respect. Man and wife should help each other by word and deed. And they must never forget that they have equal rights and that their souls are their own. I gave my solemn word not to make Nino wear the veil, and not to keep a harem. Nino came in, and I kissed her brow. She tucked her head between her shoulders, and looked like a little bird in need of protection. 'But this is not to be made public,' said the Prince. 'First Nino must finish school. Work hard, my child. If you don't pass you will have to wait another year.' Nino raised her brows, that looked as if drawn by a stroke of the pen:

'Don't worry, father. I will pass, at school and in marriage. Ali Khan will help me in both.'

Nachararyan was waiting for me, sitting in his car, when I came out of the house. His protruding eyes winked at me. 'Nachararyan,' I cried, 'shall I give you a stud or a village in Daghestan, do you want a Persian medal, or an orange grove in Enseli?' He thumped me on the back.

'Neither—nor,' he said. 'I'm happy to have changed fate. That's enough for me.'

I looked at him gratefully. We drove out of town, to the Bay of Bibi-Eibat, where black machines tortured the oil-drenched earth. The House of Nobel interfered with the eternal forms of the landscape just as Nachararyan had interfered with my fate. An immense part of the sea had been forced away from the shore. Now the new-won land was not part of the sea anymore, and not yet part of the shore. But already someone with a good head for business had built a little teahouse on the newly won ground, as far out as possible, and there we sat and drank Kyachta tea, the best tea in the world, heavy as alcohol. Drunk with the fragrant potion Nachararyan talked for a long time about the Turks, who would invade Karabagh, and of the massacres of the Armenians in Asia Minor. I hardly listened.

'Don't be afraid,' I said, 'if the Turks come to Baku I'll hide you in my house.'

'I'm not afraid,' said Nachararyan.

The stars were shining high above the sea, behind the Island of Nargin. Peaceful silence sank on the shore. 'Sea and shore are like Man and Woman, united in eternal battle.' Did I say that or did he? I did not know. He took me home. I told my father: 'Kipiani sends his thanks for the honour the House of Shirvanshir has bestowed upon his family. Nino is my fiancée. Go tomorrow and arrange the rest.' I was very tired and very happy.

14

Days turned into weeks, into months. Much had happened in the world, in the country and in my home. The nights had become long, yellow leaves lay dead and sorrowful in the Governor's garden. The horizon was dark with autumn rain. Thin ice floated on the sea, and was pulverised against the rocky shores. One morning the streets were covered with snow, white and thin as a veil, and for one short moment winter reigned. Then the nights became shorter again.

Camels came into town from the desert, with long sad steps, carrying sand in their yellow hair, looking far into the distance, with eyes that had seen eternity. They were carrying guns on their humps, the barrels hanging down their sides, crates with ammunition and guns: loot from the big battles. Turkish prisoners of war in their grey uniforms were marched through the town, tattered and bruised. When they came to the sea, little steamboats took them to the Island of Nargin, where they died of diarrhoea, hunger or homesickness. If they escaped they died in Persia's salt deserts, or in the leaden waters of the Caspian Sea. The war, that had begun so far away, had suddenly come close to us. Trains arrived from the north, packed with soldiers. Trains full of wounded arrived from the west. The Czar dismissed his uncle and was now himself leading his ten-million-strong army. The uncle now reigned over Caucasia, and his immense dark shadow lay heavy on our country. Grand Duke Nikolai Nikolayevitch! His long bony hand reached down even into the heart of Anatolia. His armies attacked wildly, driven by his rage against the Czar, that devoured his heart. Over snowy mountains and across sandy deserts thundered the wrath of the Grand Duke, towards Trapezunt, towards Stamboul. 'The Long Nikolai' people called him, and spoke fearfully of the wild frenzy in his soul, of his raging warriors' fury. Innumerable countries joined in the war. It was one long front line, from Afghanistan to the North Sea, and the names of the allied monarchs, states and generals covered the pages of the newspapers like poisonous flies sitting on the corpses of dead heroes.

And again it was summer. Scorching heat was pressing down, the asphalt on the streets was melting under our footsteps. In East and West victories were celebrated. I sat about in tea houses, coffee houses, friends' houses and at home. Many reproved me because of my friendship with the Armenian Nachararyan. Iljas Beg's regiment was still billeted in town, practising the rules of warfare on the dusty parade ground. The opera, the theatre and the cinemas were playing, as before the war. Much had happened, but nothing had changed in the world, in town and in my home.

When Nino came to me, sighing under the burden of wisdom, my hand touched her smooth skin. Her eyes were deep, filled with a curious fear. My cousin Aishe told me that the teachers, with silent forbearance, put one 'passed' after another into the book of records for the future Madame Shirvanshir. When Nino and I walked along the street the eyes of her school friends followed us as long as they could see us. We went to the City Club, the theatre, to balls, but we were hardly ever alone. Our friends surrounded us like a steep wall of apprehensive kindness. Iljas Beg, Mehmed Haidar, even pious Seyd Mustafa accompanied us. They did not always agree amongst themselves. When Nachararyan, fat and rich, sat sipping his champagne, talking of mutual love between the peoples of the Caucasus Mehmed Haidar's face became dark, and he said: 'I believe, Mr. Nachararyan, that you need not worry about that. After the war there'll be only very few Armenians left anyway.'

'But Nachararyan will be one of the ones left!' cried Nino. Nachararyan was silent, and just sipped his champagne. It was rumoured that he was transferring all his money to Sweden. I did not care one way or the other. When I asked Mehmed Haidar to be a little more friendly to Nachararyan he drew his brows together: 'I can't stand Armenians, God knows why.'

Then one day Nino stood in the Examination Hall of the Lyceum of the Holy Queen Tamar, proving her maturity by mathematical equations, classical references, historical data, and in desperate cases by imploring looks from her big Georgian eyes. And it worked—she passed.

When I took my radiant Nino home after the ball the girls of the Lyceum gave to celebrate their successes, old Kipiani said: 'Now you are engaged. Pack your trunks, Ali Khan. We are going to Tiflis. I must introduce you to the family.' So we went to Tiflis, the capital of Georgia.

*   *   *

Tiflis was like a jungle, and each tree had its own name, and was an uncle, a cousin or an aunt. It was not at all easy to know one's way about. Names that sounded like ancient steel came whirling through the air: Orbeliani, Tshavtshavadse, Zereteli, Amilachvari, Abadshidse. There was a party in the Didube Gardens, in the outskirts of the town, given by the House of Orbeliani, in honour of the new cousin. Georgian musicians played the 'Mravalyaver', the Kachetian Song of War, and the wild Chevsourian 'Lelo'. Abashidse, a cousin from Kutai, sang the 'Mgali Delia', the Storm Song of the Imereti Mountains. An uncle danced the 'Dawlour', and an old, white-bearded man jumped on the carpet that covered the green lawn and froze in the pose of 'Bouknah'. The party went on all night. When the sun rose languidly behind the hills the musicians began the hymn 'Arise, Queen Tamar, Georgia is weeping for you'. I was sitting quietly at the table, Nino beside me. Suddenly daggers and swords sparkled. This was the Georgian Dance of Knives, performed at dawn by a crowd of cousins, and it seemed a play, enacted on the stage, unreal and far away.

I was listening to my neighbours' conversations: They sounded like echoes coming from long lost centuries: 'Under Saakadse a Zereteli defended Tiflis from Ghengis Khan.' 'You know of course that we Tshavtshavadses are older than the Bagrations, the House of Kings.' 'The first Orbeliani? He came from China, three thousand years ago. He was one of the Emperor's sons. Some of the Orbelianis have slit eyes even today.' I looked shyly around. What price the few Shirvanshirs who had gone to Eternity before me, against all this? But Nino was on my side: 'Never mind, Ali Khan. Of course my cousins' family tree is very ancient and noble, but where were their ancestors when yours conquered Tiflis?' I did not say anything but looked at her thankfully. Even now, in the middle of her own kinsmen, Nino felt herself the wife of a Shirvanshir. I was very proud.

An old woman bent towards me and said: 'This wine is pure, for God is in it. Any other form of intoxication comes from the devil. There are not many who know this. Drink, Ali Khan!' The red Kachetian wine was like fluid fire. I hesitated, but in the end raised my glass in honour of the House of Orbeliani.

The sun was shining when we drove back to town. I wanted to go straight to my hotel, but a cousin—or was it an uncle?—held me back. 'Last night you were the guest of the House of Orbeliani, today you are mine. We will have breakfast in Purgvino, and our friends will come to lunch.' I was the prisoner of Georgian nobility. So it went on for a whole week. Alsanian and Kachetian wine, roast mutton and Motali cheese—again and again. The cousins took turns like soldiers on the front of Georgian hospitality. Only we two remained: Nino and I. I was full of admiration for Nino's staying power. At the end of the week she was still as fresh as dew in spring, her eyes smiled, her lips never grew tired of talking to cousins and aunts. Only a hardly perceptible hoarseness in her voice showed that for days on end she had danced, drunk wine, but hardly ever slept.

On the morning of the eighth day the cousins Sandro, Dodiko, Vamech and Soso came to my room. I dived under the cover like a frightened rabbit. 'Ali Khan,' they said mercilessly, 'today you are the guest of the Dshakelis. We're going to their estates in Kadshory.'

'Today I am nobody's guest,' I said darkly, 'today the gates of Paradise will open for me, the poor martyr. The Archangel Michael with his sword of flame will let me pass, for I died on the Path of Righteousness.'

The cousins looked at each other and laughed loud and unfeelingly. Then they said just one word: 'Sulphur.'

'Sulphur?' I repeated, 'Sulphur? That's in Hell. But me— I'm going to Paradise.'

'No,' said the cousins, 'Sulphur it is.'

I tried to raise myself up in bed. My head was very heavy, and my limbs seemed just to dangle, as if they were not part of me at all. I looked into the mirror and saw a pale, greenish-yellow face with lustreless eyes. 'Oh yes,' I said, 'fluid fire indeed,' and thought of the Kachetian wine. 'Serves me right. A Muslim should not drink.' I crept out of bed, moaning like an old man. And there were these cousins, with Nino's eyes and her slender pliant figure, fresh and upright. Georgians seem to me like noble deer, strayed amongst the jungle mixtures of the Asiatics. No other Eastern race has this charm, these graceful movements, this fantastic lust for life and healthy enjoyment of leisure. 'We'll tell Nino,' said Vamech. 'We'll be in Kadshory in about four hours time, when you're all right again.' He went out, and I heard his voice on the telephone:

'Ali Khan is not feeling too well, quite suddenly. Now we'll take him to the sulphur springs. Ask Princess Nino to start for Kadshory with her family, we'll come a bit later. No, nothing serious. Just not feeling very well.'

Lazily I dressed. I felt dizzy. All this Georgian hospitality was so completely different from the quiet, dignified receptions at my uncle's house in Teheran. There we drank strong tea and talked of sages and poetry. Here they drank wine, danced, laughed and sang, were pliant and hard like a steel spring. Was this the gate to Europe? No, of course not. This was part of us, and yet so very different from the rest of us. A gate, but leading where? Perhaps to the last stage of wisdom, that gradually becomes unheeding playfulness. I did not know. I was just terribly tired. I hardly managed to get down the stairs. We got into the carriage. 'To the bath,' shouted Sandro. The coachman cracked his whip. We drove to a big building, covered by a cupola, in the quarter called the Maidan. A gaunt man stood in the doorway, half naked, looking more like a skeleton than a living person. His eyes gazed straight through us, into Nirvana. 'Hamardshoba, Mekisse!' cried Sandro. The man jerked into consciousness. He bowed low and said: 'Hamardshoba, Tawadi. Good day, my Princes.' Then he opened the door. The big warm hall was filled with benches, one or two naked bodies on each of them. We took our clothes off, and went along the corridor into the second room. There were square holes in the floor, filled with steaming hot sulphur water. As in a dream I heard Sandro's voice: 'Once upon a time a King went hunting, and his falcon followed a mountain-cock. The King waited a long time, but neither mountain-cock nor falcon returned. When he went searching for them he came to a rivulet of sulphur-coloured waters. In it both falcon and mountain-cock had drowned. Thus the King discovered the sulphur spring, and laid the foundation stone to the town of Tiflis. So here we are in the mountain-cock's bath, and the Maidan outside is the grove through which the rivulet ran. With sulphur Tiflis began, and in sulphur it will end.' Steam and the smell of sulphur filled the domed room.

Getting into the hot bath was like stepping into a brew made of rotten eggs. The cousins' bodies were wet and glistening. I rubbed a hand on my breast, and the sulphur soaked into my skin. I thought of all the warriors and victors who had conquered this town and immersed themselves in this spring: Chwaresmir Dshellalleddin, Timur the Lame, Dshagatai, the son of Ghengis Khan. They had been drunk and heavy with the blood they had shed. Then they had stepped into the sulphur spring to become light and agile again.

'Enough, Ali Khan, get out.' The cousin's voice finished my dreams of bathing warriors. I crept out of my hole, went into the adjoining room and fell listless on the stone bench. 'Mekisse!' Sandro cried.

The man who had met us, who turned out to be the masseur, came in, wearing only his turban. I was made to lie on my stomach. With his naked feet he jumped on my back, and trampled on me, light as a dancer on a carpet. Then his fingers tore into my flesh as if they were sharp hooks. He disjointed my arms, and I heard my bones crack. My cousins were standing around, giving advice: 'Turn his arms out once more, Mekisse, he's very ill.'

'Jump on his back once more, like this, and now pinch his left side.'

I suppose it should have hurt very much, but I did not feel any pain. I was just lying there, covered with white soapy foam, relaxed under Mekisse's hard elastic blows, and the only thing I felt was that all my muscles were becoming wonderfully loose and relaxed.

'Enough,' said Mekisse, and again fell into the stance of a prophet out of this world. I got up. My whole body ached. I ran into the next room and dived into the icy cold sulphur flood of the second bath. For a moment my breath stopped. But my limbs became elastic once more, filled with new life.

I came back, swathed in a white sheet. The cousins and Mekisse looked at me expectantly. 'Hunger,' I said with great dignity, and sat down crosslegged on one of the benches.

'He's all right!' roared the cousins, 'get a watermelon, cheese, vegetables, wine—quick!'

We lay down in the anteroom and had a banquet. I forgot that I had ever been weak or tired. The taste of sulphur was chased away by the red fragrant flesh of the ice-cold watermelon. The cousins sipped their white Napareuli wine. 'Well, there you are,' said Dodiko, but did not finish his sentence, for this really meant everything: his pride of the native sulphur bath, pity for the foreigner, who broke down under Georgian hospitality, and the friendly cousinly assurance that he, Dodiko understood and excused his Mohammedan cousin's weakness. Our circle expanded. Neighbours came, naked, carrying wine bottles. Princes, and their creditors, hangers-on, servants, sages, poets, and estate owners from the mountains sat peacefully together, a gay picture of Georgian equality. It was not a bath any more, it was a club, a coffee house or just a meeting of happy naked people, their eyes carefree and laughing. But here and there I heard serious words, filled with dark foreboding. 'The Osman is coming,' said a man with small eyes. 'The Grand Duke will take Stamboul. I have heard that a German general has built a cannon there. When that goes off it will hit exactly the Zion's Dome in Tiflis.'

'You are wrong, Prince,' said a man with a face like a pumpkin. 'This cannon has not been built yet, only the plans exist. But even when it is finished, it cannot hit Tiflis. All the maps the Germans have are wrong. Russians have drawn them, even before the war. You understand? Russian maps— how can they possibly be correct?' In the corner somebody sighed. I turned and saw a white beard and a long hooked nose.

'Poor Georgia,' sighed the beard. 'We are between the two claws of a pair of red-hot tongs. If the Germans win—it's the end of the land of Tamar. If the Russians win—what then? The pale Czar has all he wants, but the fingers of the Grand Duke are gripping our throat. Even now our sons are dying in battles, the best of the best. What is left will be strangled, either by the Osman, the Grand Duke or any other enemy, it could even be a machine, or an American. It seems impossible to understand—our flame of war, and how it suddenly turned to ashes. This is the end of the Land of Tamar. Just look: our warriors are small and thin, the harvest is poor, the wine is sour.' The bearded one fell silent, wheezing softly. No one said a word. Suddenly an anxious subdued voice:

'They have killed the noble Bagration. He married one of the Czar's nieces, and the Russians never forgave him for that. The Czar himself ordered him to join the Erivan Regiment, out in the front lines. Bagration fought like a lion, and fell, pierced by eighteen bullets.'

The cousins sat, quietly sipping their wine. I stared at the floor. Bagration, I thought, the oldest noble family in Christendom. The bearded one is right. Georgia is being squeezed to death between the two claws of a red-hot pair of tongs. Another voice spoke up: 'He left a son, Teymouras Bagration, the true King. Someone is keeping him safe.'

Silence again. Mekisse's skeletal form was still standing near the door, in the same pose of a dedicated prophet. Then Dodiko broke the spell. He stretched himself and yawned happily: 'It is beautiful,' he said, 'this our country. The sulphur and the town, the war and Kachetian wine. Look at the Alasan flowing across the plain! It is wonderful to be a Georgian, even if Georgia perishes. You sound hopeless. But has it ever been otherwise in the Land of Tamar? And yet our rivers run, our vine grows, our people dance. It is a fair country, this our Georgia. And so it will remain, for all its hopelessness.' He stood up, young and slender, his eyes dancing, his skin like velvet, the descendant of singers and heroes. The bearded one in the corner smiled delightedly: 'By God, as long as we have young people like that . . .'

Vamech leaned across to me: 'Ali Khan, don't forget—
today you are the guest of the Dshakelis in Kadshory.' We
rose, dressed, and went out. The coachman cracked his whip,
and Vamech said: 'The Dshakelis are descendants of the
ancient noble family of . . .' Of course! I laughed, gay and
happy again.

15

Nino and I were sitting in the Café Mephisto in Golovinsky Street, looking out at Mount David with its big monastery. The cousins had allowed us one day of rest. I knew what Nino was thinking. Up there, on Mount David, was the grave we had visited. There lies Alexander Griboyedov, poet and Minister of the Czar. The inscription on his gravestone reads:

Your works will never be forgotten, but why must your Nino's love survive you?

Her name was Nino Tshavtshavadse, and she was sixteen years old when the Minister and poet took her for his wife. Nino Tshavtshavadse—the great aunt of Nino who was sitting next to me. She was seventeen years old when the Teheran mob surrounded the Russian Minister's house. 'Ya Ali Salavat, o Ali be praised!' the shout went up. The Minister had only his short sword and a pistol. A smith from Sülly-Sultan Street raised his hammer and crushed the Minister's breast. Days later flesh torn from a human body was still found in the streets—and a head dogs had savaged. That was all that was left of Alexander Griboyedov, poet and Minister of the Czar. Feth Ali Shah, the Kadjar, was satisfied, and Abbas Mirza, the Crown Prince, was very happy. Meshi Aga, a fanatical wise old man, who amongst others had instigated the outbreak, received a big reward, and a Shirvanshir, my great uncle, was given an estate in Giljan.

All that was a hundred years ago. And there we were, sitting on the terrace of the Café Mephisto: I, a Shirvanshir, and she, Nino, Griboyedov's great-niece. 'We ought to be blood enemies, Nino,' I nodded towards the mountain. 'Will you put up a gravestone for me as beautiful as the one up there?'

'Perhaps,' said Nino, 'it depends on how you behave during your life.' She finished her coffee. 'Come on,' she said, 'let's go for a walk.'

I rose. Nino loved this town as a child loves its mother. We walked up Golovinsky Street to the alleys of the Old Town. Nino stopped in front of the ancient Zion's Dome. We went into the dark damp room. High upon the altar stood a cross, made from the vine St. Nino had brought when she came from the West to announce to the Georgians the Saviour of the World had arrived. Nino knelt down, crossed herself and looked up to the picture of her guardian saint. She whispered: 'Holy Nino, forgive me.' By the light shining through the church windows I saw tears in her eyes.

'Come out,' I said. Obediently she rose and followed me. Silently we walked down the street. At last I said: 'What did you ask the Holy Nino to forgive you?'

'You, Ali Khan.'

She sounded sad and tired. Walking through the streets of Tiflis with Nino was a bad thing to do.

'Why me?' We had arrived at the Maidan. Georgians were sitting in the coffee houses, or in the middle of the street. Someone somewhere was playing the zurna, and far below the river Kura was rushing in its narrow bed. Nino's eyes had a faraway look, as if she was searching for her identity.

'You,' she repeated, 'and all that has been.'

I began to understand, but still I asked: 'What?' Nino

stopped. Over there, on the other side of the square rose the Cathedral Kashveti, built of stones as white and soft and tender as a virgin. Nino said:

'Walk through Tiflis. Do you see women wearing the veil? No. Do you feel the air of Asia? No. It is a different world from yours. The streets are broad, the souls are straight. I feel very wise when I'm in Tiflis, Ali Khan. No bigoted fools like Seyd Mustafa are here, and no grim scowlers, like Mehmed Haidar. Life is easy and gay here.'

'But this country is held between the two claws of a hot pair of tongs, Nino.'

'That's just why,' she was stepping lightly over the cobbled stones again, 'that's just it. Seven times Timur the Lame destroyed Tiflis. Turks, Persians, Arabs and Mongols have overrun the country. We stayed. They laid waste in Georgia, raped it, murdered it, but never really possessed it. St. Nino came from the West, carrying her vine, and it is to the West we belong. We are no Asiatics. We are the furthest eastern country of Europe. Surely you can feel that yourself?' She walked on quickly, her childish brow furrowed. 'Just because we have defied Timur, and Ghengis, Shah Abbas, Shah Tahmasp and Shah Ismail, just because of that it is that I exist, I, your Nino. And now you come along, without a sword, without trampling elephants, without warriors, and yet you are the heir of the blood-covered Shahs. My daughters will wear the veil, and when Iran's sword is sharpened again my sons and grandsons will destroy Tiflis for the hundredth time. Oh Ali Khan, we should belong to the world of the West.'

I took her hand. 'What do you want me to do, Nino?'

'Oh,' she said, 'I'm very stupid, Ali Khan. I want you to love wide streets and green woods, I want you to understand more about love, and not to cling to the crumbling wall of an Asiatic town. I am so afraid that in ten years' time you will be pious and sly, sitting there in Giljan, and that one morning you will wake up and say: "Nino, you are only an acre." Tell me: what do you love me for?'

Tiflis was making Nino all confused, she seemed intoxicated by the damp air around the Kura river.

'What do I love you for, Nino? For all of you, your voice, your fragrance, the way you walk. What more do you want? It's just you I love. Surely love is the same in Georgia as in Iran. Here, on this spot, a thousand years ago, your Rustaveli was singing of his love to Queen Tamar. And the songs of this greatest of poets are exactly like Persian rubaiyats. Georgia is nothing without Rustaveli, and Rustaveli is nothing without Persia.'

'Here, on this spot,' said Nino thoughtfully. 'But maybe Sayat Nova stood here as well, the great poet who sang of Georgian love, and whom the Shah had beheaded for it.'

There was not much I could say to my Nino today. She was saying good-bye to her homeland, feeling and showing her love for it more deeply than ever. She sighed: 'You love my eyes, my nose, my hair—all that, Ali Khan. But haven't you forgotten something: do you love my soul?'

'Yes, I love your soul too,' I said tiredly.

It was strange: when Seyd Mustafa said women have no soul I laughed. But when Nino wanted me to discover her soul I felt annoyed. What kind of thing is that, a woman's soul? She should be content that the man does not want to understand the bottomless well of her soul. 'And what do you love me for, Nino?'

Suddenly she started to cry, there, in the middle of the street. Big tears were rolling down her cheeks, making her look like a little girl: 'Forgive me, Ali Khan. I love you, just simply you, as you are. But I'm afraid of your world. I'm mad, Ali Khan. Here I am, standing on the street with you, my betrothed, behaving as if all Ghengis Khan's wars were your fault. Forgive your Nino. It is stupid of me to make you responsible for every Mohammedan who ever killed a Georgian. I'll never do it again. But you see: I, your Nino, I too am a tiny piece of this Europe that you hate, and here in Tiflis I feel it more than ever. I love you, and you love me. But I love woods and meadows, and you love hills and stones and sand. And that's why I am afraid of you, of your love and your world.'

'Well?' I asked, bewildered. I could not understand what she was trying to say.

'Well?' she dried her eyes, smiling again, turning her head to the side. 'Well? In three months time we'll be married, what more do you want?' Nino can laugh and cry, love and hate, all in one breath. She forgave me all Ghengis Khan's campaigns, and she loved me again. Taking my hand she dragged me across the Veri-Bridge to the labyrinth of the bazaar. It was a symbolic plea for forgiveness. The bazaar is the only oriental spot on the European robe of Tiflis. Fat carpet sellers, Armenians and Persians, display here the many-coloured splendour of Iran's treasures. Brass plates, wise inscriptions etched on their yellow surfaces, shone in the semi-darkness. A Kurdish girl, with light grey eyes was telling fortunes, and seemed astonished at her own knowledge. At every door leading to a wine house or a café little clusters of Tiflis' numerous idlers and loafers congregated, earnestly discussing anything and everything under the sun. This town with its eighty different peoples, each with their own language, has its own pungent smell, and we breathed it in the narrow lanes. Nino's sadness disappeared in the bazaar's many-coloured pell-mell. Armenian peddlers, Kurdish fortune-tellers, Persian cooks, Ossetian priests, Russians, Arabs, Ingushs, Indians: all the peoples of Asia meet in the bazaar of Tiflis. There is an uproar in one of the booths. The merchants are standing in a circle: an Assyrian is quarrelling with a Jew. We just hear: 'When my ancestors were taking your ancestors as prisoners to Babylon . . .' The crowd is hooting with laughter. And Nino laughs too—at the Jew, at the Assyrian, at the bazaar, at the tears she had shed. We walk on. Just a few more steps, and we have completed the circle. Again we stand in front of the Café Mephisto in Golovinsky Street. 'Shall we go in again?' I ask, but I do not really know what I want to do.

'No. Let's go up to the Monastery of St. David, to celebrate

118

our reconciliation.' We turned into the side streets, that led to the funicular railway. The little red car started to crawl slowly up the Mountain of David. The town sank away, and Nino told me the story of how the famous monastery was founded: 'Many many years ago St. David lived on this mountain. And down there in the town lived a Princess who sinfully loved a Prince. She became pregnant, but the Prince left her, and when her furious father asked for the name of the seducer she was afraid to tell him, and accused St. David. Full of wrath the King ordered the holy man to be brought to his palace. He called for his daughter, and she repeated her accusation. But the saint touched her body with his wand, and a miracle occurred. The voice of the child in her body was heard, naming the real culprit. Then the holy man raised his hands in prayer, and the Princess gave birth to a stone. The stone is still here, and from it springs the Fountain of St. David. If a woman longs for a child she bathes in the holy fountain.' Thoughtfully she added: 'Isn't it a good thing that St. David is dead, and nobody knows where his wand is, Ali Khan?' We had arrived at the monastery.

'Do you want to go to the fountain, Nino?'

'No—I think I'd rather wait for another year.' We were standing at the wall that encircled the monastery and looked down on the town. The Kura valley was filled with a blue mist. From the sea of rooftops church cupolas loomed up like lonely islands. Eastwards and westwards lay long stretches of pleasure garden: the playgrounds of Tiflis' gay set. The dark castle of Mtech rose in the distance—once the seat of Georgian kings, now one of the Russian Empire's prisons for Caucasians who dared to think about politics. Nino turned away. It was difficult for her to combine her loyalty to the Czar with the view of the famous—or infamous—place of torture and death.

'Are any of your cousins there in Mtech, Nino?'

'No, but you should be. Come on, Ali Khan.'

'Where to?'

'Let's pay a visit to Griboyedov.' We turned a corner and

stopped at the weather-beaten gravestone. Nino picked up a pebble, pressed it quickly to the gravestone and let go. The stone fell and rolled away. Nino blushed deeply. An old Tiflis superstition says that if a girl presses a pebble to the damp stone and it sticks for a moment, she will marry that same year. Hers had fallen. I looked at her embarrassed face and laughed: 'See? Three months before our marriage! Isn't our prophet right when he says "Do not believe what dead stones say" ?'

'Yes,' said Nino.

We went back to the funicular railway. 'What will we do when the war is over?' asked Nino.

'When the war is over? The same things we are doing now. Go for walks in Baku, see friends, go to Karabagh and have children. It'll be wonderful.'

'I would like to see Europe.'

'Of course. We'll go to Paris, to Berlin, wherever you like, for a whole winter.'

'Yes, for one winter.'

'Nino, don't you like our country any more? We can live in Tiflis, if you like.'

'Thank you, Ali Khan. You are very good to me. We'll stay in Baku.'

'Nino, I think there's no place like Baku.'

'Oh? have you seen so many other towns?'

'No, I haven't. But if you like I'll go round the world with you.'

'And all the time you'd be homesick for the old wall and for soulful talks with Seyd Mustafa. But never mind. Stay as you are. I love you.'

'You are right, Nino, I do love our homeland, all our town, every stone, every grain of sand in the desert.'

'I know. How strange this is—this love for Baku. To the foreigners our town is just a hot, dusty, oil-smothered dull place.'

'That's because they're foreigners.'

She put her arm round my shoulder. Her lips touched my

cheek: 'But we are not foreigners, never. Will you always love me, Ali Khan?'

'Always, Nino.'

Our carriage was back at the station in town. Again we walked along Golovinsky Street, but this time with our arms around each other. On the left was a big park enclosed by beautifully wrought iron railings. At the closed gate two soldiers were on guard, motionless, as if made of stone, they did not even seem to breathe. Hovering majestically in its gilt splendour, the Imperial Eagle hung suspended over the barred gate. This was the residence of Grand Duke Nikolai Nikolayevitch, the Czar's Governor of Caucasia.

Nino stopped suddenly. 'Look,' she said, pointing towards the park. Along an avenue of pine trees a tall, gaunt grey-haired man walked slowly past us. Now he turned and I recognised the big, coldly mad eyes of the Grand Duke. His face was long, his lips pressed together. In the shade of the pines he looked like a large noble wild animal. 'I wonder what he's thinking of, Ali Khan?'

'Of the Czar's crown, Nino.'

'It would look good on his grey hair. What is he going to do?'

'They say he's going to overthrow the Czar.'

'Come away, Ali Khan, I'm afraid.'

We turned away from the beautiful wrought iron trellis. Nino said: 'You shouldn't speak so badly of the Czar and the Grand Duke. They defend us against the Turks.'

'They're one half of the hot claws that crunch your country.'

'My country? What about yours?'

'For us it's different. We are lying on the anvil and the Grand Duke holds the hammer. That's why we hate him.'

'And you love Enver Pasha. That's stupid, you'll never see Enver coming into our town. The Grand Duke will win.'

'*Allah Barif*, only God knows,' I said peacefully.

16

The Grand Duke's armies were in Trapezunt, they conquered Erzerum, they overran the Kurdish mountains on the way to Baghdad. The Grand Duke's armies were in Teheran, in Tabriz, even in Meshed, the Holy City. Half of Turkey and half of Persia were cowering under Nikolai Nikolayevitch's dark shadow. At a meeting of Georgian noblemen he declared: 'Obeying the Czar's orders I will not rest until the golden Byzantine Cross is shining with new splendour on the cupola of the Hagia Sophia.' The countries of the Half Moon were in a disastrous state. Only the Kotshis and Ambals, who lived in the little dark alleys still talked of the Osman's might and the victorious sword of Enver Pasha. Persia had ceased to exist, and soon Turkey would cease to exist. My father had become very silent, and was often out. Sometimes he was bending over despatches and maps, whispering the names of the lost towns, then sitting for hours without moving, holding the amber rosary in his hand. I made the rounds of jewellers, florists and bookshops, buying presents for Nino. When I saw her, the war, the Grand Duke and the threatened Half Moon disappeared from my thoughts for hours on end.

One day my father said: 'Stay in tonight, Ali Khan. Some people are coming, and we will discuss important things.' He sounded a bit embarrassed, looking away. I understood, and teased him:

'Did you not make me swear, father, never to have anything to do with politics?'

'Caring for one's people does not necessarily mean politics. There are times, Ali Khan, when it is one's duty to think of one's people.'

I had arranged to take Nino to the opera that night. Shaliapin was appearing that night as a guest artist, and Nino had been looking forward to this for days. I telephoned Iljas Beg. 'Iljas, I'm busy tonight. Can you take Nino to the opera? I've got the tickets.' A surly voice answered:

'What an idea. You know I can't please myself. I'm on night duty with Mehmed Haidar.' I phoned Seyd Mustafa.

'Sorry, but I really can't. I have an appointment with the famous Mullah Hadshi Machsud. He is here from Teheran just for a few days.' I rang Nachararyan. His voice sounded very embarrassed:

'And why don't you go, Ali Khan?'

'We have guests.'

'To make plans how to kill all Armenians? I really shouldn't go to the theatre in these times when my people are bleeding to death. But as it's you—and really Shaliapin is a wonderful singer.' At last. A friend in need is a friend indeed. I told Nino and stayed at home.

Our guests arrived at seven o'clock, and they were exactly the people I had expected to see. In our great hall, sitting on the red carpets and soft divans, were assembled one thousand million rubles, or rather the men who between them commanded over one thousand million rubles. There were not many of them, and I had known them all for years. Seinal Aga, Iljas Beg's father, was the first to arrive. His back was bent, his eyes had a veiled look. He lowered himself on to a divan, put his cane down, and thoughtfully started to eat a piece of Turkish delight. Then came two brothers: Ali Assadullah and Mirza Assadullah. Their father, the late Shamsi, had left them a dozen million rubles. The sons had inherited their father's intelligence, but had also learned to read and write.

Mirza Assadullah loved money, wisdom and peace. His brother Ali was like Zarathustra's fire, burning, but not burning to death. He was always moving around, and loved war, adventure and danger. Many stories were told about him in the country, stories of fights, assaults and bloodshed. Sullen Burjat Sadé, sitting next to him, did not love adventure, but love. He was the only one of us who had four wives, always bitterly at war with each other. He was very ashamed of this situation, but could not change his nature. When asked how many children he had he would answer sadly: 'Fifteen or eighteen, how would I know, poor man that I am?' And if asked about his millions he would give the same answer. Jussuf Oghly, sitting at the other end of the hall, looked at him with disapproval, and jealousy. He had only one wife, and it was said she was not good looking. On their wedding day she had told him: 'If you squander your sperm on other women I'll cut their ears off, and their noses and their breasts. And what I'll do to you I don't even want to say.' As this woman's kinsfolk had a well deserved reputation of being quick on the draw, her threat had to be taken seriously. So the poor man collected pictures.

The man who came into the hall at half past seven was very small and very thin. The nails of his delicate hands were tinted red. We all rose and bowed to him, honouring his misfortune. Ismail, his only son, had died a few years ago. The father had built a splendid house in Nikolai Street. The name 'Ismail' shone on the front in big golden letters, and the house was dedicated to Islamic charity. His name was Aga Musa Nagi, and he was a member of our circle only by virtue of his two hundred million rubles. For he was not a Muslim any more. He belonged to the heretic sect of the Ba'haists, founded by Bab, whom Shah Nasreddin had had put to death. Only very few of us knew what Bab's teachings were. But we all knew, that Nasreddin had had red-hot needles put under the nails of

Ba'haists, burnt them alive and flogged them to death. Very evil indeed must be the teachings of a sect that deserves such punishment.

At eight o'clock all guests had assembled. There they sat, the Oil Princes, drinking tea, eating sweets, and telling each other of their booming business, of their houses, their horses, their gardens and their losses at the green table in the casino. So they talked till nine o'clock, as etiquette decreed. Then the servants cleared away the tea, closed the doors, and my father said: 'Mirza Assadullah, son of Shamsi Assadullah, has given much thought to the fate of our people. Let us hear him.' Mirza Assadullah raised his beautiful dreamy face:

'If the Grand Duke wins there will not be one single Muslim country left on the map. Heavy will be the Czar's hand. He will not touch us, who are here tonight, because we have money. But he will close our mosques and schools, and forbid us to speak our language. Strangers will overrun the land, for there will be no one to defend the people of the Prophet. If Enver wins it would be better for us, even if his victories were few. But can we do anything about it either way? I say we cannot. We have money, but the Czar has more. What shall we do? Perhaps we should give the Czar some of our money and some of our men. His hand might not be so heavy on us after the war, if we give him a batallion. Or is there another way?' His brother Ali raised himself. He said:

'Who knows, maybe after the war there won't be a Czar anymore.'

'Even so, my brother, there still would be too many Russians in our country.'

'Their number can be reduced, my brother.'

'We can't kill them all, Ali.'

'We can kill them all, Mirza.'

They were silent. Then Seinal Aga spoke, very softly, tired with age, and quite without expression: 'No one knows what is written in the Book. The Grand Duke's victories are no victories, even if he were to take Stamboul. The key to our destiny does not lie in Stamboul, but in the West. And there the Turks are victorious, even if they are called Germans there. Russians are occupying Trapezunt, Turks, are occupying Warsaw. Russians? are there any left? I have heard that a peasant—I believe his name is Rasputin—rules over the Czar, caresses the Czar's daughters and calls the Czarina Mama. And there are Dukes who want to dethrone the Czar, and people who just wait for peace, so they can start a revolution. After the war everything will be quite different.'

'Yes,' said a fat man with brilliant eyes and a long moustache, 'everything will indeed be different after the war.' This was Feth Ali Khan of Choja, a lawyer by profession. We knew that he was always thinking about The People and Their Cause. 'Yes,' he added fervently, 'and as everything will be so different we need not beg for anyone's favours. Whoever wins this war will come out of it weak and covered with wounds, and we, who will be neither weakened nor wounded, will then be in a position to demand, not to beg. We are an Islamic, a Shiitic country, and we expect the same from the House of Romanov as from the House of Osman. Independence in everything that concerns us! And the weaker the great powers are after the war, the nearer is freedom for us. This freedom will come from us, from our unspent strength, from our money and our oil. For do not forget: the world needs us more than we need the world.'

The thousand million rubles assembled in the hall were very satisfied. Wait and see was a good policy. We have got the oil, the victors will have to beg for our favours. And what will we do till then? Build hospitals, children's homes, blind people's homes, for those who fight for our faith. No one could accuse us of lack of character. I sat in a corner, silent and angry. Ali Assadullah came across the hall and sat down next to me: 'And what do you think, Ali Khan?' Without waiting for an answer he bent forward and whispered: 'Wouldn't it be wonderful to kill all Russians in our country? And not only the Russians—kill all these foreigners who talk and pray and think differently from us. We all want to do that, really, but I'm the only one who dares to say it aloud. And what then? As far as I'm concerned, Feth Ali can rule, though I prefer Enver. But first we must exterminate all foreigners.' He spoke the word 'exterminate' with such tender longing, as if it meant 'love'. His eyes shone, he smiled mischievously. I did not answer.

Now Musa Nagi, the Ba'haist, spoke: 'I am an old man,' he said, 'and I am sad to see what I see, and to hear what I hear. The Russians are killing the Turks, the Turks are killing the Armenians, the Armenians would like to kill us, and we the Russians. Is this good? I do not know. We have heard what Seinal Aga, Mirza, Ali and Feth Ali think of our people's fate. I understand they care deeply about schools, our language, hospitals and freedom. But what use is a school when what is taught there is nonsense, and what use is a hopsital, if it is the body only that is healed there, and the soul is forgotten? Our soul strives to go to God. But each nation believes they have a God all to themselves, and he is the one and only God. But I believe it is the same God who made himself known through the voices of all sages. Therefore I worship Christ and Confucius, Buddha and Mohammed. We all come from one God, and through Bab we shall all return to Him. Men should be told that there is no Black and no White, for Black is White and White is Black. So my advice is this: let us not do anything that might hurt anybody anywhere in the world, for we are part of each soul, and each soul is part of us.'

We sat silent, nonplussed. So this was the heresy of Bab. Suddenly I heard loud sobbing, turned round and saw Assadullah, his face bathed in tears, and distorted with grief. 'Oh my soul!' he sobbed, 'How right you are! What happiness to hear your words! O Almighty God! If only all men could find wisdom as profound as yours!' Then he dried his tears, sighed deeply and added, noticably cooler: 'Doubtlessly, venerated sir, the hand of God is above all our hands, but nevertheless, o fountain of wisdom, the truth is, that one cannot always depend on the Almighty's merciful intervention. We arc but men, and if inspiration fails, we have to find ways to overcome our difficulties.' It was a clever sentence, as clever as his tears had been. Mirza was looking at his brother full of admiration. The guests rose. Slender hands touched dark brows, saluting. Backs bent low, lips murmured: 'Peace be with you. May the smile remain on your lips, friend.'

The meeting was over. The thousand million rubles came out into the street and parted, nodding, saluting, shaking hands. It was half-past ten. The hall was empty and depressing. I felt very lonely. 'I'm going to the barracks,' I told the servant, 'Iljas Beg is on night duty.' Down to the sea I went, past Nino's house, to the big barracks. The guardroom windows shone brightly. Iljas Beg and Mehmed Haidar were rolling dice, and greeted me with silent nods. At last they finished. Iljas Beg threw the dice into a corner and undid his collar. 'How did it go?' he asked. 'Did Assadullah swear again to kill all Russians?'

'Just about. What's the news from the war?'

'War,' he said, bored. 'The Germans have occupied all Poland, the Grand Duke will be either stuck in the snow or occupy Baghdad. Maybe the Turks will conquer Egypt. Who knows? It's a boring world.'

Mehmed Haidar rubbed his shorn pointed skull. 'It's not boring at all,' he said. 'We have horses and soldiers, and we know how to use our weapons. What more does a man need? One of these days I will go over the mountains, lie in the trenches and see an enemy before me. He should have strong muscles and his skin should smell of sweat.'

'Why don't you volunteer for the front if that's what you want?' I said.

Mehmed Haidar's eyes were sad and lost under his low brow: 'I can't shoot at Mohammedans, even if they are Sunnites. But I can't desert either. I have sworn my Oath of Allegiance. Everything should be quite different in our country.' I looked at him and loved him. There he sat, with his broad shoulders, strong, simple face, nearly choked by his desire to fight: 'I want to go to the front, and I don't,' he said sadly.

'What should happen in our country?' I asked him. He drew his brows together, but did not reply for quite some time. Thinking was not his strong point. At last he said: 'Our country? We should build mosques. Let the earth have water. Our earth is thirsty. And it's not a good thing that all these foreigners come and tell us how stupid we are. If we're stupid, that's our business. And then: I think it would be a very good thing if we made a big fire and burnt all those oil derricks. It would look lovely, and we'd all be poor again. And instead of the oil derricks I'd build a beautiful mosque, with blue tiles. We should get buffaloes, and plant corn on the oil land.' He fell silent, dreaming of this vision. Iljas Beg laughed happily:

'And then all reading and writing should be forbidden, we'd use candles instead of electricity, and elect the most stupid man king of the country.' Mehmed Haidar did not rise to this leg-pull:

'That's all right,' he said, 'in the olden times there were many more stupid people about. And they built canals instead of oil derricks, and robbed the foreigners instead of letting them rob us. In those times people were happier then they are now.' I felt like embracing and kissing the simple fellow. He spoke as if he himself were a chunk of our poor tortured earth. But suddenly a wild knocking at the door made me jump. I looked out. Seyd Mustafa rushed into the room. His turban hung to one side over his glistening brow. His green belt had come loose, his grey cape was dusty. He fell on a chair and gasped: 'Nachararyan has kidnapped Nino. Half an hour ago. They're on the road to Mardakjany.'

17

Mehmed Haidar sprang to his feet. His eyes had become quite small. 'I'll saddle the horses.' He rushed out. The blood was pounding in my head, there was a drumming sound in my ears, and I felt an invisible hand beating my head with a stick. Iljas Beg's voice came from far away: 'Steady, Ali Khan, steady. Wait till we've got them.' His narrow face was very pale. He put a belt round my waist, a straight Caucasian dagger hanging from it. 'There,' he said, and put a revolver into my hand, and again: 'Steady, Ali Khan. Save your fury for the road to Mardakjany.' Mechanically I put the weapon into my pocket. Seyd Mustafa's pock-marked face came close to me, I saw the thick lips moving, and heard broken words: 'I left my house to see the wise Mullah Hatshi Machsud. The tent of his wisdom stands next to the theatre. I left him at 11 o'clock. The sinful play had just ended. I saw Nino get into the car, Nachararyan with her. But the car did not start. They were talking. I did not like the look on Nachararyan's face. I crept nearer, I listened. "No," said Nino, "I love him." "I love you more," said Nachararyan, "no stone in this country will be left standing. I will save you from the claws of Asia." "No," said Nino, "take me home." He started the motor. I jumped on the back. The car went to the Kipiani's house. I could not hear what they were saying, but they were talking all the time. The car stopped at the house. Nino was crying. Suddenly Nachararyan embraced her and kissed her face. "You must not fall into the hands of these savages," he cried, and then he whispered something, and I could only hear the end ". . . to my place at Mardakjany, we'll get married in Moscow, and then we'll go to Sweden." I saw Nino pushing him away. Then the motor started again, and I jumped off and ran as fast as I could to . . ." He did not finish the sentence, or maybe I just did not hear the end. Mehmed Haidar came tearing through the door, and cried: 'The horses are ready.' We ran into the yard. The moon shone on the horses, standing there, stamping and neighing softly. 'Here,' said Mehmed Haidar. I looked at the horse and was struck numb. There stood the red-golden miracle of Karabagh, the horse of Melikov, the regiment's Commanding Officer, one of the twelve golden horses in the whole world. Mehmed Haidar's face was dark. 'The Commander will go mad. No one but he ever rode this horse. It runs like the wind. Don't spare it. You'll catch them.'

I jumped into the saddle. My whip just grazed the wonderful animal's flank. One enormous jump—and I was out of the barrack yard. We chased along the sea. Full of hate I kept beating the horse. Houses danced past, as sparks flew from the horse's hooves. My wild fury grew and grew. I tore at the bridle, the horse reared up and raced on. At last—the clay huts of the suburbs were behind me. I saw the fields lying peacefully in the moonlight, and there was the road to Mardakjany. The night air made me feel a bit cooler. Melon fields, were now on our right and left, big round fruit looking like lumps of gold. The horse galloped on, with long, elastic, ravishingly even strides. I bent forward as far as I could, down to the golden mane. So that's how it was! I could see everything quite clearly . . . I heard every word they had spoken. Suddenly I could follow the alien train of thought: Enver is fighting in Asia Minor. The Czar's throne is threatened. The Grand Duke has Armenian battalions in his army. If the front breaks, Osman's army will overrun Armenia, Karabagh and Baku. Nachararyan can foresee the consequences. Therefore gold bars, heavy Armenian gold, are sent to Sweden. That's the end of the Caucasian Peoples' fraternisation. I can see the two of them in the box in the theatre: 'Princess, there's no bridge between East and West, not even the bridge of love.' Nino does not answer, but she is listening. 'We must stand together, we who are threatened by Osman's sword. We, Europe's ambassadors in Asia. I love you, Princess. We belong together. Life is easy and simple in Stockholm. There is Europe, there is the West.' And then I hear him quite plainly, as if I were there when he was saying the words: 'No stone will be left standing in this country.'

And the end: 'You yourself must decide what your fate is to be, Nino. After the war we'll live in London. We'll be presented at Court. A European must be master of his fate. I hold Ali Khan in high esteem. But he is a barbarian, forever a prisoner of the desert.'

I whip the horse. A wild cry. So howls the desert wolf when he sees the moon, with a long drawn, high mournful wail. All the night is just that one sound. I lean still further forward. My throat hurts. Why am I crying on the moonlit path to Mardakjany? I must save my fury. A sharp wind whips my face. That is what makes my tears fall, nothing else. I do not cry, not even when I suddenly know, that there is no bridge between East and West, not even the bridge of love. Smiling, radiant Georgian eyes! Yes, I'm one of the desert wolves, the grey Turkish wolves. Very nicely planned, wasn't it? 'We'll get married in Moscow, and then we'll go to Sweden.' A hotel in Stockholm, warm and clean, with white linen. A villa in London. A villa? My face touches the red-golden skin. Suddenly I bite the animal's neck. My mouth is filled with the salty taste of blood. A villa? Nachararyan has a villa in Mardakjany, like all rich people of Baku. Built of marble, standing in the fruit gardens of the oasis, near the sea. How quickly can a car go, and how swiftly runs a Karabagh horse? I know the villa. The bed is of mahogany, red and very wide. White sheets, just as in the hotel in Stockholm. He won't talk philosophy all through the night. He will . . . of course he will. I see the bed before me, and Georgian eyes, veiled by lust and fear. My teeth sink deeply into the horse's flesh. The wonderful animal races on. Go! Go! save your fury till you catch them, Ali Khan. It is a narrow road, this road to Mardakjany. Suddenly I laugh out loud. How marvellous, that we're in Asia, in wild, reactionary Asia! We have no smooth roads for Western cars here, just rough paths for Karabagh horses. How quickly can a car go on these roads, and how swiftly races a horse from Karabagh? The melons on the roadside look at me as if they had faces. 'Very bad road,' the melons are saying, 'not for English cars. Only for riders on Karabagh horses.'

Will the horse survive this ride? I don't think so. I can still see Melikov's face on that day in Shusha, when his sabre was rattling and he was saying: 'Only when the Czar calls to war I mount this horse.' Hell! Let him weep for his horse, the old man from Karabagh. Again my whip swishes through the air, and again. The wind eats on my face as if with fists. A turning —wild bushes at the roadside—and at last—far away I can hear the rattling of the motor.

Now two glaring lamps shed a white stream of light on the bumpy road. The car! Slowly it drags itself forward. A European car, helpless on Asia's roads. My whip comes down again. Now I can recognise Nachararyan at the steering wheel.

And Nino! Nino crouched in a corner. Why can't they hear the horse's hooves? Does he think there's no need to listen to the night outside? He feels so secure in his European ear, going to Mardakjany. Let it stop, this lacquered box! Now, this minute! I slip the safety catch off my revolver. Come on, dear little Belgian tool, do your duty! I fire. For a second a narrow strip of flame blazes along the road. I stop the horse. Well done, little Belgian friend. The left tyre goes down like a suddenly deflated toy balloon. The lacquered box stops. I ride up to it, blood pounding in my temples. I throw my weapon away, I don't really know any more what I'm doing. Two faces look at me, eyes staring in wild terror. A shaking alien hand clings to a revolver. So he did not feel so secure after all, in his European car. I see the fat fingers and the diamond ring. Quick, Ali Khan! Steady now. I draw my dagger. The trembling hand is not going to shoot. With a melodious whistle the dagger swishes through the air. Where did I learn to throw a dagger? In Persia? In Shusha? Nowhere! It is in my blood, in my veins, inherited from my wild ancestors, this knowledge of the exact arc the dagger must describe. Inherited from the first Shirvanshir, who went to India and conquered Delhi. A cry, surprisingly high and thin. A fat hand, spreading out its fingers, a line of blood running across the wrist. It is wonderful to see the enemy's blood on the road to Mardakjany. The revolver drops on the bottom of the car. And suddenly there are hasty creeping scramblings and a fat stomach. One jump, and the man is running across the road into the wild bushes alongside. Nino sits still and upright in the car's soft cushions. Quite without expression, her face is hard, as if made of stone. But her whole body is trembling uncontrollably, in the nightmare of this ghostly fighting in the dark. Far away I hear the thunder of hooves, drawing closer. I jump into the bushes. Sharp branches grasp me as if they were hands of unseen enemies. Leaves are rustling under my feet, dry twigs are cutting my hands. Far away in the bushes the hunted animal is breathing hotly—Nachararyan! A hotel in Stockholm! Fat greasy lips on Nino's face!

Now I see him. He is stumbling and tearing the bushes with his fat hands. Now he is running towards the sea across the melon fields. Why had I thrown away the revolver when I first saw him? I could use it now. Blood is running from my hands, torn by the thorny bushes. There—the first melon. Round fat stupid mask—are you grinning at me? I trample on it, and it bursts with a plop! under my heel. I'm running across the field. The dead face of the moon looks on. Cold golden floods of light on the melon field. You'll never take gold bars to Sweden, Nachararyan. Now. I grab his shoulder. He turns, stands there like a block of wood, his eyes hating me, because now I know him for what he is. A blow—his fist lands on my chin. And again—just below my ribs. All right, Nachararyan, you have learnt boxing in Europe. I feel dizzy. For a few short seconds my breath stops. I'm only an Asiatic, Nachararyan, and I've never grasped the art of hitting below the belt. I can only go mad like the desert wolf. I jump. My arms go round his body, as if it were a tree trunk. My feet press against his fat stomach, my hands grip his fat neck. He is hitting out at me, wildly, forgetting all European training. I bend down, and we fall together. We're rolling on the ground. Suddenly I'm under him, his hands throttling me. His mouth hangs down one side of his distorted face. My feet beat against his stomach, my heels going deep into his fat. He loosens the grip. For a split second I see the torn collar dragged to one side. My teeth sink into the fat white neck. Yes, Nachararyan, that's how we fight in Asia. Not with blows below the belt, but with the grip of the grey wolf. I feel his veins trembling.

A slight movement at my hip. Nachararyan's hand grips my dagger. I had forgotten it in the heat of the moment. A sudden glint of steel, and a piercing pain in my ribs. How warm my blood is. The thrust has slipped off my rib. I let go of his neck and tear the dagger from his wounded hand! Now he lies under me, his face turned up to the moon. I raise the dagger. He cries out—a long, thin wail, his head thrown back. All of his face is just mouth—the open gate of deadly fear. Hotel in Stockholm, you speared pig!

Why do I hesitate? There is a voice behind me:

'Kill him, Ali Khan, kill him!'

It is Mehmed Haidar. 'Just above the heart, thrusting down!'

I know where the deadly spot is. But I want to hear the enemy's pitiful voice just once more. Then: I raise my dagger. My muscles are taut. Just above the heart my dagger becomes one with the enemy's body. He writhes, again, and yet again. Slowly I get up. There is blood on my suit. My blood? His blood? What does it matter?

Mehmed Haidar bares his teeth. 'Beautifully done, Ali Khan. I'll admire you forever.' My rib hurts. He supports me. Again we dive into the bushes, and again we are standing near the lacquered box, on the road to Mardakjany. Four horses, two riders. Iljas Beg raises his hand in greeting. Seyd Mustafa pushes his green turban off his brow. He holds Nino on his saddle, tight, like a vice. Slowly and softly, his eyes half closed as if in a dream he says: 'What's to be done with the woman? Will you stab her or shall I?'

'Kill her, Ali Khan,' Mehmed Haidar holds the dagger out to me.

I look at Iljas Beg. He nods, his face as white as chalk. 'We'll throw the body into the sea.'

I stand close to Nino. Her eyes are enormous . . . she had come running across the street to our school, bathed in tears, carrying her satchel. Once I sat under her bench and whispered: 'Charlemagne was crowned in Aachen in the year 800.' Why is Nino silent? Why does she not cry, as she did on that day when she came to me for help? It was not her fault that she did not know when Charlemagne was crowned. I cling to the horse's neck and look at her. How beautiful she is, in Seyd's saddle, by the light of the moon, looking at the dagger. Georgian blood, the noblest in the world. Georgian lips—Nachararyan has kissed them. Gold bars in Sweden—he has kissed her. 'Iljas Beg, I'm wounded. Take Princess Nino home. The night is cold. Cover Princess Nino up. I'll murder you, Iljas Beg, if Princess Nino is not taken home safely. You hear me, Iljas Beg. This is how I want it. Mehmed Haidar, Seyd Mustafa, I feel very weak. Help me home. Hold me. Let me lean on you, I'm bleeding to death.'

I grasp the mane of the Karabagh horse, Mehmed Haidar helps me into the saddle. Iljas Beg comes close, takes Nino and puts her carefully on the soft cushions of his Cossack saddle. She does not resist. . . . He takes off his coat and puts it gently round her shoulders. He is still very pale. Just one look and one nod—Nino will be safe with him. Mehmed Haidar jumps into the saddle: 'You are a hero, Ali Khan. You fought brilliantly. You did your duty.' He puts his arm round my shoulder, supporting me. Seyd Mustafa's eyes are downcast.

'Her life belongs to you. You can take it, you can spare it. The Law permits either.' He smiles dreamily. Mehmed Haidar puts the reins into my hand. Silently we ride through the night, towards the softly shining lights of Baku.

18

A narrow stone terrace on the brink of an abyss. Yellow rocks, dry, weather-beaten, no trees. Stones, immense, roughly put together to form coarse walls. Close together, square and simple, the huts hang down from the rocks of the abyss. The courtyard of one hut is the flat roof of the one below. Deep down the mountain stream is rushing, the rocks gleaming in the clear air. A narrow serpentine path winds through the stones and is lost from sight down below. This is an âoul—a mountain village in Daghestan. Inside the dark hut the floor is covered with thick mats. Outside two poles carry the narrow roof. An eagle hangs in the immense expanse of the sky, his wings spread out, motionless, as if made from stone.

I am lying on the little roof, the amber mouthpiece of my nargileh between my lips, sucking the cool smoke into my lungs. My temples become cool, the blue smoke vanishes, carried away by the soft wind. A charitable hand has mixed Hashish grains into my tobacco. I look into the abyss and see faces, circling in the swimming fog. Well known faces—Rustem the Warrior and his Knights, from the rug on the wall of my room in Baku. I remember lying there, wrapped in thick silk covers. My rib hurt. The dressing was soft and white. Light steps next door. I can just hear the sound of voices. I listen. The voices become louder. My father speaks: 'I'm sorry, Inspector. I don't know myself where my son is. I suppose he has fled to Persia, to his uncle. I'm very sorry.'

The Inspector's voice is loud and angry: 'There's a warrant out for your son. This is a case of murder. We'll find him, even in Persia.'

'I would be only too pleased. Any court would find him not guilty. It was done in affect, more than justified by what had gone on before. Besides . . .'

I hear the rustle of clean crisp notes, or at least I think that is what I hear. Then silence. And again the Inspector's voice: 'Ah well, these young people. Quick at the draw with the dagger. I'm only a state servant. But I understand. The young man should not show himself in town. But the warrant has to go to Persia.' The steps became fainter, and then silence reigned again. The ornamental writing on the carpet was like a laby-rinth. My eyes followed the lines of the letters, and became lost in the lovely swirls of an N. Faces bent over me. Lips whispered words I did not understand. Then I was sitting up in bed and Iljas Beg and Mehmed Haidar were standing before me. Both smiling, both in battledress. 'We've come to say good-bye. We're posted to the front.'

'Why?'

Iljas Beg picks at his cartridges. 'I took Nino home. She never said a word. Then I rode to the barracks. A few hours later everybody knew everything. Commander Melikov locked himself in and got dead drunk. He never wanted to see the horse again, and in the evening he had it shot. Then he volunteered for the front. My father just about managed to fix the court martial. But we're posted to the front, straight to the front lines.'

'Forgive me. It is all my fault.'

Both protested vehemently. 'No, you're a hero, you did what a man has to do. We are very proud.'

'Have you seen Nino?'

They stood there, their faces stiff. 'No, we have not seen

Nino.' Their voices were cold. We embraced. 'Don't worry about us. We'll manage, front lines or no front lines.' A smile, a greeting, and the door closed.

I lay back on the pillows, looking at the red pattern of the carpet. My poor friends. It is all my fault. I sank into strange daydreams. The present had disappeared. Nino's face was hovering in a mist, sometimes laughing, sometimes serious. Strange hands were touching me. Some one said in Persian: 'Must take hashish. Very good for conscience.' Some one put an amber mouthpiece into my mouth, and words came through the rags of my waking dreams: 'My dear Khan, isn't this dreadful. What a terrible thing to happen. I think it would be best if my daughter would follow your son. They should get married at once.'

'Prince, Ali Khan cannot marry. He is Kanly now, open to the blood feud of the Nachararyans. I have sent him to Persia. He is in danger every hour of his life. He is not the right husband for your daughter.'

'Safar Khan, I implore you. We will protect the children. They must go away, to India, to Spain. My daughter is dishonoured. Only marriage can save her.'

'That is not Ali Khan's fault, my Prince. And anyway, I'm sure she'll find a Russian, or even an Armenian.'

'But please! It was just a harmless evening drive, so understandable in this heat. Your son was too hasty—quite a wrong suspicion. He must make amends.'

'Be that as it may, Prince. Ali Khan is Kanly and cannot marry.'

'I too am a father, Safar Khan.'

The voices stopped. Everything was quiet again. Hashish grains are round and look like ants. At last the bandages were taken off. I felt my scar—the first honourable scar on my body. Then I got up and paced the room, stepping hesitantly. The servants looked at me shyly, with frightened eyes. The door opened, and my father came in. My heart was beating violently. The servant disappeared. For some time my father was silent.

He paced the room, up and down, up and down. Then he stopped: 'The police come every day, and not only the police. The Nachararyans are searching for you everywhere. Five of them have already gone to Persia. I have to have twenty men to guard the house. And, by the way, the Melikovs have declared a blood-feud against you too. Because of the horse. Your friends have been sent to the front.' I looked down without replying. My father put his hand on my shoulder. His voice was soft: 'I'm proud of you, Ali Khan, very proud. I would have done exactly the same.'

'You are satisfied, father?'

'Nearly. There's just one thing,' he embraced me and looked deeply into my eyes, 'why did you spare the woman?'

'I don't know, father. I was exhausted.'

'It would have been better, my son. Now it is too late. But I won't reproach you. We all are very proud of you, all the family.'

'And what now, father?'

Again he paced up and down, sighing distractedly. 'Well, you can't stay here. And you can't go to Persia either. The police and two influential families are looking for you. The best thing is to go to Daghestan. Nobody will find you in an âoul. No Armenian and no policeman will dare to go there.'

'How long for, father?'

'For a very long time. Until the police have forgotten the whole affair. Until your enemies have made their peace with us. I'll come and see you.'

I left at night for Machatsh-Kalé, and from there went into the mountains. Small horses with long manes carried me along narrow paths to the far-away âoul, on the brink of the wild abyss. And there I was now, safely sheltered by Daghestan hospitality. 'Kanly', people said, and looked at me understandingly. Tender hands mixed hashish into my tobacco. I smoked much, and lay silent, tortured by visions. My father's friend, Kasi Mullah, who had spread the shade of his hospitality over me, talked a lot, and the splinters of his words tore

141

at the fevered dreams that again and again took me on the moonlit road. 'Don't dream, Ali Khan, don't think, Ali Khan. Listen to me. Have you ever heard the story of Andalal?'

'Andalal!' I said woodenly.

'Do you know what that is, Andalal? Six hundred years ago it was a beautiful village. A good, clever and brave prince reigned there. But so much virtue was too much for the people. So they came before the prince and said: "We are tired of you, leave us." Then the prince wept, he mounted his horse, said good-bye to his family and went far away to Persia. There he became a great man. The Shah made him his adviser, and what he said the Shah did. He conquered many cities and countries. But his heart was bitter against Andalal. Therefore he said: "In the vales of Andalal are great treasures of gold and jewels. We will conquer Andalal." And the Shah took his great army into the mountains. Then the people of Andalal said: "There are many of you, and you are down below. There are but a few of us, and we are up above. But higher still is Allah, who is but one, yet mightier than all of us." So the people of Andalal fought, men, women and children. In the first row fought the prince's sons, who had stayed in Andalal when he went away. The Persians were beaten. The Shah was the first to flee, and the traitor was the last one. Ten years passed. Then the prince grew old, and his heart yearned for his home. He left the Shah's palace and rode to his country. The people recognised the traitor, who had led the enemy into their vale. They spat at him and closed their doors. All day long the prince rode through the village, but did not find one friend. At last he went to the Kadi and said: 'I have come home to atone for the wrong I have done. Judge me according to the Law." "Bind him," said the Kadi, and announced: "The Law of our Fathers says this man shall be buried alive." And the people cried: "Let it be so." But the Kadi was a just man. "What can you say in your defence?" he asked, and the prince answered: "Nothing. I am guilty. Our fathers' laws are honoured here. That is good. But there is also the law that says: 'Whoever fights against his father, shall be killed.' I demand my right. My sons have fought against me. Let them be beheaded on my grave." "So be it," said the Kadi, and he and all the people wept bitterly. For the prince's sons were held in high esteem. But the Law must be fulfilled. So the traitor was buried alive, and his sons, the bravest warriors in the country, were beheaded on his grave.'

'Silly nonsense,' I grumbled. 'Is that your best story? Your hero was the last one in this country, and he's been dead for six hundred years, and on top of that he was a traitor.'

Kasi Mullah sniffed, his feelings were hurt. 'Have you heard of Imam Shamil?'

'I know all about Imam Shamil.'

'That is now fifty years ago. People were happy under Shamil, there was no wine, no tobacco. When a thief was caught his right hand was cut off, but there were hardly any thieves. Until the Russians came. Then the Prophet appeared to Imam Shamil and ordered him to start the Gasawat, the Holy War. All mountain peoples were tied to Shamil by terrible oaths, amongst them the people of the Tshetshen. But the Russians were strong. They threatened the Tshetshen, burnt their villages and destroyed their fields. Then the wise men of the tribe sent to Dargo, the Imam's residence, to implore him to unbind them from their oath. But when they came to face him they did not dare to speak of what was in their hearts. Instead they went to the Imam's mother, and she wept for the Tshetshen's sorrow and said: "I'll ask the Imam for you." For the Imam had always been a good son, and his mother's influence over him was great. He had said once: "Cursed be he, who brings sorrow to his mother." When the Hanum spoke to him he said: "The Koran forbids treason. The Koran forbids the son to contradict his mother. My wisdom is not enough for this problem. I will fast and pray, so that Allah may enlighten my thoughts." The Imam fasted for three days and three nights. Then he appeared before the people and said: "Allah has enlightened me and given me his Law:

143

The first one who talks about treason to me shall be sentenced to one hundred strokes of the rod. The first one to talk to me about treason was the Hanum, my mother. I sentence her to one hundred strokes of the rod." They brought the Hanum. The warriors tore off her veils, threw her on the steps of the mosque and raised their rods. But she received only one stroke. Then the Imam fell on his knees, wept and cried: "The Laws of the Almighty are unbreakable. No one can revoke them, not even I. But the Koran allows this: children can take upon themselves the parent's punishment. Therefore I take upon me the rest of my mother's punishment." The Imam took off his robe, lay down on the steps of the mosque in front of all the people and cried: "Now hit me, and as sure as I am Imam, I'll have your heads cut off if I feel that you do not use all your strength." The Imam suffered ninety-nine strokes. He lay there bathed in blood, his skin in tatters. The people, beholding this, were horrified, and nobody ever dared to talk about treason again. That is how the mountains were governed fifty years ago. And the people were happy.' I was silent.

The eagle had disappeared from the sky. Twilight was falling. The Mullah appeared on the minaret of the little mosque. Kasi Mullah unfolded the prayer rug, and we prayed, our faces turned to Mecca. The Arabic prayers sounded like old war songs. 'Go now, Kasi Mullah. You are a friend. I'll sleep now.' He looked at me suspiciously. Then he sighed and mixed the hashish grains. When he went out I heard him saying to a neighbour: 'Kanly very ill.' And the neighbour answered: 'Nobody is ill for very long in Daghestan.'

19

A single file of women and children was walking through the village, their faces drawn and tired. They had walked a very long way. In their hands they carried small satchels, filled with earth and manure, clasping the precious burden tightly, like a golden treasure. They had collected it in far-away villages, giving in exchange sheep, silver coins and handwoven lengths of material. Now they were going to spread the dearly bought earth on the bleak rocks, so the poor acres could bear corn to feed the people. The fields hung on a slant over the abyss. Strapped on a chain, men slid down on to the little platforms, and carefully crumbled the new earth over the rocky ground. A rough wall was put up over the future field, to protect it from wind and landslides. These acres, three paces long, four paces wide, were the mountain people's most treasured possession. Early in the morning the men went out to the fields. They said a long prayer, and only then bent over the good earth. When the wind was strong the women brought their blankets to cover the dear land. They caressed the seeds with slender brown fingers and later cut the few blades with little scythes. They ground the grains and baked flat long loaves. Into the first loaf a coin was put, the people's thanksgiving for the miracle of the seed.

I was walking along the wall of one of the tiny acres. Up on the rocks sheep were stumbling about. A farmer, wearing a broad white felt hat, came driving along on a two-wheeled cart. The wheels were squeaking like screaming babies, I had heard the noise when he was a long way off. 'Little brother,' I said, 'I'll write to Baku for somebody to send you some grease for your axles.' The farmer grinned.

'I'm just a simple man, why should I hide myself? They can all hear my cart coming, that's why I don't grease my axles. Only the Abreks do that.'

'The Abreks?'

'Yes, the Abreks, the outcasts.'

'Are there many of them?'

'Enough. They are robbers and murderers. Some of them murder for the good of the people, others for their own good. But they all must swear a terrible oath.'

'What oath?'

The farmer stopped his cart and got off. He leaned against the wall of his field, took a piece of sheep's cheese from his bag, broke it with his long fingers and gave me half of it. Dark hairs were in the glutinous mass. I ate. 'The oath of the Abreks. You don't know it? At midnight the Abrek creeps into the mosque and swears: "By this holy place, that I venerate, I swear that from today on I will be an outcast. I will shed human blood and have pity for no one. I will wage war on everybody. I swear to rob people of everything dear to their hearts, their conscience and their honour. I will stab the child on his mother's breast, put fire to the poorest beggar's hut and bring sorrow to all places where men rejoice. If I do not fulfill this oath, if love or pity ever creep into my heart, may I never see my father's grave again, may water never quench my thirst nor bread my hunger, may my body be cast on to the road and a dirty dog relieve himself on it."' The farmer's voice was solemn, his face turned towards the sun, his eyes were green and deep. 'Yes,' he said, 'that is the oath of the Abreks.'

146

'Who swears this oath?'

'Men who have suffered much injustice.' He fell silent. I went home. The square of the âoul looked like dice. The sun was beating down on us. Maybe I myself was an Abrek, an outcast, driven into the wild mountains? Should I swear this bloodthirsty oath, like the robbers of Daghestan? The words were still ringing in my ears, tempting me. Then I saw three strange saddled horses in front of my cottage, one of them with silver reins. On the terrace sat a sixteen-year-old fat boy, a golden dagger in his belt. He waved at me and laughed. It was Arslan Aga, a boy from our school. His father owned rich oil wells, and the boy was not very strong, so he often went to the spas of Kislovodsk. I hardly knew him, for he was much younger than I. But here, in the lonely mountains, I embraced him like a brother. He blushed with pride and said: 'I happened to pass this way with my servants, so I thought I'd come and see you.'

I clapped my hand on his shoulder. 'Be my guest, Arslan Aga. Tonight we'll celebrate, in honour of our home town.' Then I shouted into the hut: 'Kasi Mullah, prepare a feast. I have a guest from Baku.' Half an hour later Arslan Aga was sitting crosslegged on the mat, eating roast mutton and cake, absolutely overcome with delight.

'I'm so happy to see you, Ali Khan. You live like a hero, in this far village, hiding from the blood-feud. But don't worry. I won't give you away.' I was not at all worried. It was obvious all Baku knew where I was.

'How did you find me?'

'Seyd Mustafa told me. I saw that your village is practically on my way, and he asked me to give you his regards.'

'And where are you going, Arslan Aga?'

'To Kislovodsk. These two servants are going with me.'

'Oh.' I smiled. He looked very innocent. 'Tell me, Arslan Aga, why didn't you go the direct way, by rail?'

'Well, I wanted a bit of mountain air. I got off at Machatsh-

Kalé and took the direct road to Kislovodsk.' He crammed his mouth full of cake and chewed happily.

'But the direct road to Kislovodsk is a three-day journey from here.'

Arslan Aga pretended to be very surprised: 'Is it really? Then they've given me the wrong information. But I'm glad, because at least I have had the chance to see you.' It was quite obvious that the imp had made the detour on purpose, so he could tell them at home he had seen me. It seemed I had quite a reputation in Baku. I poured wine for him, and he drank with big gulps. Then he came a bit closer: 'Have you killed anybody since then, Ali Khan? Please tell me, I swear I won't give you away.'

'Oh yes, a few dozen.'

'Have you really?' He was delighted, kept on drinking wine, and I kept pouring it out. 'Are you going to marry Nino? They're betting on it all over the town. People say you still love her.' He laughed gaily and went on drinking: 'You know, we were all so surprised. We didn't talk of anything else for weeks and weeks.'

'Didn't you? Well, what's the news in Baku, Arslan Aga?'

'Oh, in Baku—nothing. There's a new newspaper. The workers are on strike. Our teachers say you've always been very impulsive. Tell me—how on earth did you find out?'

'Dear Arslan, dear friend, enough of your questions. Now it's my turn. Have you seen Nino? Or any of the Nachararyans? What do the Kipianis say?'

The poor boy nearly choked on his cake. 'But I know nothing, absolutely nothing. I haven't seen anybody. I hardly ever went out.'

'Why, my friend? Have you been ill?'

'Yes, yes. I was ill. Very ill. I had diphtheria. Just imagine—I had to have three clysters a day.'

'For diphtheria?'

'. . . yes . . .'

'Go on, drink, Arslan Aga. It's very good for you.'

He drank. Then I leaned towards him and asked: 'My dear friend, when have you last spoken the truth?'

He looked at me with big innocent eyes and said honestly: 'At school, when I still knew how much is three times three.' The sweet wine had made the dear boy quite drunk. He was still very young, and had now reached the stage where he would answer my questions more or less truthfully. He confessed to have come here because he was curious, he confessed that he had never had diphtheria, and that he knew all Baku gossip inside out. 'The Nachararyans are going to murder you,' he chatted happily, 'but they are waiting for a suitable occasion. They're not in a hurry. I went to see the Kipianis once or twice. Nino was ill for a long time. Then they took her to Tiflis. Now she's back. I've seen her at the Club ball. You know—she was drinking wine as if it was water, and she was laughing all the time. She danced only with Russians. Her parents wanted to send her to Moscow, but she did not want to go. She goes out every day, and all the Russians are in love with her. Iljas Beg has been decorated and Mehmed Haidar has been wounded. Nachararyan's villa has been burnt down, and I have heard that was your friends' doing. Oh yes, another thing. Nino has a little dog, and she beats him every day, mercilessly. Nobody knows what she calls him, some say Ali Khan, others say Nachararyan. I think she calls him Seyd Mustafa. I've seen your father too. He says he's going to box my ears if I keep on gossiping so much. Kipianis have bought an estate in Tiflis. Maybe they'll go there for good.' He was a pathetic little thing.

'Arslan Aga, what on earth will become of you?'

He returned my look drunkenly: 'I'll become a king.'

'You will what?'

'I want to become a king of a beautiful country with lots of cavalry.'

'Anything else?'

'Die.'

'What for?'

'When I'm conquering my kingdom.'

I laughed and he was very hurt. 'They've given me three day's detention, the swine.'

'At school?'

'Yes, and guess why. Just because I've written to the newspaper again, about the brutal way the children are treated. My God, what a fuss they made about that.'

'But Arslan, no respectable person writes to newspapers.'

'Yes they do, and when I'm back I'll write something about you. Without mentioning your name, of course. I'm your friend, and I'm discreet. Something like this: "Flight from blood-feud—a deplorable custom in our country."' He finished off the rest of the bottle, dropped on the mat and was asleep at once. His servant came in and gave me a disapproving look, as if to say: You should be ashamed Ali Khan, to make the poor child drunk like that. I went out into the night. What a degenerate little rat he was, that Arslan Aga. Surely half the stories he had told must be lies. Why should Nino beat her dog? God knows what she calls the cur!

I went up the village street and sat down at the edge of the fields. Grimly the rocks looked down on me, dark in the shadow of the moon. Did they remember the past, or the dreams of men? High up in the sky the stars glittered like the lights of Baku. Thousands of light rays from the universe—and they met in my eyes. Dazedly I sat and looked at the sky, for an hour or more. 'So she's dancing with Russians,' I thought, and suddenly wanted to be back in town, to finish that ghostly night. A lizard rustled by, and I caught it. Frightened to death the little heart beat against my hand. I caressed the cold skin. Small eyes were looking at me, rigid with fear or maybe with wisdom. I raised the tiny creature to my face. It was like a living stone, ancient, weather-beaten, covered with dried-up skin. 'Nino,' I said, and thought of the dog, 'Nino, shall I beat you? But how does one beat a lizard?' Suddenly the little thing opened its mouth. A small pointed tongue shot out and disappeared again, all in one second. I laughed, the tongue was so small and so quick. I opened my hand, and the lizard was gone. There were just the dark stones. I got up and went back to the hut. Arslan was still lying on the floor, sleeping, his head on the devoted servant's knees. I went up to the roof and smoked hashish until I heard the call to prayer.

20

I don't know myself how it all happened. One day I woke up
and there was Nino standing before me. 'You've become a
lazybones, Ali Khan,' she said, and sat down on my mat, 'and
what's more, you snore, and that's bad manners.'

'It's the hashish in my tobacco that makes me snore,' I said
darkly.

Nino nodded. 'Then you'll just have to stop smoking
hashish.'

'Why do you beat the dog, you wretch?'

'The dog. Oh. I grab him by the tail with my left hand, and
beat him on the back with my right until he cries.'

'And what do you call him?'

'I call him Kilimandsharo,' said Nino softly. I rubbed my
eyes, and suddenly saw everything clearly before me again:
Nachararyan, the horse from Karabagh, the moonlit road, and
Nino in Seyd's saddle. 'Nino,' I shouted and jumped up. 'How
did you get here?'

'Arslan Aga told everybody in town that you wanted to
murder me. So I've just come.' Her face bent towards me, her
eyes full of tears. 'Ali Khan, I've missed you so terribly.' My
hand sank into the darkness of her hair. I kissed her, and her
lips opened, intoxicating me by her warmth. I put her on the

mat, and with one grip tore away the flowered silk that covered her. Her skin was soft and fragrant. I caressed her tenderly, she breathed heavily, looked up into my eyes, and her small bosom was trembling in my hand. I held her, and she groaned under my close embrace. Her ribs showed under her skin, narrow and tender. I put my face on her breast. 'Nino.' I said, and it seemed this word had a magical power, that made all the tangible world disappear. There were only two big moist Georgian eyes, mirroring all: fear, joy, curiosity and sudden tearing pain. She did not cry. But suddenly she grabbed the cover and crept under the warm feathers. She hid her face on my breast, and every movement of her slender body was like the call of earth, thirsting for the fulfilling benediction of rain. Tenderly I moved the cover down. Time stood still. . . .

We lay there quietly, tired and happy. Then Nino said: 'Now I'm going home. I see you're not going to kill me after all.'

'Did you come all by yourself?'

'No, Seyd Mustafa brought me. He said he'd take me and kill me if I disappointed you. He's sitting outside, his gun ready. You can call him if I've disappointed you.' I did not call him, but kissed her instead.

'And that is all you came for?'

'No,' she said honestly.

'Tell me, Nino.'

'Tell you what?'

'Why were you silent that night, when you were sitting in Seyd's saddle?'

'That was pride.'

'And why are you here now?'

'That too is pride.'

I took her hand and played with her rosy fingers: 'And Nachararyan?'

'Nachararyan,' she said slowly, 'you must not think he kidnapped me against my will. I knew what I was doing, and I thought it was the right thing to do. But it was wrong. It was my fault, and I deserved to die. That is why I was silent, and that is why I am here. Now you know all.' I kissed her palm. She spoke the truth, even though the other was dead, and the truth was dangerous for her. She got up, looked around the room and said gloomily: 'Now I'm going home. You needn't marry me. I'm going to Moscow.' I went to the door and opened it wide enough to see my pock-marked friend sitting outside, his legs crossed, his gun in his hand. His green belt was wrapped tightly round his stomach. 'Seyd,' I said, 'call a Mullah and another witness. I'm getting married in an hour's time.'

'I'm not calling any Mullah,' said Seyd, 'just two witnesses. I'll marry you myself. I'm entitled to do that.'

I closed the door. Nino was sitting up in bed, her black hair tumbling over her shoulders. She laughed: 'Ali Khan, do you realise what you're doing? You're marrying a fallen woman.'

I lay down with her, our bodies close together. 'You really want to marry me?' Nino asked.

'If you'll have me. You know I'm Kanly. Enemies are searching for me.'

'I know. But they won't come here. We'll just stay where we are.'

'Nino—you mean you'll stay here with me? In this mountain village, in this hut, without any servants?'

'Yes,' she said, 'I want to stay here, because you must stay here. I'll do the housework, bake bread and be a good wife to you.'

'And you won't be bored?'

'No,' she said simply, 'how could I—when we'll be lying together under one cover?' Someone knocked at the door. Nino slipped into my dressing gown. Seyd Mustafa came in, his green turban newly bound, and introduced the two witnesses. He sat down on the floor. From his belt he took a brass inkpot and a pen. On the inkpot was the inscription: 'Only in Praise of God.' He unfolded a sheet of paper and put it on his left palm. Then he dipped the bamboo pen into the ink.

154

Daintily he wrote: 'In the Name of God, the All-Merciful'. Then he turned to me: 'What is your name, sir?'

'Ali Khan Shirvanshir, son of Safar Khan of the House of Shirvanshir.'

'What is your religion?'

'Mohammedan, Shiite, in the interpretation of Imam Dshafar.'

'What is your desire?'

'To make public my wish to take this woman for my own.'

'What is your name, my lady?'

'Princess Nino Kipiani.'

'What is your religion?'

'Greek Orthodox.'

'What is your desire?'

'To be this man's wife.'

'Do you wish to retain your religion, or to change it to that of you husband?'

Nino hesitated for a while, then she raised her head and said proudly and decidedly: 'I wish to retain my religion.' Seyd was writing. The sheet was sliding over his palm, gradually getting covered with beautifully ornamented Arabic script. The marriage contract was ready. 'Now you sign,' said Seyd. I signed my name.

'Which name do I sign now?' asked Nino.

'Your new name.'

With a steady hand she wrote: 'Nino Hanum Shirvanshir'. Then the witnesses signed. Seyd Mustafa brought out the seal with his name on it and pressed it to the paper. There it was, in lovely Kufi script: 'Hafis Seyd Mustafa Meshedi, Slave to the Lord of the World.' He gave me the document. Then he embraced me and said in Persian: 'I am not a good man, Ali Khan. But Arslan Aga told me that without Nino you're going to ruin in the mountains, and becoming a drunkard. That is a sin. Nino asked me to take her here. If it is true what she says, love her. If it is not true we'll kill her tomorrow.'

'It is not true anymore, Seyd, but we won't kill her, even so.'

155

He gave me a puzzled look. Then he looked round the room and laughed. One hour later we cast the hashish pipe ceremoniously into the abyss. And that was all there was to our wedding.

Quite unexpectedly life was wonderful again. The whole village smiled when I was walking along the street, and I smiled back, because I was happy, happier than I had ever been. I would have loved to spend all my life here on our roof-yard, alone with Nino who had such tiny feet and was wearing the full bright red Daghestan pantaloons, gathered at the knees. She adapted herself perfectly. Nobody would have guessed that she was used to another life, to think and act quite differently from all the other women in the âoul. No one kept servants in our village, so Nino refused to have any. She prepared our meals, chatted with the women and told me all the village gossip. I rode, hunted, brought game home to her and ate all the strange dishes her imagination concocted, and her taste discarded.

This was a day in our life: Early in the morning I watched Nino running barefoot to the well, carrying an empty earthen-ware jug. Then she came back, carefully placing her bare heels on the sharp stones. She carried the water jug on her right shoulder, her slender hands holding the jug tightly. Once only, on one of her first days, she stumbled and the jug fell. She wept bitterly—it was so humiliating. But the other women comforted her. Every day Nino fetched the water, together with all the other village women. They walked in single file up the mountain, and I could see from afar Nino's bare legs, and her eyes looking seriously ahead. She did not look at me, and I too looked past her. She had immediately understood the law of the mountains: never, under any circumstance, to show one's love in front of other people. She came into the dark hut, closed the door and put the jug on the floor. She gave me a cup of water, and from a corner she fetched bread, cheese and honey. We ate with our hands, the way all people ate in the âoul. Nino

156

soon mastered the difficult art of sitting on the floor cross-legged. When we had finished eating Nino licked her fingers, showing white, gleaming teeth: 'The custom here,' she said, 'demands I should now wash your feet. But as we are alone, and I have gone to the spring, you will now wash my feet.' I put the funny little toys she called her feet into the water, and she splashed about, drops flying into my face. Then we would sit on the roof-yard, I on the cushions, and Nino at my feet, humming a song or just sitting silent, looking at me; while I never tired of looking at the face of my Madonna.

Every evening she would huddle under the bedclothes like a little animal: 'Are you happy, Ali Khan?' she asked me one night.

'Very happy. And you? Don't you want to go back to Baku?'

'Oh no,' she said seriously, 'I want to show that I can do what all Asian women can: serve my husband.'

When the oil lamp was put out she would lie, staring into the darkness, contemplating important matters: whether she really ought to put so much garlic into the roast mutton, and whether the poet Rustaveli had had an affair with Queen Tamar? And what would happen if, while living in this village, she should suddenly get a terrible toothache? And why, did I think, had the woman next door taken her broomstick and beaten her husband so terribly? 'Life is full of mysteries,' she said sadly and fell asleep. During the night she woke up, bumped against my elbow and murmured very proudly and conceitedly, 'I'm Nino'. Then she slept on, and I covered her slim shoulders with the blanket. 'Nino,' I thought, 'you really deserve a better life than this in a Daghestan village.'

One day I went to the nearest small town, called Chunsach. I came back loaded with the fruits of civilisation: an oil lamp, a lute, a gramophone, and a silk scarf. Her face lit up when she saw the gramophone. It was a pity that in the whole of Chunsach I had not been able to find more than two records: a dance of the mountain people and an aria from Aida. We played and played them until we could not tell them apart. News from

Baku was few and far between. Nino's parents kept imploring us to go to a more civilised country, when they were not threatening to put a curse on us. Nino's father came, but once only. When he saw how his daughter lived he exploded: 'For God's sake, get away from here at once! Nino will certainly fall ill in this wilderness!'

'I've never felt better,' said Nino. 'Can't you understand, father, we cannot go away. I don't want to become a widow yet.'

'But there are neutral countries, Spain, for instance. No Nachararyan can get at you there.'

'But father, how can we get to Spain?'

'Via Sweden.'

'I'm not going to Sweden,' said Nino furiously. The Prince returned to Baku and started sending monthly parcels of lingerie, cakes and books. Nino kept the books and gave the rest away. One day my father came. Nino received him with a shy smile, the smile of her schooldays, when confronted by an equation with too many foreign factors. This equation was soon solved: 'You cook?'

'I do.'

'You fetch the water?'

'I do.'

'The long way has made me tired. Will you wash my feet?' She fetched the jug and washed his feet.

'Thank you,' he said, took a long row of pink pearls from his pocket and put them round Nino's neck. Then he ate a meal she had prepared and pronounced his judgment: 'You have a good wife, Ali Khan, but a bad cook. I'll send you a cook from Baku.'

'Please don't,' cried Nino,' I want to serve my husband.' He laughed and sent her a pair of big diamond earrings.

It was very peaceful in our village. Only once Kasi Mullah came running with big news: an armed stranger had been caught on the outskirts of the âoul, obviously an Armenian. The whole village was in an uproar—I was their guest. My death would have been an everlasting blot on everyone's honour. I went out to take a look at the man. He really was an Armenian. But of course it was impossible to tell whether he was a Nachararyan or not. The wise men of the village held a meeting, talked the matter over and decided to give the man a good hiding and chase him from the village. If he was a Nachararyan he would warn the others, if he was not, God would see the farmers' good intentions and forgive them.

Somewhere on another planet war was raging. We neither heard nor saw anything of it. Our mountains were full of legends and fairy tales from the days of Shamil. War news never came our way. From time to time friends would send us newspapers, but I just threw them away unread. 'Do you still remember there's a war on?' Nino asked one day. I laughed. 'To be honest, Nino, I had forgotten all about it.' There really could be no better life for me, even if it was just an interval between past and future: God's incidental gift to Ali Khan Shirvanshir.

Then the letter came. An exhausted rider on a foam-covered horse brought it to our house. It was not from my father, nor from Seyd. 'Arslan Aga to Ali Khan' was written on it.

'What can he want?' said Nino astonished.

The rider said: 'Many letters are on the way to you, Khan. Arslan Aga gave me a lot of money because he wanted his letter to be the first.'

'This is the end of life in the âoul,' I thought and opened the letter. I read: 'In the Name of God. I greet you, Ali Khan. How are you, your horses, your wine, and the people you are living with? I am well, and so are my horses, my wine and my people. Hear me: Great things have happened in our town. The prisoners have left prison and are now walking about freely. "Wheré are the police?" I hear you asking. Behold—the police are now, where the prisoners used to be: in the prison near the sea. And the soldiers? There are no soldiers any more, either. I can see you shaking your head, my friend, and wonder how the Governor can allow all this? So let me tell you: yesterday our wise Governor decided to run away. He was getting tired of ruling over such bad people. He left behind a few old pairs of trousers and a cockade. Now you're laughing, Ali Khan, and think I'm lying. But surprise, surprise! this time I'm not lying. I can hear you asking: "Why doesn't the Czar send a new police force and a new Governor?" Let me tell you: there isn't a Czar any more either. There just isn't anything any more. I don't know what the whole thing is called, but yesterday we gave the headmaster a good thrashing and nobody interfered. I am your friend, Ali Khan, and so I want to be the first one to tell you all this, even though many people in town are writing to you today. So here it is: all Nachararyans have gone home, and there are no police any more. Peace be with you, Ali Khan. I am your friend and servant Arslan Aga.'

I looked up. Nino had gone quite pale. 'Ali Khan,' she said, and her voice trembled, 'the road is clear, we'll go! we'll go!'

In a strange ecstasy she kept repeating these words over and over again. She hung on my neck, sobbing 'We'll go!' and her naked feet beat a tattoo on the sand in the courtyard. 'Yes. Nino, of course we'll go.' I was happy and sad at the same time. The bare rocks of the mountains glistened in yellow splendour, There were the little huts, hanging over the abyss like beehives, and there was the little minaret, calling mutely for prayer and contemplation. That was our last day in the âoul.

21

The faces in the crowd showed a mixture of fear and joy. Scarlet banners with rather senseless slogans were stretched from one side of the street to the other. Market women gathered at street corners, demanding freedom for America's Indians and Africa's Bushmen. The tide had turned on the front: the Grand Duke had disappeared and crowds of ragged soldiers were lounging about the town. There was some shooting during the night, and during the day the crowd was looting the shops.

Nino was bending over the atlas. 'I'm looking for a country that is at peace,' she said, and her finger crossed the many-coloured border lines. 'Maybe Moscow. Or Petersburg,' I said, mocking her. She shrugged her shoulders, and her finger discovered Norway.

'I'm sure that's a peaceful country,' I said, 'but how do we get there?'

'We don't,' sighed Nino. 'America?'

'U-boats,' I said cheerfully.

'India, Spain, China, Japan?'

'Either they're at war, or we can't get there.'

'Ali Khan, we're in a mousetrap.'

'You are quite right, Nino. There's no sense in running away.

We will have to find a way to get a bit of common sense into our town, at least till the Turks come.'

'What's the use of having a hero for a husband!' said Nino reproachfully. 'I don't like banners and slogans and speeches. If this goes on I'll run away to your uncle in Persia.'

'It won't go on,' I said, and left the house.

At the Islamic Benevolent Society a meeting was in progress. The fine gentlemen who at my father's house a few months ago had cared so much for the future of our people were not amongst those present. Strong-muscled young men crowded the room. I met Iljas Beg at the door. He and Mehmed Haidar had come back from the front. The Czar's abdication had released them from their oath, and here they were back, brown, proud and strong. The war had done them good. They seemed like people who had had a glimpse of another world, and would carry it in their hearts forever. 'Ali Khan,' said Iljas Beg, 'we must do something. The enemy is at the gates of the city.'

'Yes, we must defend ourselves.'

'No, we must attack.' He went up to the dais and spoke in a loud commanding voice: 'Mohammedans! I'll make our town's position clear just once more. Since the beginning of the revolution the front has fallen to pieces. Russian deserters of all political parties are camping around Baku, armed and lusting for loot. There is only one Mohammedan military formation in town: we, the "Wild Division" Volunteers. We are fewer than the Russians, and we have fewer weapons. The second military formation in our town is the Military Association of the Armenian Nationalist Party *Dashnak-Tütün*. Stepa Lalai and Andronik are the leaders, and they have approached us. They are forming an army composed of the Armenians living here, and they want to take this army back to Karabagh and Armenia. We have agreed to the formation of this army and their exodus to Armenia. Therefore the Armenians will, together with us, offer an ultimatum to the Russians. We demand that no more Russian soldiers and refugees should be passed through our town. If the Russians reject our ultimatum, we can, together with the Armenians, get what we want by military means. Mohammedans, join the "Wild Division", take up your arms. The enemy is at our door.' I listened. It smelt of blood and war. For many days I had practised handling a machine-gun on the parade ground. Now my new knowledge was to be put to use. Mehmed Haidar was standing next to me, playing with his cartridge belt. I turned to him: 'Come to my house with Iljas Beg after the meeting. Seyd Mustafa is coming too. We'll have to talk this over.' He nodded and I went home.

My friends came armed, even Seyd Mustafa wore a dagger in his green belt. Nino prepared the tea. There was a strange silence in us. On the eve of the battle the town was unfamiliar and depressing. People were still walking along the streets, going about their business or just for a walk. But somehow all this seemed unreal and ghostly, as if they already felt that everyday life would soon become absurd.

'Have you got enough weapons?' asked Iljas Beg.

'Five guns, eight revolvers, one machine-gun and ammunition. And there's a cellar for the women and children.'

Nino raised her head. 'I'm not going into the cellar,' she said firmly. 'I'll defend my home with you.' Her voice sounded hard and firm.

'Nino,' said Mehmed Haidar quietly, 'we'll do the shooting and you'll dress the wounds.'

Nino bent her head, her shoulders sagged. 'Oh God—our streets will become battlefields, the theatre will be the H.Q., soon it will be as impossible to cross Nikolai Street as to go to China. We'll have to change our politics or conquer an army to be allowed to go to the Lyceum of the Holy Tamar. I can see you creeping on your stomachs through the Governor's garden, armed to the teeth, and there'll be a machine-gun near the lake where Ali Khan and I used to meet. We live in a strange town.'

'I'm sure there won't be any fighting,' said Iljas Beg. 'The Russians will accept our ultimatum."

Mehmed Haidar laughed grimly. 'I forgot to tell you that I

met Assadullah when I was on my way here. He says the Russians refuse. They demand that we surrender all our weapons. They won't get mine.'

'Then it's war,' said Iljas Beg, 'For us and our Armenian allies.'

Nino was silent, looking to the window. Seyd Mustafa adjusted his turban. 'Allah, Allah,' he said, 'I have not been to the front. I'm not as clever as Ali Khan. But I do know the Law. It is a bad thing if Mohammedans have to depend on the loyalty of unbelievers in a fight. In fact it is always bad to depend on anybody. Thus says the Law, and thus is life. Who is the leader of the Armenian troops? Stepa Lalai! I know him. In 1905 his parents were killed by Mohammedans. How can he ever forget that? And I don't believe that the Armenians will fight with us against the Russians anyway. Who are these Russians? Just rabble, anarchist robbers. Their leader's name is Stephan Shaumian, and he too is an Armenian. Armenian anarchists and Armenian Nationalists will make friends much quicker than Mohammedan Nationalists and Armenian Nationalists. That is the Mystery of the Blood. There'll be a rift, as sure as the Koran is always right.'

'Seyd,' said Nino, 'there is not only blood, there is also common sense. If the Russians win they won't treat Stepa Lalai and Andronik very kindly.'

Mehmed Haidar laughed out loud. 'Sorry, friends,' he said, 'I just thought how we will treat the Armenians if we win. If the Turks should overrun Armenia, surely you cannot imagine us defending it.'

Iljas Beg was furious: 'That's no way to talk or even to think. The Armenian question will be solved very simply: Lalai's battalions emigrate to Armenia, and their families with them. A year later there won't be a single Armenian left in Baku. They will have their own country and we will have ours. We'll simply be two peoples living side by side.'

'Iljas Beg,' I said, 'Seyd is right. You forget the Mystery of the Blood. Stepa Lalai's parents have been killed by Mohammedans, and he would be a knave if he forgot the duty of his blood.'

'Or a politician, Ali Khan, who can govern the call of his blood to save his people from bleeding to death. If he is clever he'll be on our side, in his and his people's interest.' We quarrelled until twilight fell. Then Nino said: 'Whoever you are, politicians or just men, I hope that in a week's time you'll all be here again, safe and sound. Because, if there should be fighting in town . . .' She fell silent.

In the night she was lying beside me, but she did not sleep. Her lips were parted and moist. Silently she stared at the window. I embraced her. She turned to me and asked: 'Are you going to fight, Ali Khan?'

'Of course, Nino.'

'Yes,' she said, 'Of course.' Suddenly she took my face into her hands and pressed it to her breast. She kissed me, silently, her eyes wide open. Wild passion gripped her. She was straining against me, full of lust, submission and fear of death. Her face looked as if she were in another world, a world she had to go to alone. Suddenly she fell back, held my head close to her eyes and said, so softly that I could hardly hear her: 'I will call the child Ali.' Then she was silent again, her veiled eyes turned to the window. Slender and dainty the old minaret rose in the pale light of the moon. Dark and threatening crouched the shadows of the old fortress wall. From far away came the sound of iron on iron—somebody was sharpening his dagger, and it sounded like a promise. Then the telephone rang. I got up and stumbled through the darkness. Iljas Beg's voice came through the receiver: 'The Armenians have joined the Russians. They demand that all Mohammedans surrender their weapons not later than three o'clock tomorrow afternoon. We refuse of course. You'll be at the machine-gun at the wall, left of Zizianashvili's Gate. I'm sending you another thirty men. Prepare everything for the defence of the Gate.' I put the receiver down. Nino was sitting up in bed, staring at me. I took up my dagger and tried its sharp edge.

'What is it, Ali?'

'The enemy is at the gate, Nino.' I dressed and called the servants. They came, broad-shouldered, strong and clumsy. I gave each of them a gun, then I went down to my father. He was standing in front of the mirror, a servant brushing his Tsherkess coat.

'Where is your position, Ali Khan?'

'At the Zizianashvili Gate.'

'Good. I'm in the hall of the Benevolent Society, on the Staff.' His sabre rattled, he fingered his moustache. 'Be brave, Ali. The enemy must not come over the wall. If they reach the Square outside the wall use your machine-gun. Assadullah is bringing in the farmers from the villages, they will attack the enemy from the rear in Nikolai Street.' He put his revolver into its holster and blinked tiredly. 'The last boat to Persia sails at eight o'clock. Nino must be sure to go. If the Russians win they will rape all women.'

I went back to my room. Nino was talking on the telephone. 'No, Mama,' I heard her say, 'I'm staying here. There is really no danger, you know. Thanks, Papa, don't worry, we've got enough food. Yes, thank you. But please don't worry. I'm not coming, I'm not!' She raised her voice on the last word, it was a cry. She put the receiver down. 'You are right, Nino,' I said, you wouldn't be safe at your parents' house either. At eight o'clock the last boat leaves for Persia. Pack your things.'

She blushed deeply. 'You're sending me away, Ali Khan?'

Never had I seen Nino blush like this. 'You'll be safe in Teheran, Nino. If the enemies win they'll rape all women.'

She raised her head and said defiantly: 'They won't rape me, Ali Khan—not me. Don't worry.'

'Go to Persia, Nino, please! There's still time.'

'Stop it,' she said severely. 'Ali, I'm terribly afraid, of the enemy, of the battle, of all the terrible things that are going to happen. But I'm staying here. I can't help you, but I belong to you. I have to stay here, that's all there is to it.' That was all. I kissed her eyes and felt very proud. She was a good wife, even when she defied me. I left the house. Dawn was breaking. Dust was in the air. I mounted the wall. My servants were crouching behind the stone battlements, their guns at the ready. Iljas Beg's thirty men were watching the empty Duma Square. There they were, with their black moustaches and brown faces, clumsy, silent and tense. The machine-gun with its small muzzle looked like a Russian nose, snub and broad. All was quiet around us. From time to time the liaison patrols came running silently along the wall, bringing short messages. Somewhere old men and priests were still trying to negotiate for the miracle of a last minute reconciliation.

The sun rose, and heat flooded from the leaden sky to sink into the stones. I looked across to my house. Nino was sitting on the roof, her face turned to the sun. At midday she came to the wall, bringing food and drink. She looked at the machine-gun with frightened curiosity, then she crouched silently in the shade until I sent her home. Now it was one o'clock. From the minaret Seyd Mustafa sang his prayer, plaintive and solemn. Then he joined us, awkwardly dragging his gun behind. He had stuck the Koran into his belt. I looked across to Duma Square, outside the wall. A few people were hurrying across the dust, anxiously bent low, as if in fear of an immediate attack. A veiled woman ran shouting and stumbling after her children, who were playing in the middle of the square. One, two, three. The bells of the Town Hall roared, shattering the silence. And at the same moment, as if these bells had miraculously opened the door to another world, we heard the first shots from the outskirts of the town.

22

There was no moon that night. Softly the sailing boat glided over the dull waters of the Caspian Sea. Little sprays of foam splashed us from time to time, bitter and salty. Like the wings of a huge bird the black sail was spread out above us. I was lying on the wet planks of the boat, swathed in sheepskins. The boatman, a Tekine, had his broad beardless face turned towards the stars. I raised my head, and my hand touched the curly fur. 'Seyd Mustafa?' I asked. His pock-marked face bent over me. The red stones of his rosary were gliding through his fingers . . . as if his hand, so well cared for, was playing with drops of blood. 'I am here, Ali Khan, just lie quietly,' he said. I saw the tears in his eyes and sat up. 'Mehmed Haidar is dead,' I said, 'I saw his body in Nikolai Street. They had cut off his nose and his ears.'

Seyd's face turned to me: 'The Russians came from Bailov and surrounded the Esplanade. You just brushed them off Duma Square.'

'Yes?' I remembered, 'and then Assadullah came and gave the order to attack. We came forward with bayonets and daggers. You sang the prayer "Ya sin."'

'And you—you drank the enemies' blood. Do you know who

stood at the corner of Ashoum? The whole family of the Nachararyans. They're wiped out.'

'They're wiped out,' I repeated. 'I had eight machine-guns on the roof of Ashoum House. We were masters of the whole quarter.'

Seyd Mustafa rubbed his brow. His face looked as if strewn with ashes: 'Up there the rattling went on all day. Some one said you were dead. Nino heard it, but did not say a word. She sat in her room, silent. And the machine-guns rattled. Suddenly she covered her face with her hands and cried: "Stop it! Stop it! Stop it!" and the machine-guns rattled. Then we ran out of ammunition, but the enemy did not know that. They thought it was a trap. Musa Nagi is dead, too. Lalai strangled him.' There was nothing I could say. The Tekine from the Red Sand Desert stared at the sky. His many-coloured silk kaftan fluttered in the breeze. Seyd said: 'I heard you were in the skirmish at the Zizianashvili Gate. Were you? I was on the other side of the wall.'

'I was. There was a black leather jacket. I pierced it with my dagger and it turned red. My cousin Aishe is dead, too.' The sea was like a mirror, the boat smelt of tar. It had no name, and it floated along the nameless coast of the Red Sand Desert. Seyd said softly: 'We put on shrouds, we of the Mosque. Then we took our daggers and fell on the enemy. Most of us are dead. But God did not let me die. Iljas too is alive, hiding in the country. How they looted your house! Not one carpet, not one piece of furniture, no crockery is left. Just the bare walls.' I closed my eyes. I was just one burning pain. I saw carts crammed with dead bodies, and Nino carrying a bundle in the dark, on the oil-saturated shore of Bibi-Eibat. Then the boat with the man from the desert. The tower of the Island of Nargin shedding its light. The town disappeared in the dark. The black oil derricks looked like grim prison guards. And now I was lying here, swathed in sheepskins, a throbbing pain tearing my chest. I rose. Nino was lying in the shade of a little piece of sailcloth. Her face was narrow and very pale. I took her cold hand and felt her fingers trembling slightly. Behind us my father was sitting next to the boatman. I heard a sentence here and there: '. . . so you really think that in the Oasis Tshardshui one can change the colour of one's eyes at will?'

'Yes, Khan. There is only one place in the world where one can do that—the Oasis Tshardshui. A holy man made a prophesy . . .'

'Nino,' I said, 'my father is having a conversation about the miracles of the Oasis Tshardshui. That's the way to be if one has to live in this world.'

'I can't,' said Nino, 'I can't Ali Khan, the dust on the street was red with blood.' She covered her face with her hands and cried soundlessly. Her shoulders were trembling. . . . I sat beside her, thinking of Duma Square outside the great wall, of Mehmed Haidar, lying dead in Nikolai Street—the same street he had walked all these years going to school—and of the black leather jacket, that had suddenly turned red. It hurt to be alive. My father's voice sounded as if from afar: 'There are serpents on the Island of Tsheleken?'

'Yes, Khan, immensely long, poisonous snakes . . . but no human eye has ever seen them. Only one holy man from the Oasis of Merv told once . . .' I could not stand it any longer. I went up to the steering wheel and said: 'Father, Asia is dead, our friends are dead, and we are exiles. God's anger is upon us, and you talk of the serpents on the Island of Tsheleken.' My father's face was serene. He leaned against the little mast and looked at me for a long time: 'Asia is not dead. Its borders only have changed, changed forever. Baku is now Europe. And that is not just a coincidence. There were no Asiatics left in Baku any longer.'

'Father, for three days I have defended Asia with machine-gun, bayonet and dagger.'

'You are a brave man, Ali Khan. But what is bravery? Europeans are brave too. You and all the men who fought with you—you are not Asiatics any more. I do not hate Europe. I am indifferent to it. You hate it, because there is something

European in you. You went to a Russian school, you have learnt Latin, you have a European wife. How can you still be an Asiatic? If you had won, you yourself would have introduced Europe in Baku, even without realising it, or intending to. It does not really matter whether we or the Russians build the new factories and highways. Things could not go on as they were. Being a good Asiatic does not mean killing many enemies, wildly lusting for blood.'

'Then what is being a good Asiatic?'

'You are half European, Ali Khan, that is why you ask this. I cannot explain it to you, because you see the visible things in life only. Your face is turned towards the earth. That is why your defeat pains you, and why you show it.' My father fell silent, his eyes looked withdrawn. He knew more than this our world of reality: he was, like all older people in Baku and in Persia, aware of another world, into which he could withdraw, and where he was unassailable. I had only a vague feeling of this realm of otherworldly peace, where one could bury friends, and yet talk to a boatman about the miracles of the Island of Tshardshui. I knocked at the door of this world, but I was not admitted. I was too involved in our painful reality. So I was not an Asiatic any more. No one blamed me for it, but they all seemed to know it. I longed to be at home again, in Asia's world of dreams, but I had become a stranger. Alone I stood in the boat, looking into the black mirror that was the sea. Mehmed Haidar is dead, Aishe is dead, our house is destroyed. And I was sailing in a little boat to the land of the Shah, to the great quiet that is Persia. Suddenly Nino stood beside me. 'Persia', she said, 'what are we going to do there?'

'We'll rest.'

'Yes, rest—I want to sleep, Ali Khan, for a month or a year. I want to sleep in a garden full of green trees. And there must be no shooting.'

'You're coming to the right country. Persia has been asleep for a thousand years, and not many shots are fired there.' We went on deck. Nino fell asleep at once. I lay awake for a long time, looking at Seyd's silhouette, the drops of blood in his fingers. He was praying. He knew the hidden world, the world that begins where reality ends. The sun was rising, and behind it was Persia. We could feel its breath while we were eating fish and drinking water, crouching on the boat's planks. The wild Tekine was talking to my father, looking at me indifferently, as if I were just a thing.

On the evening of the fourth day we saw a yellow strip on the horizon. It looked like a cloud, but it was Persia. The strip broadened. I saw clay huts and poor moorings. That was Enseli—the Shah's port. We dropped anchor on a mouldy wooden pier. A man wearing a morning coat came to meet us. On his high sheepskin hat shone the Silver Lion, his foot raised, the Rising Sun behind him. Two marine policemen strolled behind the official, barefoot and in rags. He looked at us with big round eyes and said: 'I greet you as a child greets the first rays of the sun on the day of his birth. Have you got documents?'

'We are Shirvanshirs,' said my father.

'Is Assad es Saltaneh Shirvanshir, for whom the Shah's Diamond Gate is opened, so fortunate as to have the same blood in his veins as yours?'

'He is my brother.' We disembarked. The man accompanied us. When we came to the storehouse he said: 'Assad es Saltaneh divined your coming. He has sent his machine which is stronger than the lion, faster than the stag, more beautiful than the eagle, more secure than a castle on a rock.' We turned a corner. There on the street, gasping asthmatically, stood an old rickety Ford. The tyres were mended in several places. We got in, and the engine started to tremble. The driver's eyes looked into the far distance, as if he were the captain of an ocean liner. It took only half an hour for the car to start, and then we began our journey to Teheran via Resht.

23

Enseli—Resht—streets and villages, the desert's breath hot on them. From time to time Abi-Jesid appears on the horizon like a ghost, Abi-Jesid, the Devil's Water, the Persian Fata Morgana. The grand road to Resht carries us along a river bed, but there is no river, and the bed is caked with mud. There is no running water in Persia's rivers, just pools and puddles here and there. On the dry shores stand rocks, throwing their shadows on the sand, and they look like prehistoric giants with fat stomachs, sleepy and content. The sound of a caravan's bells comes from afar. Our car slows up, and we see camels striding along the steep mountain range. The leader walks in front, carrying a rod in his hand, followed by men in black garments. The camels stride on, strong and tense. The little bells on their necks tinkle slowly with every measured step. Long dark sacks are hanging down on both sides from the camels' backs. Are they carrying silks from Ispahan? Or wool from Giljan? The car stops. Dead bodies are hanging there. A hundred, two hundred dead bodies, wrapped in black sheets. The camels pass us, heads nodding like stalks in a cornfield, when the wind brushes them. Through deserts and mountains, through the white glare of the salt steppe, through many a green oasis, passing great lakes, the caravan carries its load.

Far away, on the Turkish border, the camels will kneel down. Civil Servants, wearing the red fez, will prod the bodies, and then the caravan will move on again to the cupolas of the Holy Town of Kerbela. They will halt near the vault of the Martyr Hussein. Careful hands will carry the bodies to their prepared graves, where they can rest in Kerbela's sands till the Last Trumpet will wake them from their sleep. We bow to them, our hands covering our eyes: 'Pray for us at the saint's grave!' we cry, and their leader answers: 'We are ourselves in need of prayer!' And the caravan moves on, silently, like a shadow, like Abi-Jesid, the Fata Morgana of the great desert. . . .

We are driving through the streets of Resht. Wood and clay hide the horizon. Here one can feel the long centuries that have passed since this town was founded. The clay houses huddle in narrow alleys, as if afraid of wide expanses. Clay and glowing coal are the only colours. Everything is tiny, perhaps symbolically submitting to fate. It comes as a surprise to see a mosque rising up suddenly among all these cowering huts. The men wear round caps, which look like pumpkins, on their shorn heads, and their faces are like masks. Dust and dirt everywhere. It is not that Persians particularly like dust and dirt, they just leave things as they are because they know that in the end all returns to dust. We rest in a little tea house. The room smells of hashish. The men look at Nino with sidelong glances. A dervish stands in a corner, wrapped in rags, his mouth open, his lips covered in spittle, a copper bowl in his hand. He looks at everyone and no one, as if listening to an invisible presence, as if waiting for a sign from this unseen. He radiates an unbearable silence. Suddenly he leaps up, his mouth open, and cries out: 'I see the sun rise in the West!' The crowd shudders. A Governor's Messenger appears at the door: 'His Excellency has ordered a guard because of the naked woman.' He means Nino, who is not wearing a veil. Nino remains impassive, she does not speak Persian. We spend the night at the Governor's house. In the morning our guards saddle their horses. They will accompany us all the way to Teheran, because Nino refuses to wear the veil, and therefore is considered naked, but also because of the bandits roaming the country. Slowly, slowly the car drags itself through the desert. We pass Kasvin with its ancient ruins. Here Shah Shapur drew his armies together. The frail Sefevids, artists, artists' protectors, and apostles, held court here.

Another eighty, seventy, sixty miles—the road winds like a long serpent. And then—there is the Gate of Teheran, with its soft many-coloured tiles. Starkly the four towers stand against the snow of far-off Demavend. The black Arabic archway with its wise inscription looks at me like a demon's eye. Beggars with horrifying sores, wandering dervishes in filthy rags are lying in the dust under the big gate. Their hands with the slender aristocratic fingers are stretched out, to us. They sing of the splendour of the kingly town of Teheran, their voices mournful and sad. Long ago they too came with high hopes to the town of many cupolas. Now they are dust, lying in the dust, and sing sorrowful melodies of this town that has rejected them. The little car finds its way through the maze of alleys, across Cannon Square, passing the Imperial Diamond Gate, and then outside again, on to the wide road to the suburb of Shimran. The gate of the Shimran palace stood wide open, and as we passed through it the perfume of roses came towards us like a cloud. The blue tiles on the walls looked cool and friendly. Quickly we walked through the garden, where the fountain threw silver water into the air. The dark room with its curtained windows was like a cool well. Nino and I dropped on the soft cushions and immediately fell into an endless sleep.

We slept, woke up, slumbered, dreamed and slept on. It was wonderful to be in this cool room with its draped windows. The floor and the low divans were covered with innumerable cushions, mats and bolsters. In our dreams we heard the nightingales sing. It was strange to slumber in this big quiet house, far away from all danger, far from Baku's weatherbeaten wall. The hours passed quietly. From time to time Nino sighed, rose sleepily, and then put her head back on my stomach. I dropped my face into the soft cushions, perfumed with the sweet scent of a Persian harem. I felt infinitely lazy. For hours I was suffering, because my nose itched, and I was too indolent to raise my hand to scratch it. At last the itching stopped and I fell asleep again. Suddenly Nino woke up, rose and said: 'Ali Khan, I'm dying of hunger.' We went out into the garden. Rose bushes were in bloom around the fountain, cypresses reached up to the sky. A peacock, his tail an enormous coloured circle, stood motionless, looking at the setting sun. Far away the white peak of Demavend rose against the red and gold. I clapped my hands. A eunuch with a bloated face rushed up to us, followed by an old woman, stumbling under a load of rugs and cushions. We sat down in the shade of a cypress. The eunuch fetched bowls and water and covered the rugs with delicacies of the Persian cuisine. 'Well—I suppose I'd rather eat with my fingers than listen to machine-guns,' said Nino, and put her left hand into the steaming rice bowl. The eunuch's face was a study in horror—he looked away, so as not to see his master's shame. I showed Nino how to eat rice in Persia: by using three fingers of her right hand. She laughed for the first time since we had left Baku, and I felt calm and tranquil. It was wonderful to be in the Shimran palace, in the Shah's quiet peaceful land of devout poets and sages. Suddenly Nino asked: 'Where is your uncle, Assad es Saltaneh, and all his harem?'

'In his city palace, I suppose, and his four wives with him. And the harem? But this is the harem, this garden, and the rooms around it.'

Nino laughed: 'So I'm imprisoned in a harem after all. I thought it would come to that.' A second eunuch, a skinny old man, came to ask us whether we would like him to sing to us. We declined. Three girls rolled up the rugs, the old woman carried the left-overs away, and a little boy started feeding the peacock.

'Who are all these people, Ali Khan?'

'They're servants.'

'Good God, how many servants have we here then?' I did not know and called the eunuch. He pondered for a long time, his lips moving silently. It came out that about twenty-eight people were looking after the harem.

'And how many women are living here?'

'As many as you order, Khan. At present there is only the one sitting next to you. But we have plenty of room. Assad es Saltaneh is in town with his women. This is your harem.' He squatted down on his haunches and continued with great dignity: 'My name is Jahja Kuli. I am the guard of your honour, Khan. I can read, write, and do sums. I know all about management and how to treat women. You can depend on me. I can see this is a wild one, but in time I will teach her how to behave. Tell me when she has her periods, so I can make a note of it and remember. I'll have to know this, so I can judge her moods. For I'm sure she can be ill-tempered. I'll wash and shave her myself. I see she has even got hair in her armpits. It is really terrible how in some countries women's education is neglected. Tomorrow I'll dye her nails red, and before she goes to bed I'll look into her mouth.'

'Good heavens, what for?'

'Women with bad teeth have foul breath, so I must see her teeth and smell her breath.'

'What's the creature jabbering about?' asked Nino.

'He's recommending a dentist. Seems a queer character.' That came out sounding rather embarrassed. I told the eunuch: 'Jajha Kuli, I see you are an experienced person, who knows all about culture. But my wife is pregnant, and must be treated very carefully. Therefore we'll leave the education until she has had the child.' I could feel myself blushing. It was true that Nino was pregnant, and yet I had lied. 'You are very wise, Khan,' said the eunuch. 'Pregnant women are very slow to learn. By the way, there is a potion for making it a boy. But—' he looked searchingly at Nino's slender figure—'I think there's plenty of time for that.'

Outside, on the verandah, many slippers were shuffling along. Eunuchs and women made mysterious signs. Jahja Kuli went out and came back, his face in serious folds. 'Khan, His

Reverence, the learned Hafis Seyd Mustafa desires to greet you. I would not dare to disturb you, Khan, while you are enjoying the pleasures of your harem, but the Seyd is a learned man from the House of the Prophet. He is awaiting you in the Master's Suite.' At the word 'Seyd' Nino raised her head. 'Seyd Mustafa?' she repeated, 'let him come in, we'll have tea together.' The House of Shirvanshir's reputation escaped utter ruin only by the fact that the eunuch did not understand Russian. It beggars imagination—a Khan's wife receives another man in the harem!! Embarrassed and a bit shamefacedly I said: 'But Seyd can't come in here. This is the harem.' 'Oh. Haven't they got funny customs here. All right, we'll see him outside.'

'Nino, I'm afraid . . . I don't quite know how to explain . . . you see here in Persia things are rather different. What I mean, is . . . Seyd really is a man, isn't he?'

Nino's eyes opened wide. 'Do you mean to say that Seyd mustn't see me—that same Seyd who took me all the way to Daghestan?'

'I'm afraid that's about it, Nino, at least for the time being.'

'All right,' said Nino, suddenly quite cold, 'you'd better go now.'

I went, rather dejectedly. Then I sat in the big library with Seyd, drinking tea. He told me about his plans to go to Meshed, to stay there with his famous uncle, until Baku would be free of unbelievers. I agreed this was a good plan. Seyd was a polite man, he did not ask about Nino, did not even pronounce her name. Suddenly the door opened. 'Good evening, Seyd.' Nino's voice was controlled, but she sounded depressed. Seyd Mustafa jumped up. His pock-marked face showed something like terror. Nino sat down on the mats: 'Another cup of tea, Seyd?' From the corridor we heard innumerable slippers scurrying to and fro. The House of Shirvanshir's honour had collapsed for ever. It took Seyd several minutes to recover from his horror. Nino made a little face at him: 'I was not afraid of machine-guns, and I won't be afraid of your eunuchs.' And so we stayed together for hours, for Seyd was not only a polite, but also a very tactful man. Before we went to bed the eunuch approached me humbly: 'Lord, punish me. I should have watched her. But who could have foreseen that she would be so wild—so wild. It is my fault.' His fat face expressed deepest self-reproach.

24

It was strange—when the last shots had been fired on the oil-drenched shore of Bibi-Eibat I had thought I could never be happy again. And now, after only four weeks in the fragrant gardens of Shimran I was wholly at peace. I felt at home, and just lived like a plant, breathing the cool air of this tranquil place near Teheran. I did not drive to town very often, just to see friends and relatives from time to time, and to stroll through the dark labyrinths of the bazaar, accompanied by my servants. Narrow alleys, booths like tents, lamps burning in dark corners, people dressed in flowing garments, in wide trousers, in rags, and all of it covered by a domed roof, like an umbrella made of clay. I rummaged in roses, nuts, carpets, scarves, silks and jewels. I found gold-patterned jugs, ancient filigree necklaces and bracelets, choice perfumes, and cushions made of Morocco leather. Heavy silver tomans glide into the merchants' pockets. My servants are loaded with all the marvels of the Orient—all for Nino. I cannot bear it when her little face looks so terrified out there in the rose garden. The servants' backs are bent under their loads. I walk on. In one corner they are selling Korans bound in soft leather, and miniature paintings: a girl sitting under a cypress, next to her a Prince with almond eyes— a king hunting, a lance and a fleeing stag. Again the silver tomans clink. A bit further on two merchants crouch at a low table. One of them takes big coins from his pocket and gives them to the other, who scrutinises them carefully, bites them, weighs them on small scales and then puts them into a big bag. A hundred, a thousand maybe ten thousand times the merchant puts his hand into his pocket, before the debt is paid. His movements are sedate and dignified. Tshidaret! Trade! Was not Mohammed himself a merchant?

The bazaar is a maze. Next to the two merchants a sage sits in his booth, turning over the leaves of a book. His face looks like a rock on which a weather-beaten inscription is overgrown with moss. His long slender fingers are patient and delicate. From yellow moulding pages arises the perfume of the roses of Shiras, the song of Persian nightingales, joyous melodies, the vision of almond eyes and long lashes. The old man's beautiful hands turn the pages lovingly. Whispers, noises, cries. I started to haggle for an ancient soft-coloured carpet from Kerman. Nino loves the smooth lines of these woven gardens. Near me somebody is selling rose water and rose oil. Thousands of roses are blended in one drop of the precious rose oil, just as thousands of people are brought together in the narrow lanes of Teheran's bazaar. In my mind's eye I see Nino bent over a small bowl filled with rose oil.

The servants are exhausted. 'Take all this to Shimran, quickly, I'll come later.' They disappear in the crowd. I stoop and enter through a low door into a Persian tearoom, crowded with people. A red-bearded man sits in the middle.His eyes are half closed, he recites one of Hafis' love poems. The listener sigh enraptured. Then he reads from a newspaper: 'In America someone has invented a machine that can bring the spoken word to the listener. His Imperial Majesty, The King of Kings, whose splendour outshines the sun, whose hand reaches up to Mars, whose throne is higher than the world, received the resident of the monarch who at present reigns over England in his palace at Baghashah. In Spain a child was born that has three heads and four feet. The populace believe this to be a bad omen.' The listeners click their tongues in astonishment. Red-beard folds his newspaper. Another song! this time about the Knight Rustem and his son Sorab. I hardly listen, but look into the hot golden tea and ponder: things are not what they should be.

I am content, I am in Persia and live in a palace. But Nino lives in the same palace, and she is far from content. She was quite happy in Daghestan, though she had to bear all the dis-comforts of life in the wilderness. Here she just cannot come to terms with Persian etiquette. She wants to walk along the streets with me, even though the police forbid this strictly. Man and wife simply cannot go out together, neither can they receive guests together. She asks me to show her the town and is upset when I try to talk her out of it: 'I would love to show you the town, Nino. But I must not show you to the town.' Her big dark eyes look at me reproachful and bewildered. How can I make her understand that a Khan's wife simply cannot walk along the streets unveiled? I buy the most expensive veils: 'Look Nino, how beautiful. How they protect the face from sun and dust. Honestly, I would like to wear one myself.' She smiles sadly and puts the veils away: 'It degrades a woman to cover her face, Ali Khan. I would despise myself if I put this on.' I show her the police regulations. She tears them up and I order a closed coach with crystal windows. So I drive her through the town. On Cannon Square she saw my father and wanted to say hello to him. It was terrible, and I had to buy up half the bazaar to make it up with her. . . . And now I'm sitting here all by myself, looking into my teacup. Nino is dying of boredom, and I cannot help her. She wants to meet the wives and daughters of the European colony. But that would not do. A Khan's wife must not mix with the women of the unbelievers. They would be sorry for her, because she has to live in a harem, and in the end she would feel she really could not bear it any longer.

A few days ago she went to see my aunts and cousins, and came back terribly distracted. 'Ali Khan,' she cried in despair, 'they wanted to know how many times a day you honour me by making love to me. They say you are always with me. Their men tell them so—and they cannot imagine we're doing anything else. They gave me a charm against demons and an amulet that is certain to safeguard me against any rival. Your aunt Sultan Hanum asked me whether it wasn't too tiring to be the only wife of such a young man, and they all wanted to know what I do to keep you from going to the dancing boys. Your cousin Suata wanted to know whether you had ever had a dirty illness. They say I'm to be envied. Ali Khan, I feel as if they had thrown filth at me.' I comforted her as well as I could. She was crouching in the corner like a frightened child, and kept looking over her shoulder, terrified. It took her a long time to calm down.

My tea is getting cold. I'm sitting here in a tearoom so that people can see I do not spend my whole life in the harem. It is bad form to be with one's wife all the time—already my cousins are pulling my leg. Certain hours of the day only belong to the woman, all the rest to the man. But to Nino I am everything: newspaper, theatre, café, circle of friends and husband, all at the same time. That is why I just cannot let her sit at home all alone, that is why I buy practically the whole bazaar, for tonight my uncle holds a big reception in my father's honour. An Imperial Prince will be there, and Nino must stay at home, alone except for the company of the eunuch who wants to educate her.

I leave the bazaar and drive to Shimran. Nino sits in the big, rug- and carpet-covered hall, deep in thought, looking at a mountain of earrings, bracelets, silk scarves and bottles of scent. She kisses me quietly and gently, and my heart sinks in despair. The eunuch brings cool sorbet and looks at me disapprovingly. A man should not pamper his wife like that. In Persia life begins at night. The day is oppressive with heat, dirt and dust. But when night falls new life seems to seep into people, thoughts become free and easy, words come with new fluency. Teshachüt, Persia's strange ritualistic etiquette, begins to emerge. I love and admire this way of life, so different from

183

the world of Baku, Daghestan and Georgia. At eight o'clock my uncle's gala coaches drove up to our door, one for my father, one for me. Thus etiquette decreed. Three Peshemeds stood in front of each coach, heralds and runners, holding lanterns that shed their light on those dedicated faces. When these men had been small boys their spleens had been cut out, and now their only task in life was to run before a coach and call out importantly: 'Beware!' The streets were empty, but even so the runners had to keep calling 'Beware!' for this was etiquette as well. We drove along narrow alleys, past endless grey clay walls. Huts or palaces might be behind these walls, barracks or offices. But clay walls only face the streets, sheltering the privacy of Persian life. In the white light of the moon the bazaar's round cupolas looked like innumerable toy balloons, held together by an invisible hand. We stopped at a beautifully curved brass gate, set into a broad wall. The gate opened and we passed into the palace courtyard.

On ordinary days, when I came to this house by myself, an old man in a tattered coat would be standing at the gate. But tonight the front of the palace was covered with garlands and paper lanterns, and eight men bowed low when our coaches stopped. The immense courtyard was divided into two parts. On one side was the harem, where the fountain splashed and the nightingales sang. On the men's side was just a rectangular pool, with goldfish swimming lazily about.

We stepped out. My uncle came to the door to receive us. His small hand covered his face as he bowed low and escorted us into the house. There were carved wooden walls and gilt pillars in the big hall, and it was crowded with people, wearing black sheepskin caps, turbans, and wide robes of thin dark material. In the middle sat an elderly man with an immense curved nose, grey hair and eyebrows like birds' wings—His Imperial Highness the Prince. They all rose when we entered. After we had greeted the Prince first, and then all the others, we sank into soft cushions. The others followed suit. For a minute or two we sat silently. Then we all jumped up and bowed to each other again. At last we sat down for good, and a dignified silence reigned. Servants brought pale blue cups of fragrant tea. Baskets of fruit were handed round. His Imperial Highness broke the silence: 'I have travelled far and know many countries. But nowhere are peaches and cucumbers as good as in Persia.' He peeled a cucumber, sprinkled it with salt and ate it slowly, his eyes very sad.

'Your Highness is right,' said my uncle, 'I have travelled in Europe and have been amazed to see how small and ugly the fruits of the unbelievers are.'

'I am always absolutely content when I come back to Persia,' said a gentleman who represented the Persian Empire at a European court. 'There is nothing on earth we Persians need be jealous of. One can really say there are only Persians and barbarians in the world.'

'One could count in a few Indians, perhaps,' said the Prince. 'When I was in India a few years ago I met some people who were quite civilised and nearly came up to our standards of culture. But then again—it is so easy to make a mistake. A high born Indian I knew, and whom I took to be one of us, proved to be a barbarian after all. He invited me to his house for a meal, and just imagine, he ate the outer leaves of a green salad.'

We were horrified. A Mullah with sunken cheeks, wearing a heavy turban, said in a soft tired voice: 'The difference between Persians and non-Persians is this: We are the only ones who can appreciate beauty.' 'True—true,' said my uncle. 'I prefer a beautiful poem to a noisy factory any day. I forgive Abu Said his heresy, because he was the first to introduce our most lovely form of verses, the Rubaiyat, into our literature.'

He cleared his throat and recited:

"*Te medressé ve minaré viran neshúd*
In kar kalendari bisman neshúd
Ta iman kafr ve kaft iman neshüd
Ek bendé hakikata musulmán neshúd."

"Before not mosque and school are closed for good
The men who search for Truth cannot in truth be good
Before not Faith and Unbelief are one for good
No man can be Mohammedan for good."

'Terrible,' said the Mullah. 'Terrible. But this rhythm . . .' and he repeated lovingly: '*Ek bendé hakikata musulman neshúd.*' He rose, took a slender silver water-can with a long slim neck and staggered out. After a while he came back and put the can on the floor. We all rose to congratulate him, for his body had cleared itself of superfluous matter. Now my father asked: 'Is it true, Your Highness, that Vossough es Dawleh, our Premier, is about to make a new treaty with England?'

The Prince smiled: 'You'll have to ask Assad es Saltaneh about that—though it is not really a secret.'

'He is,' said my uncle. 'It is a very good treaty. For from now on the barbarians are going to be our slaves.'

'Are they? How?'

'It's like this: the English love work, and we love security. They love fighting, we love peace. So we have come to an agreement: we don't have to worry about the security of our borders any more. England is going to protect them, to build roads and houses and on top of it to pay us for all that. For England knows that it is mainly we who have brought culture to the world.'

My cousin Bahram Khan Shirvanshir was sitting next to my uncle. He raised his head and said: 'Do you think England appreciates us because of our culture or because of our oil?'

'Both lighten the world and need protection,' said my uncle indifferently. 'And surely we could not possibly be soldiers?'

'Why not?' This time it was I who put the question. 'I for one have fought for my people, and might well fight again.' Assad es Saltaneh looked at me disapprovingly, and the Prince put his teacup down. 'I did not know,' he said, haughtily, 'That there are soldiers amongst the Shirvanshirs.'

'But your Highness! Actually, he was an officer.'

'It's all the same, Assad es Saltaneh. Officer,' he repeated mockingly and pushed his lips out. I kept silent. I had forgotten that in the eyes of a noble Persian to be a soldier is to be low class. My cousin Bahram Khan Shirvanshir seemed to be the only one who had different ideas from those of the others. He was young. Mashir es Dawleh, a much decorated nobleman, sitting next to the Prince, told him at great length that Iran was under God's special protection, and did not need the sword any more to shine in the world. It had proved its valour in days long gone by. 'In the King's treasure chamber,' he finished, 'there is a globe made of gold. Every country on this globe is inlaid with jewels, each country with a different stone. But Iran is the only one covered with the clearest and most brilliant diamonds. This is more than a symbol—this is Truth.' I thought of all the foreign soldiers stationed in the country and of the policemen, covered in rags, in the port of Enseli. That was Asia, laying down its weapons before Europe, afraid to become European itself. The Prince despised soldiers—yet he himself was a descendant of the Shah under whom my forefather had been one of the conquerors of Tiflis. In those days Iran knew how to use weapons without losing face. But times had changed, and Iran had degenerated, as it had when ruled by the artistic Sefevids. The Prince preferred a poem to a machine-gun, maybe because he knew more about poems than about machine-guns. The Prince was old, and so was my uncle. Iran was dying, but dying gracefully. A poem by Omar the Tentmaker came suddenly to my lips:

'A chessboard made of Night and Day
Is used by fate, on which his game to play
With men, put up and push around and then
Return each one to where before he lay.'

I had not realised that, deep in thought, I had spoken the verses aloud. The Prince's face softened. 'I suppose you became a soldier more or less just by coincidence,' he said condescendingly. 'I see you are an educated person. If you had the choice to decide your fate, would you seriously consider becoming a soldier?' I bowed. 'You ask what I would choose, Your Highness? Just four things: Ruby-red lips, the sound of guitars, wise counsel and red wine.' Dakiki's famous verse put me back in favour with every one. Even the Mullah with the sunken cheeks smiled graciously.

It was midnight when the doors of the dining room opened, and we entered. An enormous sheet had been put on the carpets. In the middle stood a big brass bowl, filled with pilav. All around lay big flat white loaves of bread, and innumerable bowls of all sizes, either empty or filled with various delicacies tempted us. Servants, standing in the corners motionless like statues were holding lanterns, spreading soft light. We sat down and began to help ourselves, each in any sequence he liked. We ate quickly, as custom decreed, for eating is the one thing a Persian does quickly. The Mullah said a short prayer. My cousin Bahram Khan sat next to me. He ate little, and looked at me curiously: 'Do you like Persia?'

'Yes, I do, very much.'

'How long will you stay here?'

'Until the Turks have taken Baku.'

'I envy you, Ali Khan.' His voice was full of admiration. He made a roll of a flat piece of bread and filled it with rice. 'You sat behind a machine-gun and saw tears in the faces of your enemies. Iran's sword is rusty. We enthuse over poems Firdausi wrote four hundred years ago, and we can easily distinguish between a verse by Dakiki and one by Rudaki. But we don't know how to build a road fit for motor cars, or how to lead a regiment.'

'Roads fit for motor cars,' I repeated, and thought of melon fields in the moonlight on the road to Mardakjany. It was very good that nobody in Asia knew how to build these roads. If they did a horse from Karabagh could never, never catch up with a European car.

'What do you need motor roads for, Bahram Khan?'

'To transport soldiers on trucks, even though our statesmen

188

say we don't need soldiers. But we do! We need machine-guns, schools, hospitals, a well-organised system of taxation, new laws, and people like you. The last thing we need is old verses. Iran is falling to pieces while old men sit about reciting poetry. But we have other songs now: do you know the poet Ashraf's verses, the one who lives in Giljan?' He bent forward and recited softly: '"Our country is attacked by Sorrow and Grief. Rise up, follow Iran's coffin. Persia's Youth was slain in this wake. Red are the moon, the fields and hills and valleys—red with their blood."'

'Terrible rhymes, the Prince would say. His sense of beauty would be deeply offended.'

'There is another poem, even more beautiful,' said Bahram Khan stubbornly, 'by a poet called Mirza Aga Khan. Listen to this: "May Iran be spared the fate of being ruled over by an unbeliever. Iran the Bride must never share the bed of the Russian bridegroom. Her unearthly beauty must never be the plaything of English lords."'

'Not too bad,' I said, and smiled. Young Persia seemed to differ from Old Persia mainly by composing bad poems. 'But tell me, Bahram Khan, what do you really want to accomplish?'

He sat stiffly on the pale red carpet and answered: 'Have you seen Maidani Square? A hundred old rusty cannons are standing there, their muzzles turned to all four corners of the earth. Do you realise that these stupid dusty relics are the only guns in all Persia? And that there's not one single fort, not one single man-of-war, practically not one single soldier—except of course the Russian Cossacks, the English Redcoats, and the four hundred fat Bahaduran of the Palace Guard? Just look at your uncle, or the Prince, or all these honourable noblemen, with their marvellous titles: dim eyes, weak hands, old and rusty like the cannons on Maidani-Sipeh Square. They haven't got many more years to live, and it's high time for them to go. Far too long has our country been in the tired hands of Princes and poets. Persia is like the outstretched hand of an old beggar. I want it to be the clenched fist of a young man. Stay here, Ali

Khan. I have heard about you. How you were the last to stay with your machine-gun, defending the old wall of Baku, how you killed an enemy by biting his throat in the moonlight. Here you would have more than an old wall to defend, and you would have more than one machine-gun. Wouldn't that be better than sitting about in the harem, or buying up all the treasures in the bazaar?' I was silent, deep in thought. Teheran! The oldest city in the world. 'Roga Rey' the Babylonians called her, Roga Rey, the City of Kings. The dust of old legends, the faded gold of old palaces—twisted pillars of the Diamond Gate, faded lines on old carpets, and calm rythms of old Rubaiyats—here they were before me, in past, present and future.

'Bahram Khan,' I said, 'Suppose you get what you want. When you have built your asphalt roads and forts, and when you have sent the worst servants to the most modern schools—what will become of the soul of Asia?'

'The soul of Asia?' he smiled. 'We'll build a big house on the far end of Cannon Square. There we'll house the Soul of Asia: the flags of the mosques, the manuscripts of the poets, miniature paintings, and dancing boys, for they too are a part of the soul of Asia. And on the front of the building we'll write in the most ornamental Kufi script: the word "Museum". Uncle Assad es Saltaneh can be the museum's manager and His Imperial Highness its director. Will you help us to build this magnificent edifice?'

'I'll think about it, Bahram Khan.'

The meal came to an end. The guests were sitting about in loose groups. I got up and went out to the open verandah, where the air was cool and fresh. From the garden came the fragrance of Persia's roses. I sat down, a rosary gliding through my fingers, and looked out into the night. Over there, behind the clay cupolas of the bazaar, was Shimran. There my Nino was lying, covered by rugs and pillows. She was probably asleep, her lips just open, her eyelids swollen by tears. Deep sadness engulfed me. All the treasures of the bazaar put together were not enough to bring back the smile to Nino's eyes.

Persia! Should I stay? Among eunuchs and Princes, dervishes and fools? To build asphalt roads, to form armies, to bring Europe still further into the heart of Asia? Suddenly I felt that nothing, nothing in the world was as dear to me as the smile in Nino's eyes. When had I last seen that smile? One day, long ago, in Baku near the old wall. A wave of wild homesickness swept over me. In my mind's eye I saw the dusty wall again, and the sun setting behind the Island of Nargin. I heard the jackals howling at the moon under the Gate of the Grey Wolf, in the desert sand covering the steppe around Baku. Merchants were haggling near the Maiden's Tower, and when you walked along Nikolai Street you came to the Lyceum of the Holy Queen Tamar. And under the trees in the court of the Lyceum stood Nino, her exercise book in her hand, her eyes big and astonished. The fragrance of the Persian roses had suddenly vanished, and instead the clear desert air of Baku and the faint scent of sea, sand and oil was around me. I called to my homeland as a child calls for its mother, and this homeland, I felt dimly, was no more. Never, never should I have left this town, where God let me be born. I was chained to the old wall, like a dog to his kennel. My eyes turned to the sky. There Persian stars were big and far away, like the jewels in the Shah's crown. Never had this feeling of being a stranger here come over me as strongly as at this moment. I belonged to Baku, where Nino's eyes looked smiling at me in the shade of the old wall.

Bahram Khan touched my shoulder. 'Ali Khan, are you dreaming? Have you thought about what I said—will you help to build the house of New Iran?'

'Cousin Bahram Khan,' I said, 'I envy you. Only a refugee knows what his homeland means to him. I cannot build Iran. My dagger was sharpened on the stones of Baku's wall.'

He looked sadly at me. '*Madjnoun*' he said in Arabic, and that meant Lover as well as Madman. He was of my blood and had guessed my secret. I rose. The dignitaries were bowing before the Prince in the big hall. I saw his hands with the long withered fingers and red finger-nails. No, I was not made to display Firdausi's verses, Hafis' sighs of love and Sa'adi's quotations. I went into the hall and bent over the Prince's hand. His eyes were sad and absent, filled with foreboding of a threatening destiny. Then I drove to Shimran and thought of the Square where the rusty cannons stood, of the Prince's tired eyes. Nino's submissive calm and the puzzle of ruin without escape.

25

Glaring and entangled the colours on the map ran into each other. Names of towns, mountain ranges and rivers were mixed up and practically unreadable. The map was spread out on the divan, and there I sat, little coloured flags in my hand. I had a newspaper too, and in those columns the names of towns, mountain ranges and rivers were just as confused as on the coloured map. I was bending over both pieces of paper, trying industriously to get the correct solution from the mistakes in the newspaper and the unreadability of the map. I put a little green flag into a little circle, next to which was printed 'Elisabethpol (Gandsha)'. But the last five letters were overprinted on to the mountains of Sanguldak. According to the newspaper the solicitor Feth Ali Khan of Choja in Gandsha had proclaimed the Free Republic of Azerbeidshan. The row of little green flags east of Gandsha represented the army Enver Bey had sent to liberate our country. From the right Nuri Pasha's regiments were moving towards the town of Agdash. On the left Mursal Pasha occupied the valleys of Elissu. The New Azerbeidshan Volunteers' Battalions were fighting in the middle. Now the map was quite clear and understandable. Slowly the Turkish ring was closing round Russian-occupied Baku. The little green flags needed just a little more readjusting—and then the red flags would be squeezed together in one lump on the big spot that was marked 'Baku'.

Jahja Kuli, the eunuch, stood silently behind me and followed my strange game most interestedly. It seemed to him, that all this moving around of little flags on coloured paper must be some dark and strange magic of a mighty sorcerer. Maybe he mistook cause and effect and thought that all I had to do to free my home from the unbelievers was to ensure help of unearthly powers by sticking little green flags into the red spot that was Baku. He did not want to disturb me in this secret work, but only made his report, as bound in duty, in a monotonous serious voice: 'Oh Khan, when I tried to dye her nails with henna she overthrew the bowl and scratched me, even though I had bought the most expensive henna. Early in the morning I led her to the window, took her head very gently into my hands and asked her to open her mouth. Surely it is my duty, Khan, to look after her teeth. But she drew back harshly, raised her right hand and beat me on my left cheek. It did not hurt very much, but I lost face. Forgive your slave, Khan, but I dare not remove the hair on her body. She is a strange woman. She will not wear any amulets, and does not take any precautions to safeguard her child. Be not angry with me, Khan, if it is a girl, be angry with Nino Hanum. She must be possessed by an evil spirit, for she trembles when I touch her. I know an old woman who lives near the Mosque Abdul-Asim. She is an expert in exorcising evil spirits. Maybe it would be a good idea if I asked her to come here. Just think Khan, in the morning she washes her face in cold water, to spoil her skin. She brushes her teeth with hard brushes, that make the gums bleed, instead of cleaning them with the right forefinger, dipped into scented salve, like everybody else. Only an evil spirit can have given her these ideas.'

I did not really listen. Nearly every day he came to my room to give me these monotonous reports. He was really troubled, for he was an honest person and wanted to do his duty, and he felt responsible for my future child. Nino had a running battle with him, playful but tenacious. She threw cushions at him, walked on the wide top of the wall of the house without wearing a veil, threw his amulets out of the window, and covered the walls with photos of her Georgian cousins—male cousins! He reported all this to me, sad and frightened, and every evening Nino sat with me on the divan and made her plans for the battle of next day. 'What do you think Ali Khan,' she said, and rubbed her chin thoughtfully, 'shall I pour water on his face at night from a thin hose, or throw a cat at him during the day? No, I know. I'll do exercises every day in the garden by the fountain. And I'll make him do them too, he's getting too fat. Or even better: I'll tickle him till he dies. I've heard you can kill people by tickling them, and he's awfully ticklish.' She was sunk in dark plans of revenge, till she fell asleep, and the next day the eunuch reported horrified: 'Ali Khan, Nino Hanum is standing by the fountain, making very strange movements with her arms and legs. I'm afraid, O Lord. She bends her body backwards and forwards, as if she had no bones. Maybe she is praying to an unknown god. She wants me to copy her movements. But I am a devout Muslim, Khan, and I only throw myself into the dust before Allah. I am greatly afraid for her bones and for the welfare of my soul.'

To dismiss the eunuch would not solve anything. Another would have to come in his place, for a household without an eunuch is unthinkable. No one else can supervise the women who do the housework, no one else can do the accounts, keep the money and check the expenses. Only the eunuch can do that, he who has no desires and cannot be bribed. Therefore I did not say anything, but looked at the green line of little flags around Baku. The eunuch cleared his throat, eager to do his duty. 'Shall I ask the old woman from the Mosque of Abdul-Asim to come?'

'What for, Jahja Kuli?'

'To exorcise the evil spirits from Nino Hanum's body.' I sighed, for I did not think it possible that the wise woman from the Mosque Abdul-Asim could be a match for the spirits of Europe.

'I don't think that is necessary, Jahja Kuli. I myself know how to ban spirits. I will arrange everything in my own good time. But just now my force must be concentrated on these little flags.' Curiosity and fear shone in the eunuch's eyes.

'When the green flags have crowded out the red ones, then your hometown is free? Is that so, Khan?'

'That is so, Jahja Kuli.'

'Then why do you not just put the green flags where they should be?'

'That I cannot do, Jahja Kuli, my force is not strong enough.'

He looked at me with concern: 'You should pray to God to give you strength. Next week begins the festival of Moharram. If you offer your prayer to God during Moharram he will certainly give you strength.' I folded up the map, and was bewildered and sad. Listening to the eunuch's chatter was beginning to get on my nerves. Nino was not at home. Her parents had come to Teheran, and Nino spent long hours in the little villa the illustrious family had rented. There she met other Europeans, and tried to keep this a secret. But of course I heard about it, and as I felt very sorry for her, I pretended to know nothing. The eunuch stood motionless, waiting for my orders. I thought of Seyd Mustafa, my friend, who had come to Teheran for a few days. I saw him but seldom, for he spent his days in mosques, saints' graves and having wise discussions with tattered dervishes. 'Jahja Kuli,' I said at last, 'go to Seyd Mustafa. He lives next to the Mosque of Sepahlesar. Ask him to honour me with his visit.' The eunuch went, and I was alone. Indeed my strength was not enough, to bring the green flags to Baku. Somewhere in the steppes of my homeland the Turkish battalions were fighting, and with them our Volunteer Troops assembled under New Azerbeidshan's banner. I knew the banner, I knew the number of troops and the battles they fought. Iljas Beg was with them, and I longed to be on the battlefield with him in the cool of the morning. But the road to the front was closed to me. English and Russian troops were guarding the borders. The broad bridge across the river Araxes, which joined Iran to the theatre of war was now barricaded with barbed wire, machine-guns and soldiers. The country of the Shah retreated into its calm like a snail into its shell. No man, no mouse, not even a fly was allowed to cross into the pestilential area where only disgusting fighting and shooting was going on, but hardly any poetry was recited. Many refugees came from Baku, amongst them Arslan Aga, the chatterbox. He was rushing from one tea house to another and writing articles in which he likened the Turk's victories to those of Alexander the Great. One of these articles was banned, because the censor had the nasty suspicion that in glorifying Alexander, Persia, once vanquished by Alexander, was secretly being run down. Since that day Arslan Aga referred to himself as a martyr of his convictions. He came to see me, and told me in great detail all the heroic deeds I was supposed to have done during the defence of Baku. In his mind's eye he saw legions of enemies marching past my machine-gun, with the sole purpose of being mowed down by me. He himself had spent the time of battle in the cellar of a printing office, where he had been busy writing rousing patriotic speeches, which had never been delivered. He read them to me, and asked me to describe to him a hero's feelings in a hand-to-hand fight. I choked him with sweets and saw him to the door. He left behind the smell of printers' ink, and a fat new copy book in which I was supposed to enter the hero's feelings. I looked at the white pages, thought of Nino's sad absent looks, of my entangled life and took up the pen. Not to describe the hero's feelings, but to record on paper the road that had led us, Nino and me, to the fragrant garden of Shimran, where she had lost her smile.

There I sat, writing with the Persian pen of slit bamboo. I put the loose leaves in the order that I had started when I was still at school, and the past rose up again, until Seyd Mustafa came into the room, and pressed his pock-marked face against my shoulder. 'Seyd,' I said, 'my life has become a tangle. The road to the front is barred, Nino has forgotten how to laugh, and I shed ink instead of blood. What shall I do, Seyd Mustafa?' My friend looked at me quietly and searchingly. His robe was black, his face had become thin. His slender body seemed bowed under the weight of a mystery. He sat down and said:

'With your hands you cannot do anything, Ali Khan. But man has more than just hands. Look at my robe, and you'll know what I mean. Man is ruled by the Unseen. Brush against the Mystery, and its might will descend on you.'

'I cannot understand you, Seyd Mustafa. My soul is in pain, and I search for a road out of the darkness.'

'You are turned towards the world, Ali Khan, and you forget the Unseen, who rules the world. In 680, the Year of the Flight, Hussein, the Prophet's grandson, fell near Kerbela, pursued by enemies. He was the Saviour and the Mystery. With his blood the All-Mighty marked the rising and the setting sun. Twelve Imams reigned over the community of Shia, over us Shiites: the first one was Hussein, and the Last One is the Imam of the Last Day, the Invisible One, who even today is secretly leading the people of Shia. Visible in his work, and yet unassailable is the Hidden Imam. I see him in the rising sun, in the miracle of the seed, in the stormy sea. I hear his voice in the rattling of a machine-gun, a woman's sigh, in the blowing of the wind. And the Unseen ordains: mourning be Shia's fate! Mourning for Hussein's blood, shed in the desert sands of Kerbela. One month of the year is dedicated to mourning: the month of Moharram. Whoever is suffering—let him cry in the month of Mourning. On the tenth day of Moharram the fate of Shia fulfils itself, for this is the day of the martyr's death. This suffering, that the young Hussein took upon his shoulders, this suffering must be taken on their shoulders by his devout followers. Whoever takes upon himself a part of this suffering will be blessed with part of the blessing. Therefore the devout man chastises himself in the month of Moharram, and in the self-inflicted pain the man entangled in the problems of this world is shown the road to grace, and the joy of salvation. This is the secret of Moharram.'

'Seyd,' I said, tired and irritable, 'I asked you how I can bring back happiness to my house, for I feel full of dim terror, and you feed me with wise tales from religious instructions we learned at school. Should I then run to the mosques and flay my back with iron chains? I am devout and fulfil our religious duties. I believe in the Mystery of the Unseen, but I do not believe the road to my happiness goes through the martyrdom of the Holy Hussein.'

'But I believe that, Ali Khan. You ask me for the road, and I show it to you. I do not know of any other. Iljas Beg sheds his blood on the front at Gandsha. You cannot go to Gandsha. Therefore you should dedicate your blood to the Unseen, who asks you for it on the tenth day of Moharram. Do not say the Holy Sacrifice does not make sense—there is nothing in this vale of tears that does not make sense. Do battle for the homeland during Moharram, as Iljas Beg does at Gandsha.' I was silent. The coach drove into the courtyard, and Nino's face was a blur through the crystal windows. The door of the harem opened, and Seyd Mustafa was suddenly eager to go. 'Come tomorrow to the Mosque Sepahlesar. We will talk again.'

26

We were lying on the divan, between us the Nardy board, inlaid with mother of pearl, covered with ivory pieces. Ever since I had taught Nino this Persian game we had been throwing dice for tomans, earrings, kisses and names of our future children. Nino lost, paid her debts and threw the dice again. Her eyes shone with excitement, her fingers touched the ivory pieces as if they were precious jewels. 'You'll be the ruin of me, Ali,' she sighed, sliding towards me the eight tomans I had just won. She pushed the board away, put her head on my knees, looked thoughtfully up to the ceiling and sank into a dream.

It was a wonderful day, for Nino was happy with the deep content of fulfilled revenge. This is what had happened: Early in the morning the house reverberated with moaning and groaning. Her enemy, Jahja Kuli, came into the room, his cheek swollen, his face contorted. 'Toothache,' he said, with a face as if on the brink of suicide. Triumph and joy shone in Nino's eyes. She led him to the window, looked into his mouth, and raised her eyebrows. Then she shook her head, as if worried, got a strong piece of string and wound it round Jahja Kuli's hollow tooth. She then fastened the other end of the string to the handle of the open door. 'Now,' she said, rushed to the door and banged it closed. A terrific howl—the eunuch fell to the ground, frightened to death, and stared at his tooth flying towards the door in an elegant arc. 'Tell him, Ali Khan, that's what comes from cleaning one's teeth with the forefinger of the right hand!' I translated word for word, and Jahja Kuli picked his tooth up from the floor. But Nino's thirst for revenge was not settled yet. 'Tell him Ali Khan, that he is not cured yet, not by a long way. He must go to bed and for six hours he must put a hot poultice on his cheek. And on no account must he eat sweets for at least a week.' Jahja Kuli went away, relieved but shattered. 'You should be ashamed of yourself, Nino,' I said, 'taking away the last thing this poor soul can enjoy.' 'Serves him right,' said Nino heartlessly, and fetched the Nardy board. She lost the game, and the balance of justice was restored.

Now she looked up and her fingers caressed my chin: 'When will Baku be liberated, Ali?'

'I would say in about two weeks' time.'

'Fourteen days,' she sighed. 'You know, I just can't wait for Baku and the Turks. Everything has turned out so differently. You like it here, but I am dishonoured every day.'

'What do you mean, dishonoured?'

'Everybody treats me like a very expensive and fragile thing. I don't know how expensive I am, but I am neither fragile nor a thing. Remember Daghestan? There it was quite different. No, I don't like it here at all. If Baku is not liberated very soon we must go somewhere else. I don't know anything about all these poets this country is so proud of, but I do know that on the feast of Hussein men scratch their breasts, beat their heads with daggers and whip their backs with iron chains. Many Europeans have left town today, because they don't want to see these things. The whole thing makes me sick. I feel that here I am exposed to a malignant force, impervious to reason, that can attack me any time.' Her tender face looked up at me. Her eyes were deep and dark as never before, the pupils were big and her glance seemed directed inwards. Only Nino's eyes gave away the secret of her pregnancy.

'Are you afraid, Nino?'

'What of?' her voice sounded genuinely astonished.

'Some women are.'

'No,' she said seriously, 'I am not afraid. I'm afraid of mice, of crocodiles, exams and eunuchs. But not of that. I might as well be afraid of a cold in the head in winter.'

I kissed her cool eyelids. She stood up and brushed her hair back. 'I'll go to see my parents, Ali Khan.' I nodded, though I knew only too well that in the Kipiani's villa all the harem rules were disregarded. The Prince received Georgian friends and European diplomats. Nino drank tea, ate English biscuits and talked to the Dutch Consul about Rembrandt and the problem of Oriental Women. She went, and I saw the coach with the crystal windows leave the courtyard.

I was alone, thinking about the little green flags, and the few inches of coloured paper that separated me from my home. Slowly the room became darker and darker. The faint fragrance of Nino's scent still lingered in the soft cushions of the divan. I slid to the floor, my hand searching for the rosary. The Silver Lion, holding the sword in his left paw, shone on the wall. I looked up to him, and a sudden feeling of weakness and hopelessness overwhelmed me. It was shameful to sit here in the shade of the Silver Lion, while my people were bleeding to death in the steppes of Gandsha. I too was just a thing. An expensive, sheltered thing, looked after and cared for, a Shirvanshir, whose fate it was to receive some sort of splendid title sooner or later, and to express elegant feelings in elegant classical sentences. I was helpless, and the Silver Lion grinned at me from the wall. The border-bridge over the Araxes was closed, and no road led from the land of Iran to Nino's soul. I fingered the rosary. The thread snapped, the amber beads rolled to the floor.

From far off the dull beats of a tambourine came through the twilight, calling and threatening, like a warning of the Unseen. I went to the window. The dusty road lay glowing in the last rays of the sun. I became aware of drumbeats, coming closer, their rhythm accompanied by staccato shouts, repeated over and over again, thousands of times: 'Shah—ssé ... Wah—ssé—Shah Hussein ... Woe Hussein!' Round the corner erupted the procession. Three immense standards, embroidered in heavy gold, swayed above the crowd, carried by strong hands. On one of them was written 'Ali' in gold letters—the name of the Prophet's friend on earth. On the second flag of black velvet were the broad outlines of a left palm, blessing and rejecting, the Hand of Fatima, the Prophet's daughter. And on the third flag, with letters that seemed to cover the sky, was one word only: 'Hussein'—the Prophet's grandson, martyr and inheritor. Slowly the crowd passed along the street. First came the devout penitents, with naked backs, wearing black mourning robes, carrying heavy iron chains, and the chains hit their bleeding red shoulders. Behind them came a wide half circle of broad-shouldered men, taking two steps forward and one step back. Huskily their cry sounded along the road: 'Shah—ssé ... Wah—ssé ...' and with each cry their fists beat hard and hollow on their naked hairy breasts. The Prophet's descendants followed, wearing the green belt of their rank, their heads bent. And behind them the Martyrs of Moharram in the white robes of death, their faces dark and mute, carrying daggers in their hands. 'Shah-ssé ... Wah-ssé ...' The daggers blinked and came down on the shorn heads. The Martyrs' robes were covered with blood. One of them stumbled and was carried away by friends, a beatific smile on his lips.

I stood at the window. Suddenly I was overcome by a new and irresistible feeling—the cry gripped my soul with its warning, and I was filled with the desire for utter submission. I saw the drops of blood in the dust of the street, and I heard the sound of the tambourine, calling and liberating. This was it: the Mystery of the Unseen, the Gate of Sorrow, that leads to the Grace of the Redeemer. I pressed my lips together, and my hands gripped the windowsill. I saw the Hand of Fatima, and all the visible world sank away from me. Once more I heard the hollow sound of the drum—then the rhythm of the wild cries was in me. I had become part of the crowd. I walked with the broad-shouldered men, and my fists hammered against my naked breast. Later I sensed the cool darkness of a mosque around me, and heard the Imam's plaintive call. Someone put a heavy chain into my hand, and I felt the burning pain on my back. Hours passed. A wide square lay in front of me, and from my throat came wild and joyous, the old cry: 'Shah-ssé ... Wah-ssé ...' A dervish with a crushed face stood in front of me. His ribs showed under the dry skin. The thousand eyes of the praying crowd were staring ahead in a trance, and the crowd was singing. Across the square walked a horse, carrying a bloodstained saddle, the horse of the young Hussein. The dervish with the crushed face gave a sudden yell, high-pitched and long drawn out. His copper bowl flew aside, and he threw himself under the horse's hooves. I stumbled. Heavy fists drummed against the naked breast. 'Shah-ssé ... Wah-ssé ...' the crowd cried out, rejoicing. A man was carried past, his white robe bespattered with blood. From afar innumerable torches came to join us in the dark, and I had to follow them. Then I was sitting in the courtyard of a mosque again, and the people round me were wearing high round caps, and their eyes were full of tears. Some one sang the Song of the Young Hussein, and choked in sudden sorrow. I rose. The crowd was flowing back. The night was cool. We passed the Administration Buildings, black flags flying on the masts on the roofs. The endless row of torches was like a river, mirroring the stars. The roofs were crowded to capacity. Shrouded figures peered round corners. The Consulate's gates were guarded by soldiers, their bayonets at the ready. A camel caravan passed the rows of figures sunk in prayer. Plaintive cries rose, women fell to the ground, their limbs jerking in the pale moonlight. The Holy Young Man's family sat in sedan chairs, carried by camels. Behind them, on a black horse, rode the grim Khalif Jesid, his face covered by a Saracen visor—the Holy Hussein's murderer. When he came into view stones flew across the square, just missing his visor. He rode faster and hid in the courtyard of the Exhibition Hall of Nasreddin Shah. Tomorrow the Passion Play of the Holy Hussein would begin.

We came to the Diamond Porch of the Emperor's Palace—black flags flying at half mast there too. The Bahadurs, the Palace Guard, were standing with bowed heads, wearing black mourning crêpe. The Emperor was not in residence, but staying in his Summer Palace in Baghashah. The crowd flowed into Ala'ed Dawleh Street, and suddenly I was alone on dark Cannon Square. The muzzles of the rusty guns looked at me indifferently. My body hurt, as if torn by a thousand strokes with the whip. I touched my shoulder and felt a thick crust of blood. The square flickered before my eyes. When it steadied again I saw an empty coach. The coachman looked at me with understanding and pity. 'Take a bit of pigeons' dung and mix it with oil, then put it on the wounds. That is very good,' he said, obviously an expert. I fell on the cushions, feeling very tired. 'To Shimran,' I cried, 'to the House of Shirvanshir.' The coachman cracked his whip and we drove through the rough uneven streets. From time to time he turned around and said: 'You must be a very pious man. Pray for me too, please. I can't do it myself, I have no time, I must work. My name is Sorhab Jussuf.'

Tears were streaming down Nino's face. She was sitting on the divan, her hands folded helplessly, crying without hiding her face. Her mouth was open, the corners drawn down, deep creases between cheeks and nose. She sobbed just once, her little body was trembling. She did not say a word, but bright teardrops fell from her lashes, on her cheeks, disintegrating on her defenceless face. I stood before her, torn by the force of her sorrow. She did not move, did not wipe off her tears, her lips trembled like leaves in the autumn wind. I took her hands and they were cold, lifeless and withdrawn. I kissed her wet eyes, and she looked at me absently, without understanding. 'Nino,' I cried, 'Nino—what is it?' She raised her hand to the mouth, as if to close it. When she dropped it again I could see clearly her toothmarks on the back of it.

'I hate you, Ali Khan.' Her voice sounded deeply frightened.
'Nino—are you ill?'

'No, I hate you.' She drew her lower lip between her teeth,
and her eyes were the eyes of a hurt child. She looked with
horror at my tattered clothes and my raw red naked shoulders.

'What is it, Nino?'

'I hate you.' She crawled into the corner of the divan, drew
her legs up and put her chin on her knees. Her tears had
stopped. She looked at me with sad eyes, quiet, like a stranger.

'What have I done, Nino?'

'You have showed me your soul, Ali Khan.' She spoke
monotonously, softly, as if in a dream. 'I was at my parents'
house. We were having tea, and the Dutch Consul invited us to
his house on Cannon Square. He was going to show us the
most barbaric rites of the Orient. We stood at the window, and
the stream of fanatics passed underneath. I heard the tambourine, saw the wild faces and felt sick. "An orgy of flagellantism,"
said the Consul, and closed the windows, because the stink of
sweat and dirt came in from the street. Suddenly we heard a
wild cry and a dervish threw himself under a horse's hooves.
And then—then the Consul stretched out his hand and said:
"Isn't that——" he didn't finish the sentence. I looked where he
pointed and saw a native beating his breast and whipping his
back amongst all those madmen. And that native was you, Ali
Khan! I was ashamed, ashamed to death to be the wife of a
fanatical barbarian. I could see all your movements and felt
the Consul's pitying glance. I believe we had tea later, or
dinner. I can't remember. I just managed to stay on my feet,
for I had suddenly seen the abyss dividing us. Ali Khan, the
Young Hussein has destroyed our happiness. I see you as a
fanatic barbarian, and I'll always see you like that.' She sat
there, silent, broken and suffering, because I had tried to find
home and peace with the unseen.

'What now, Nino?'

'I don't know. We can never be happy again. I want to go
away—to a place where I can look you in the face again, and

not see the madman of Cannon Square. Let me go, Ali Khan.'

'Go where, Nino?'

'Oh, I don't know,' her fingers touched my wounded back. 'Why, oh why did you do it?'

'I did it for you, Nino, but you wouldn't understand that.'

'No,' she said disconsolately, 'I want to go away. I'm so tired, Ali Khan. Asia is disgusting.'

'Do you love me?'

'Yes,' she said in despair, and let her hands fall into her lap. I took her into my arms and carried her into the bedroom. I undressed her, and she spoke confusedly in feverish terror.

'Nino,' I said, 'just a few more weeks, and then we'll go home to Baku.'

She nodded tiredly and closed her eyes. Overcome with sleep she took my hand and pressed it against her ribs. I sat a long time like that, feeling her heart beating against my palm. Then I too undressed and lay down next to her. Her body was warm, and she lay there like a child, on her left side, knees drawn up, her head hidden under the cover.

She woke up early, leapt over me and ran into the bathroom. There she took a long time washing and splashing about, but would not let me come in. . . . Then she came out, avoiding my eyes. She carried a little bowl containing some salve. Guiltily she treated my back with it. 'You should have beaten me, Ali Khan,' she said, like a very good little girl.

'I couldn't. I had beaten myself all day long, and hadn't any strength left.'

She put the salve away, and the eunuch brought the tea. She drank hastily and looked out into the garden, silent and embarrassed. Suddenly she looked firmly into my eyes and said: 'It's no use, Ali Khan. I hate you, and I will go on hating you as long as we're in Persia. I can't help it.' We rose, went out into the garden and sat silently by the fountain. The peacock paraded before us, and my father's coach drove noisily into the courtyard of the men's part of the house. Then Nino looked at me sideways and said timidly: 'I can throw dice even with a man I hate.' I fetched the Nardy board, and sadly and dispiritedly we started throwing dice. Then we bent over the fountain's rim and looked at our faces mirrored in the water. Nino dipped her hand in, and our images were distorted by little ripples. 'Don't be so sad, Ali Khan. It's not you I hate, it's this strange country and its strange people. It will pass as soon as we're home again, and as soon as . . .' She put her face on the water for a moment. When she raised her face again clear drops ran down her cheeks to the chin: 'I'm sure it will be a boy—but it's still seven months to go,' she finished, and looked a little proud and superior. So now our fate depended on the regiments marching over the sunglazed plain of Azerbeidshan to the old town of Baku, the town that already suffered enemy occupation and perpetual torture by the oil derricks. I dried Nino's face and kissed her cool cheeks. And she smiled. Then the drums of Holy Hussein called again from afar. I grabbed Nino's hand, dragged her quickly into the house, and put the strongest needle on the gramophone. A loud voice started to shout deafeningly the 'Gold' aria from Gounod's 'Faust'. It was surely the loudest record ever, and while Nino clung to me trembling with fright the immense bass drowned the ancient cry 'Shah-ssé—Wah-ssé. . . .'

27

During the first days of Persia's autumn, Enver Bey's army had marched in to occupy Baku—thus ran the news through bazaars, tea houses and Ministries. The town's last Russian defenders landed in the ports of Persia and Turkestan, starved and cut off from their units. They told of the red flag with the white half-moon fluttering victoriously on the old citadel. Arslan Aga published highly coloured reports in Teheran's newspapers of the Turks marching in, and uncle Assad es Saltaneh banned these newspapers, because he thought he was doing the English a favour by doing so, and because he hated the Turks. My father went to see the Prime Minister, and after some hesitation the Prime Minister allowed the shipping line between Baku and Persia to be re-opened. We travelled to Enseli, and the steamboat Nasreddin took the crowd of refugees, us amongst them, to their liberated home town.

Soldiers with high fur caps stood on Baku's pier. Iljas Beg saluted us, raising his sword, and the Turkish Colonel made a speech, trying to make his soft Stamboul-Turkish sound as much as possible like our own rough dialect. We came to our completely destroyed and raided house, and for days and weeks on end Nino became nothing but a housewife. She had long discussions with carpenters, rooted about in furniture shops, and, frowning with concentration, took measurements of our rooms. She had mysterious sessions with architects, and our house became filled with workmen's noises and the smell of paint, wood and plaster. And in the middle of this domestic hullabaloo was Nino, radiant and conscious of her responsibility, for she had carte blanche for the selection of furniture, wallpaper, and decoration in general. In the evening she reported, ashamed but happy: 'Don't be angry with your Nino, Ali. I have ordered beds, real beds instead of divans. The wallpaper will be light coloured, and we'll have fitted carpets on the floor. The nursery is going to be all in white. Everything will be quite, quite different from the Persian harem.' She put her arms round my neck and rubbed her face against my cheek, for she had a bad conscience. Then she turned her head to the side, drew her little tongue across her lips and tried to reach the tip of her nose with it. She always did that when she was facing a difficult situation, exams, doctors or funerals. I thought of Hussein's Night, and let her have her way, though it hurt my feelings that I had to step on carpets with my shod feet, and to sit at a European table. The flat roof with the view over the desert was all that was left to me. Nino had not proposed any structural alterations there. Mortar dust and noises filled the house.

I sat on the roof with my father, turned my head to the side, let my tongue glide across my lips the way Nino did, and felt that I looked guilty. My father said gently: 'Well—that's how it is, Ali Khan. The house is the woman's domain. Nino has been very good in Persia, even though it was not at all easy for her. Now it's your turn. Don't forget what I told you: Baku is now part of Europe. For ever! The cool darkness of the rooms and the red carpets on the wall belong to Persia.'

'And you, father?'

'I too belong to Persia, and I'll go there as soon as I have seen your child. I'll live in our house in Shimran, and wait until even there white walls and beds will be introduced.'

'I have to stay here, father.'

He nodded seriously. 'I know. You love this town, and Nino loves Europe. But I don't like our new flag, and the noise of the new state, nor the smell of godlessness that hangs over the town.' He looked down quietly, and suddenly seemed very like his brother, Assad es Saltaneh: 'I'm an old man, Ali Khan. I can't stand all these new things. You are young and brave, you must stay here, and the country of Azerbeidshan will need you.'

When twilight fell I was strolling around the streets of our town. Turkish patrols were standing at the corners, hard, upright and deadpan. I spoke to the officers, and they told me of Stamboul's mosques and the summer nights of Tatly-su. The new flag was fluttering on the old Governor's Palace, and Parliament assembled in our school. The old town seemed to have turned its everyday life into a fancy dress party. Feth Ali Khan, the solicitor, was the new Prime Minister, and made laws and gave orders. Mirza Assadullah, the brother of that Assadullah who wanted to kill all Russians, was Foreign Minister and signed treaties with our neighbouring countries. I became enthusiastic about the transformation of our country. The unaccustomed feeling of political independence stirred me profoundly, and I loved the new coat of arms, the uniforms and laws. For the first time in my life I was really at home in my own country. The Russians slunk timidly past me, and my former teachers saluted me reverently. In the City Club the orchestra played native songs all through the evening, we could keep our hats on, and Iljas Beg and I entertained the Turkish officers there, who were either coming from or going to the front. They told us of the siege of Baghdad, and the trek through the Sinai desert. They knew Tripolis' sand dunes, Galicia's muddy lanes and the snow storms in Armenia's mountains. They drank champagne, blatantly disregarding the Law of the Prophet, and spoke of Enver and the coming of the Empire of Turan, in which all people of Turkish blood would be united. I drank in their words full of wonder and reverence, for all this was unreal and like a shadow, like a beautiful unforgettable dream.

Then came the day of the big parade. Military bands marched through the town. The Pasha, his breast covered with decorations, rode on his steed along the rows of soldiers and saluted the new flag. We were full of pride and gratitude, forgot all differences between Shiites and Sunnites, and would have been prepared to kiss the Pasha's lean hand and to die for the Osman Khalif. Seyd Mustafa alone stood apart from the crowd, his face expressing hate and contempt. He had seen a Bulgarian military cross amongst all the stars and half moons covering the Pasha's tunic, and he resented deeply this symbol of an alien creed on a Muslim's breast.

After the parade Iljas, Seyd and I sat on the Esplanade, where autumn leaves were fluttering from the trees. My friends were quarrelling violently about the basic ideas of the new state. From the campaigns and battles at Gandsha, from talks with Young Turk officers, and from his war experiences, Iljas Beg had become convinced that the only way our country could be saved from another Russian invasion was to carry out European reforms as quickly as possible. 'I say it is possible to build forts and roads, introduce reforms, and still stay a good Mohammedan!' he cried boisterously. Seyd's brow was furrowed and his eyes tired:

'Take it just one step further, Iljas Beg,' he said, coolly, 'say it is possible to drink wine, eat pork and yet stay a good Mohammedan. The Europeans have discovered long ago that wine is good for you, and that pork is nourishing. Of course one may stay a good Mohammedan, only the Archangel at the Gate of Paradise will not believe that.'

Iljas laughed: 'Surely there's a difference between marching on parade and eating pork.'

'But not between eating pork and drinking wine. The Turkish officers drink wine quite openly, and they have crosses pinned to their uniforms.'

I was listening to my friends. 'Seyd,' I asked, 'is it possible to be a good Mohammedan, and yet to sleep in beds and eat with knife and fork?'

212

Seyd's smile was tender. 'You will always be a good Moham-medan. I saw you on the day of Moharram.' I was silent. Iljas Beg pushed his cap back.

'Is it true that your house will be quite European, with modern furniture and light coloured wallpaper?'

'Yes, that is true, Iljas Beg.'

'That's good,' he said, decidedly. 'We are now a Capital. Foreign Consuls will come to our country. We'll need houses where we can receive them, and we'll have to have ladies of our own who can talk to the diplomats' wives. You have exactly the right kind of wife, Ali Khan, and you're getting the right kind of house. You should work in the Ministry for Foreign Affairs.'

I laughed. 'Iljas Beg, you're judging my wife, my house and myself as if we were horses about to start for the race of inter-national understanding. You seem to believe that I am only rebuilding my house in the national interests.'

'That's how it should be,' said Iljas Beg in a hard voice, and it came as a revelation to me that he was quite right, that every-thing and everybody had to serve this new state we wanted to grow from the poor sunglazed soil of Azerbeidshan. I went home, and when Nino saw that I had no objection to parquet floors and oil-paintings she laughed happily and her eyes shone as they had on that night in the woods at the spring of Pechapür.

During this time I often rode out into the desert, and lay there for hours, covered by the soft sand, while the sun sank into the west as if into a river of blood. Turkish troops passed me. But now the officers' faces were troubled and tense. For us the noise of our new state had deadened the far-away thunder of the guns and the world war. But somewhere, far, far away, the Bulgarian troops, the Turks' allies, retreated from the enemies' onslaught. 'Breakthrough,' said the Turks, 'impossible to repair the front again,' and they stopped drinking champagne. News came but rarely, and when it did it was like strokes of lightning. In the far-away port of Mudros a man whose back was bent and whose eyes looked down, came aboard the British battleship *Agamemnon*. This was Hussein Reuf Bey, Sealord of the High

Ottoman Empire, Plenipotentiary of the Khalif for the cease-fire. He bent over a table, signed his name on a piece of paper, and the eyes of the Pasha, who was still Lord of our town, filled with tears. Once more the song of the Realm of Turan was played in the streets of Baku, but this time it sounded like a dirge. The Pasha, very upright in his saddle, in full-dress uniform, with white kid gloves, rode once more along the lines of his soldiers. The Turkish faces were numb and expressionless. The flag of the Holy House of Osman was rolled up, the drum sounded and the Pasha saluted with his white-gloved hand. Then the column of soldiers marched out of town, leaving behind them the dream pictures of Stamboul's mosques, the graceful palaces on the Bosphorus, and the lean man, who was the Khalif and wore the Prophet's mantle on his shoulders.

A few days later I was standing on the Esplanade when the first ships carrying English occupation troops appeared from beyond the Island of Nargin. The General had blue eyes, a clipped moustache and strong broad hands. New Zealanders, Canadians and Australians flooded our town. The Union Jack fluttered over our country next to our flag, and Feth Ali Khan telephoned, asking me to come and see him in his Ministry. When I came into his room he was sitting in a deep armchair, his fiery eyes looking at me. 'Ali Khan, why are you not serving your country yet?' I really did not know myself. I looked at the thick files on his desk and answered guiltily:

'I belong wholeheartedly to our country, Feth Ali Khan. I am at your service.'

'I hear you have a monkey-like ability to pick up foreign languages. How long will it take you to learn English?'

My smile was a bit embarrassed: 'Feth Ali, I haven't got to learn English, I speak it already.' At first he was silent, leaning his large head on the back of his easy chair. Then he asked suddenly: 'How is Nino?' I was shocked. Our Prime Minister asking about my wife, disregarding all rules of decent behaviour!

'Thank you, your Excellency, my wife is very well.'

'And does she speak English too?'

'Yes.'

Again he was silent, caressing his big moustache.

'Feth Ali Khan,' I said quietly, 'I know what you want. In two weeks' time my house will be ready, Nino's wardrobe is full of evening dresses. We speak English, and I'll pay for the champagne myself.'

A quick smile under the moustache. 'I beg your pardon, Ali Khan,' his smile grew soft, 'I did not intend to hurt your feelings. We do need people like you. There are not too many who have a European wife, an old name, and a presentable house. Take me for instance: I have never had the money to learn to speak English, let alone own a house or a European wife.' He seemed to be tired and took up his pen: 'As from today you are attaché in the Department for Western Europe. Present yourself to the Foreign Minister Assadullah. He'll explain the work to you. And . . . but please don't be annoyed . . . do you think your house could possibly be ready in five days' time? I'm really ashamed to have to ask you this.'

'Yes, Excellency,' I said firmly, and felt as if I had just betrayed and forsaken an old and trusted friend. I went home. Nino's fingers were covered with clay and paint. She was standing high on a ladder, hammering at a nail that was to hold an oil-painting. She would have been very surprised to hear that she was serving the country. So I did not tell her, but kissed her dirty fingers and allowed her to buy a Frigidaire to keep the foreign wines cool.

28

Have you got an aunt? No, I have not got an aunt, but my servant has broken his right leg. Do you like travelling? Yes, I do like travelling, but in the evening I prefer to eat just fruit. These sentences in our *Teach yourself English* book were of a vicious idiocy. Nino closed the book: 'I think our English is good enough to win the battle, but have you ever tried to drink whisky?'

'Nino,' I cried aghast, 'you talk just like the book.'

'That would mean easily understandable mental deterioration, Ali Khan, caused by a misunderstood desire to serve the homeland. Who is coming tonight?' She tried to sound as if she did not care, but she could not quite bring it off. I told her all the names of the English Civil Servants and officers who would honour us with their presence tonight. Nino looked down, quietly proud. She knew—no Minister and no General in Azerbeidshan had what her husband had: a sophisticated wife, with a Western upbringing, royal parents and a knowledge of English. She plucked at her evening dress and looked into the mirror. 'I have tried to drink whisky,' she said darkly, 'it tastes horrible, really disgusting. That's probably why they mix it with soda water.' I put my arm round her shoulder, and she looked at me gratefully: 'We do lead a strange life. Ali Khan.

Either you shut me up in a harem or else I'm the proof of our country's cultural progress.'

We went down to the reception rooms. Servants were standing around, their expressions carefully controlled, pictures of landscapes and animals hung on the walls. Soft easy-chairs stood in the corners, and vases with flowers on the tables. Nino buried her face in fragrant rose petals: 'Do you remember, Ali Khan? How I served you, carrying water from the valley to the âoul?'

'Which service do you like better?'

Nino's eyes became soft and dreamy and she did not answer. The bell rang, and her lips trembled with excitement. But the first ones to come were only her illustrious parents, and Iljas Beg in full gala uniform. He went round the hall, examining everything and nodded enthusiastically: 'I really think I should get married too, Ali Khan,' he said weightily, 'has Nino got any cousins?'

We stood at the door, Nino and I, shaking strong English hands. The officers were tall and red-faced. The ladies wore gloves, had blue eyes, and smiled graciously but full of curiosity. Maybe they had expected to be served by eunuchs and entertained by belly-dancers—but instead well-trained servants appeared, the dishes were served from the left, and pictures of racehorses and green meadows hung on the walls. Nino caught her breath when she saw a young lieutenant drink down a whole glass of whisky in one go, without taking any notice of the offered soda water. Scraps of conversations were floating round the room, and they sounded just as idiotic as the sentences in our *Teach Yourself English* book:

'Have you been married very long, Mrs. Shirvanshir?' 'Nearly two years.'

'Yes, we went to Persia for our honeymoon.' 'My husband likes riding.' 'No, he does not play polo.'

'Do you like our town?' 'I'm so glad.' 'Oh, but please! We are not savages! To have many wives has been forbidden long ago in Azerbeidshan. And of eunuchs I have only read in novels.' Nino looked at me across the table, and her rosy nostrils were trembling with suppressed laughter. A major's wife had even asked her whether she had ever been to the opera. 'Yes I have,' she had answered gently, 'and I can read and write too.' First round to Nino, as she offered the lady a plate with biscuits.

Young Englishmen, Civil Servants and officers, bowed before Nino, their hands touched her tender fingers, and their eyes looked at Nino's naked back. I looked away. Assadullah was standing in a corner, smoking a cigarette, as if nothing was wrong. He would never have exposed his own wife to the eyes of all these strangers, but Nino was a Georgian and a Christian, and so it did not matter if her hands, her eyes, her back were a prey to all other men's glances. I was overcome with shame and fury. Bits of conversations brushed past my ears and sounded shameless and vulgar. I dropped my eyes. Nino was standing at the other end of the hall, surrounded by strangers. 'Thank you,' she said suddenly, her voice hoarse, 'thank you, you are very kind.' I looked up and saw her blushing deeply, looking frightened. She crossed the hall and came to me. Her hand touched my sleeve, as if asking for help. 'Ali Khan,' she said softly, 'you feel now the way I felt when I went to see your aunts and cousins in Teheran. What are all these men to me? I don't want them to look at me like that.' Then she turned away and took the major's wife's hand. I heard her say: 'You should really see our National Theatre. Just now Shakespeare is being translated into our Tartar language. Next week will be the first night of "Hamlet"'. I wiped the sweat off my brow and thought of the severe laws of hospitality: There is an old saying: 'If a guest enters your house holding the severed head of your only son in his hand, you must still receive him, offer him food and drink and honour him as a guest.' That is a wise law. But sometimes it is very difficult to keep.

I poured whisky and cognac into many glasses. The officers smoked cigars, but no one put his feet on the table, though that was the one thing we had expected them to do. 'You have a charming wife and a charming home, Ali Khan,' a young officer prolonged my torture. It would probably have surprised him very much to learn that political considerations only saved him from having his ears boxed. A dog of an unbeliever dared to praise openly my wife's beauty! My hand shook as I poured him a glass of cognac, and some drops spilled over. An elderly Civil Servant with a white moustache, wearing a white shirt under his dinner jacket, was sitting in a corner. I offered him some biscuits. His teeth were long and yellow and his fingers short. He looked at me searchingly: 'There seems to be an immense cultural difference between Persia and Azerbeidshan.'

'Oh yes. We are centuries ahead. You must remember that we have an enormous amount of industry here, and a railway. Unfortunately the Russian administration has suppressed our cultural evolution. We have not enough doctors and teachers. But I hear the Government plans to send gifted young people to Europe, to learn there what they have missed under the Russian yoke.' I went on like that for some time, and was about to pour him some more whisky, but he refused.

'I was a Consul in Persia for twenty years,' he said, 'and I feel it is a great pity to see the old solid forms of oriental culture crumble, and the orientals of today trying to imitate us, and despising their ancestors' customs. But they may be right. After all, it is their affair to choose how they want to live. In any case I'll admit that your country is just as ripe for independence as, shall we say, the Republics of Central America. I think our Government will soon recognise your state.' I was an idiot, but the object of the evening had been achieved. Foreign Minister Assadullah was standing at the other end of the hall, with Nino's illustrious parents and Iljas Beg. I joined them.

'What did the old one say?' Assadullah asked quickly.

'He says I am an idiot, but that England will soon recognise us.'

Mirza Assadullah sighed with relief: 'You are not an idiot, Ali Khan, far from it.'

'Thank you, sir, but I believe I am.'

219

He shook my hand and took his leave. When he kissed Nino's hand at the door I heard her whisper something to him, smiling mysteriously. He nodded—he had understood. The guests left at midnight, and the big hall smelt of tobacco and alcohol. . . . Tired and content we went upstairs to our bedroom, and suddenly a strange exhuberance came over us. Nino threw her evening shoes into the corner, jumped on the bed and standing on the mattress, let the springs throw her up into the air again and again. She crinkled her nose, pushed her lower lip out and looked like a playful little monkey. She puffed her cheeks out, then pushed her forefinger against them, so her lips opened with a 'plop!' 'How do you like me in my role as saviour of the country?' she cried. Then she jumped down, ran to the mirror and looked at herself admiringly: 'Nino Hanum Shirvanshir, Azerbeidshan's Jeanne d'Arc! Fascinates majors' wives and pretends never to have seen a eunuch!' She clapped her little hands, laughing. She wore a light-coloured evening dress, very low cut at the back. Long earrings hung from her delicate ears. The rope of pearls round her neck shimmered in the lamplight. Her arms were slender and girlish, and her dark hair fell on her neck. Standing in front of the mirror she was ravishing in her new beauty. I stepped close to her and looked into the happy eyes of a European Princess. I embraced her, feeling as if this was the very first time. Her skin was soft and fragrant, and her teeth glistened behind her lips like little white stones. For the first time we sat down on a bed, and I held a European woman in my arms. She blinked quickly—the intimate caress of her long curved lashes against my cheek—and it had never been so wonderful before. I took her chin into my hand and raised her head. I saw the soft oval of her face, moist thirsty lips and dreaming eyes behind half closed Georgian lashes. I caressed her neck, and her little head fell weakly into my hand. She was all longing and submission. Her evening dress, and the European bed with its turned-down covers and cool linen disappeared before my eyes—there she was, in the âoul, in Daghestan, half-undressed on the narrow mat, covering the clay floor. My hands gripped her shoulders and then we were lying fully dressed on the pale carpet from Kerman, at the foot of the proud European bed of state. I looked into Nino's face over the soft carpet, her eyebrows contracting in painful joy. I heard her breathe, felt the hard roundness of her slender thighs, and forgot the old Englishman, the young officers and the future of our republic.

Later on we were lying quietly side by side, looking into the big mirror over our heads. 'That dress is ruined,' said Nino, and it sounded as if she were confessing great happiness. She cradled her head in my lap and thought aloud: 'What would Madam Major say if she saw us now? She would say: "Doesn't Ali Khan know what beds are for?" She got up and kicked my knee with her little foot: 'Would the honourable attaché be so good as to decide to undress and take his place in the marital bed, following the general customs of the diplomatic world? Whoever heard of attachés rolling about on the carpet?' I got up, grumbling and sleepy, threw off my clothes and lay down between the sheets with Nino.

Days passed, weeks passed, guests came, drank whisky and praised our home. Nino's Georgian hospitality unfolded like a flower. She danced with the young lieutenants and talked about gout to older majors. She told the English ladies stories from the days of Queen Tamar, and left them in their belief that the great Queen had ruled over Azerbeidshan as well as over Georgia. I sat in the Ministry, alone in the big room, wrote reports for diplomats, read the reports of our foreign representatives and looked at the sea. Nino came to meet me in the evening, and was wifely and gay, full of careless charm. She began a rather surprising friendship with the Foreign Minister Assadullah. She served him food and drink when he came to visit us, gave him advice about how to behave in European society, and sometimes I came across the two of them whispering mysteriously in some secluded corner of our house. 'What's going on between you and Mirza?' I asked, but she just smiled and said she wanted to be the first female Chief of Protocol.

More and more letters, reports and memoranda piled up on my desk. The new state was being built up as quickly as possible, and I liked to unfold letters and forms headed with our coat of arms.

One day, shortly before lunch the courier brought me the newspapers. I opened our Government's official paper and saw on the third page my name in bold print: 'Ali Khan Shirvanshir, attaché in the Ministry for Foreign Affairs has been posted to our Consulate in Paris.' Followed a long paragraph, obviously written by Arslan Aga, praising my outstanding abilities. I jumped up, rushed through the communicating rooms to the Minister's office, and crashed the door open: 'Mirza Assadullah,' I cried, 'What is this?'

'Ah,' he smiled, 'a surprise for you, my friend. I promised your wife. Nino and you will be the right people for Paris.' I threw the paper on the floor, overcome by a wild rage.

'Mirza,' I shouted, 'there's no law in this country that can force me to leave my homeland for years on end!'

He looked at me dumbfounded. 'What on earth is the matter, Ali Khan? Most people in our service would be only too happy to get a foreign posting. And you're just the right man for it.'

'But I don't want to go to Paris, and if you force me I'll resign. I hate this Western world, these strange roads, peoples and customs. But I don't suppose you'll ever understand that.'

'No, I don't,' he said politely, 'but if you insist you can stay here.'

I ran home, up the stairs, and arrived out of breath. 'Nino,' I said, 'I can't do it, I just can't.' All colour drained from her face, and her hands trembled.

'But why not, Ali Khan?'

'Nino, please try to understand. It's just that I love this flat roof over my head, the desert and the sea. I love this town, the old wall and the mosques in the little alleys, and I would die

away from the Orient, like a fish out of water.' For a moment
she closed her eyes.

'I'm sorry,' she said, and it sounded so sad and forlorn that
it tore at my heartstrings. I sat down and took her hand:

'Look—I would be just as unhappy in Paris as you were in
Persia. This time it would be I who would feel exposed to some
malignant force. Remember how you felt in the harem of Shimran. For me it would be just as impossible to live in Europe as
it was for you to live in Asia. Let's stay in Baku, where Asia and
Europe meet. I cannot go to Paris where there are no mosques,
no old wall, and no Seyd Mustafa. I must feel Asia once in a
while if I have to bear with all these strangers who are coming
here. I would hate you in Paris as you hated me after Moharram. Not immediately when we get there, but some day, after a
fancy dress party, or a ball, I would suddenly start to hate you
in this strange world you're trying to force me into. And that's
why I want to stay here, come what may. I was born in this
country, and I want to die here.' She had not said a word.
When I stopped she bent over me, and her hand caressed my
hair: 'Forgive your Nino, Ali Khan. I have been very stupid. I
don't know why I should think that it would be easier for you
to change than for me. We'll stay here, and not say another
word about Paris. You keep your Asiatic town, and I'll
keep my European house.' She kissed me tenderly, her eyes
shining.

'Nino, is it very difficult, being my wife?'

'No, Ali Khan, not difficult at all. It just needs some sense
and understanding.' Her fingers caressed my face. She was a
strong woman, my Nino. I knew I had shattered her life's
dream. I took her on my knees: 'Nino, when the child is born
we'll go to Paris, London, Berlin or Rome. We still have a
honeymoon to come. And we'll stay wherever you like, for a
whole long summer. And every year we'll go to Europe again,
you know that I'm no tyrant. But my home I want to be in the
country I belong to, because I'm the son of our desert, our sun
and our sand.'

'Yes,' she said, 'and a very good son too. We'll forget Europe. But your child that I carry shall not be a child of the desert or the sand, but just the child of Ali and Nino.'

'Yes,' I said, and knew that I had agreed to be the father of a European.

29

'Your birth was a very difficult one, Ali Khan, and in those days we did not call European doctors to our women.' My father was sitting with me on the roof of our house, his voice was soft and plaintive: 'When the birthpains became too bad we gave your mother turquoises and diamonds, ground to a powder. But that did not do much good. When you were born we put the navel cord close to the eastern wall of the room, together with a sword and the Koran, so you should become devout and brave. Later you wore it round your neck as an amulet, and you were always a healthy child. But when you were three you threw it away, and then you started to become sickly. At first we tried to lure the illness away, and put wine and sweets into your room. We had a coloured cock run across and out of the room, but the illness did not run out after it. Then a wise man from the mountains came and brought a cow. We slaughtered the cow, and the wise man cut her stomach open and took the innards out. He then put you into the cow's stomach. When he took you out after three hours your skin was quite red. But you've never had a day's illness since then.' A long muffled cry came from the house. I sat straight and motionless, my whole being concentrated in listening. The cry came again, long drawn out and plaintive. 'Now she's cursing you,' my father said quietly. 'All women curse their husbands when they give birth. In former times after the child had been born, the woman had to slaughter a ram and to spray her husband's and the child's mats with the blood, to turn away the disaster she had called down on them during her labour.'

'How long can it take, father?'

'Five hours, six hours, maybe ten hours. Her hips are slim.' He fell silent. Perhaps he was thinking of his own wife, my mother, who had died when I was born. Then he got up. 'Come,' he said, and we went to the two red prayer rugs lying in the middle of the roof, the top ends turned towards Mekka, towards the Kaaba. We took our shoes off, stood on the carpets and folded our hands, covering the back of the left hand with the palm of the right: 'This is all we can do, but it is more than all the doctors' wisdom.' He bent forward and spoke the Arabic prayer: '*Bismi Ilahi arrahmani rahim*—In the name of God, the All-Merciful, the All-Compassionate . . .' I followed his lead. I knelt on the prayer rug, my forehead touching the floor: '*Ahamdu lillahi rabi-l-alamin, arrahmani, rahim, maliki jaumi din* —Praised be God the Lord of All the Worlds, the All-Merciful, the All-Compassionate, the Lord of the Last Judgment . . .' I was sitting on the rug, my hands covering my face. Nino's cries still sounded from below, brushing my ears, but I was past comprehension. My lips formed the sentences of the Koran, as if they were not part of me any more: '*Ijjaka na budu waijjaka nastain*—it is you we worship, and it is you we beg for mercy . . .' My hands were on my knees. It was very quiet, and I heard my father whispering: '*Ihdina sirata-lmustaqim sirata lladina anammta alaihim*—lead us on to the right way, on to the way of those in your grace . . .' My face touched the prayer rug, I was lying on it, the red patterns disappearing before my eyes.

'*Gaira lmagdumi alaihim wala ddalin*—of those against whom your wrath is not turned, those whom you do not lead astray . . .' Thus we lay in the dust before the Lord's face. Again and again we spoke the words of prayer, the words God gave to the Prophet in the foreign tongue of the Arab nomads. I sat on the rug crosslegged, the rosary gliding through my fingers, my lips whispering the thirty-three names of the Lord.

Someone touched my shoulder. I raised my head, saw a smiling face and heard words I did not comprehend. I rose. I felt my father's glance on me and walked slowly down the stairs. In Nino's room the curtains were drawn. I came to the bed. Nino's eyes were full of tears, her cheeks sunken. She smiled quietly and then said in Tartar, in the simple language of our people, that she hardly spoke at all:

'*Kis dir, Ali Khan, Tshoch gusel bir kis. O kadar bahtiarim—* It's a girl, Ali Khan, a wonderful girl, I'm so happy.' I took her cold hand and she closed her eyes.

'Don't let her go to sleep, Ali Khan, she must stay awake a little longer,' some one said behind me. I caressed her dry lips, and she looked up to me, tired and serene. A woman wearing a white apron came to the bed and held out a bundle to me. I saw a tiny wrinkled toy with little fingers and big expressionless eyes. The toy was crying, its small face distorted. 'How beautiful she is,' said Nino delightedly, and spread out her fingers, imitating the toy's movements. I raised my hand and timidly touched the bundle, but the toy was already asleep, its face now very serious. 'We'll call her Tamar, in honour of the Lyceum,' whispered Nino, and I nodded, for Tamar is a beautiful name, used by both Christians and Muslims. Someone led me from the room. Curious glances met me, and father took my hand. We went out into the courtyard.

'Let's ride into the desert,' said my father, 'Nino will soon be allowed to sleep.' We mounted our horses and chased through the yellow sand dunes in a wild gallop. My father was saying something, but I could not really understand what. It seemed he was trying to comfort me, and I could not understand why, for I was very proud to have a sleeping wrinkled daughter with a serious face and big expressionless eyes

Days passed like pearls on a rosary. Nino held the Toy at her breast, at night she sang soft Georgian songs to it, and pensively shook her head looking at her small wrinkled double. To me she was cruel and haughty as never before, for I was only a man, who could neither bear children, nurse them or even change them. So I sat in my office in the Ministry, and she would graciously phone me to tell of great events and revolutionary deeds: 'Ali Khan, the Toy has laughed, and it's spreading its hands towards the sun.'

'It's a very clever Toy, Ali Khan, I showed it a glass ball, and it really looked at it.'

'Listen, Ali Khan, the Toy is drawing lines on its stomach with its fingers. It seems to be a very talented Toy.'

But while the Toy was drawing lines on its stomach, and excitedly followed a glass ball with its eyes, people in far-away Europe played with borders, armies and states. I read the reports on my desk and looked at the maps, on which questionable future borders were drawn. Mysterious men, with names difficult to pronounce, were gathered at Versailles, ordering the Orient's fate. One man only, a fair-haired Turkish General from Ankara, desperately tried to oppose the victors. Even though our country, Azerbeidshan, was now recognised by the European powers as a sovereign state, I could not share Iljas Beg's enthusiasm, and it was rather awkward for me to have to disillusion him with the news that the English regiments would be withdrawn for good from the area of our now sovereign Republic.

'Now we're free forever,' he cried joyfully, 'no more foreigners on our country's soil!'

'Look here, Iljas Beg,' I said and took him to the map, 'our natural allies should be Turkey and Persia, but now they are both powerless. We're hanging in mid-air, and from the north one hundred and sixty million Russians are pressing down on us, thirsting for our oil. As long as the English are here, no Russian, Red or White, dares to cross our borders. But once the English have left there's just you and me, and our few regiments to defend our country.'

'Never mind,' Iljas Beg shook his head optimistically, 'we've got our diplomats to make friendship treaties with the Russians.

The army has other things to do. Here,' he pointed to the south, we must go to the Armenian border. There is trouble in that area. General Mechander, the Minister of War, has already given the order.' It was hopeless to try and convince him that diplomacy can only work if supported intelligently by the military forces. So the English regiments went, the streets were full of festive flags, our troops marched to the Armenian border, and in Jalama, our station at the Russian border, only a border control and a few Civil Servants remained. We at the Ministry started working on the treaties with both Red and White Russians, and my father went back to Persia. Nino and I saw him off the pier. He looked at us sadly and did not ask whether we would follow him.

'What will you do in Persia, father?'

'I'll probably marry again,' he said offhand. Then he kissed us ceremoniously and added thoughtfully: 'I'll come to see you from time to time, and if this state should fall apart—well, I've got some estates in Mazendaran.' He stepped upon the gangway, and waved for a long, long time, to us, to the old wall, to the Maiden's Tower, the town and the desert, all fading slowly from his view. It was hot in town, and the blinds in the Ministry were half drawn. The Russian delegates came, their faces bored and cunning. Quickly and indifferently they signed the endless treaty, consisting of paragraphs, columns and footnotes.

Dust and sand covered our streets, the hot wind let torn pieces of paper flutter in the air, my illustrious inlaws went to Georgia for the summer, and at Jalama was nothing but the border control and a few Civil Servants. 'Assadullah,' I turned to the Minister, 'thirty thousand Russians are standing opposite Jalama.'

'I know,' he said darkly, 'our City Commandant thinks it's just a scheme.'

'And if it isn't?'

He looked at me irritated. 'We can't do more than make treaties. Everything else is in God's hand.' A few staunch guardsmen, their bayonets at the ready, were guarding the

Parliament building. Inside the political parties were quarrelling, and in the suburbs the Russian workers threatened to strike if the government would not allow oil exports to Russia. The coffee houses were crowded with men reading newspapers, and playing Nardy. Children were scuffling in the hot dust. The sun's flames poured over the town, and from the minaret came the call: 'Rise for prayer! Rise for prayer! Prayer is better than sleep!'

I did not sleep, I was lying on the carpet, my eyes closed, but I kept seeing the dreaded vision of the border station of Jalama threatened by thirty thousand Russian soldiers. 'Nino,' I said, 'it is hot, the Toy is not used to the sun, and you love trees, shadows and water. Would you like to go to your parents for the summer?'

'No,' she said severely, 'I would not.'

I did not say another word, but Nino wrinkled her brow thoughtfully. 'But we could go together, Ali Khan. It's hot here in town, and your estate in Gandsha is surrounded by gardens and vineyards. Let's go, you're at home there, and the Toy can lie in the shade.' I could not but agree. And so we took the train, the coaches of which were decorated with the full glory of the new Azerbeidshan coat of arms.

A long, wide, dusty road took us from the station to the town of Gandsha. Churches and mosques were surrounded by low-built houses. A dried-up river divided the Mohammedan quarter from the Armenian one, and I showed Nino the stone on which my ancestor Ibrahim had died a hundred years ago, killed by Russian bullets. On our estate, out of town, lazy bullocks were lying motionless in the water, only their heads showing. The smell of milk was in the air, and each grape in the big bunches was as big as a cow's eye. The farmers had their heads shaved down the middle, and long hair combed forward right and left. The little house with the wooden verandah was surrounded by trees, and the Toy laughed when it saw the horses, dogs and chickens.

We settled down, and for weeks on end I forgot all about the

230

Ministry, treaties and the border station of Jalama. We lay in the grass, and Nino chewed the bitter stalks. Her face caught the sun, and it was clear and peaceful like the sky over Gandsha. She was now twenty years old, and still far too slim for the Oriental taste. 'Ali Khan, this Toy is mine alone. Next time it will be a boy, and you can have him.' Then she made plans for the Toy's future in great detail, with tennis, Oxford, English and French language courses, all European. I did not say anything, for the Toy was still very small, and there were thirty thousand Russians at Jalama. We played in the grass and had our meals on big carpets in the shade of the trees. Nino swam in the little river above the spot where the buffaloes took their bath. Farmers came to us, little round caps on their heads, bowed before their Khan, and brought baskets of peaches, apples and grapes. We did not read any newspapers, and did not get any letters. For us the world finished on the borders of our estate, and it was nearly as wonderful as in Daghestan.

One late summer evening we were sitting in our room when we heard a horse galloping wildly. I went out on the verandah, and a slim man in a black Tsherkess coat jumped off his horse. 'Iljas Beg!' I cried, and stretched out both hands in greeting. He did not reply, but stood there in the light of the oil lamp, his face ashen.

'The Russians are in Baku,' he said hastily.

I nodded, as if I had known all the time. Nino was standing behind me, and I heard her faint cry: 'How did it happen, Iljas Beg?'

'Trains came down from Jalama during the night, full of Russian soldiers. They surrounded the town, and the Parliament capitulated. All Ministers who could not get away were arrested and Parliament dissolved. The Russian workers joined their countrymen. There were no soldiers in town, and the army is in a lost position on the Armenian border. I'm collecting partisans.' I turned round. Nino had disappeared into the house, while the servants came running to put horses to the carriage. She was packing, and talking softly to the Toy in the language of her ancestors. Then we were driving through the fields, Iljas Beg riding at our side. The lights of Gandsha were shining far away, and for a moment I felt past and present merging into one. I saw Iljas Beg, the dagger at his belt, pale and serious, and Nino, composed and proud, as she had been in the melon field at Mardakjany, a long long time ago. We arrived at Gandsha in the middle of the night. The streets were crowded, peoples' faces excited and tense. Soldiers, their guns at the ready, were standing on the bridge that separated the Armenians' and the Mohammedans' quarters, and torches shed their light on the Banner of Azerbeidshan on the balcony of the Government building.

Here I sit, leaning my back against the wall of the big mosque of Gandsha, a plate of soup in my hand, looking at the tired soldiers, lying about the courtyard. Machine-guns are barking, and their vicious sound forces its way into the courtyard, and the Republic of Azerbeidshan has only a few more days to live. I'm sitting here by myself. My book lies in front of me, and I'm filling it with hasty lines, so as to record the past once again. That's how it was, eight days ago, in our little hotel in Gandsha:

'You're mad,' said Iljas Beg. It was three o'clock in the morning, and Nino was asleep in the next room. 'You're mad,' he repeated, walking up and down. I was sitting at the table, and Iljas Beg's opinion was the least important thing in the world to me.

'I'm staying here. The Partisans will come. We'll fight, I'm not fleeing my country.' I spoke softly, as in a dream. Iljas Beg stood before me, looking at me, sad and proud.

'Ali Khan, we went to school together, and together we fought the Russians in the big breaks. I was riding behind you when you went after Nachararyan. I took Nino home on my saddle, and we fought together at Zizianashvili's Gate. Now you must go—for Nino's sake, for your own sake, for the sake of our country, that might need you again.'

'You're staying here, Iljas Beg, and I'm staying too.'

'I'm staying because I'm alone in the world, because I know

how to lead soldiers, and because I can offer our country the experience of two campaigns. Go to Persia, Ali Khan.'

'I can't go to Persia, and I can't go to Europe either.' I went to the window. Below on the street torches were burning and iron was clinking.

'Ali Khan, our Republic has only a few more days to live.' I nodded indifferently. People were passing the window, carrying weapons. I heard steps in the next room, and turned. Nino was standing in the door, sleepy-eyed.

'Nino,' I said, 'the last train to Tiflis goes in two hours' time.'

'Yes. Let's go, Ali Khan.'

'No, you go with the child. I'll come later. I have to stay here a little longer. But you must go. It's not like that time in Baku. It's all different now, and you can't stay here, Nino. You've got your child now.' I was talking, in the streets the torches were burning, and Iljas Beg stood in a corner, his head bowed. Sleep disappeared from Nino's eyes. Slowly she went to the window and looked out. She looked at Iljas Beg, and he looked away. She came into the middle of the room and hung her head.

'The Toy,' she said, 'and you're not coming?'

'I can't, Nino.'

'Your ancestor died on the bridge of Gandsha. I have known that stone since I took my exam.' Suddenly Nino collapsed on the floor and cried out like a wounded animal in the throes of death. Her eyes were dry, and her whole body was trembling. She cried at the top of her voice and Iljas Beg ran out of the room.

'I'll come, Nino. I'll come, I promise, it's just for a few days.' Her cries continued, on the street people were singing the wild song of the dying republic. All at once she calmed down and looked straight ahead with dead eyes. Then she got up. I took the suitcase. The bundle with the Toy was in my arms, and we walked down the stairs silently. Iljas Beg was waiting in the carriage. We drove through the crowded streets to the station.

'Just for three or four days,' said Ilas Beg, 'just three or four days, and then Ali Khan is with you again.'

'I know,' Nino nodded quietly, 'we'll stay in Tiflis and then go to Paris. We'll have a house with a garden, and the next child will be a boy.'

'That's how it will be, Nino, that's just how it will be.' My voice was clear and optimistic. She clasped my hand and looked far into the distance. The rails were like long snakes, and the train came out of the dark like an evil monster. She kissed me quickly. 'Good-bye Ali Khan. We'll meet again in three days' time.'

'Of course we will, Nino, and then off to Paris.'

She smiled, and her eyes were like soft velvet. I just stood there on the platform, unable to move, as if nailed to the hard asphalt. Iljas Beg took her into the compartment. She looked out of the window, quiet and lost, like a little frightened bird. When the train started to move she waved, and Iljas Beg jumped off.

We drove to town, and the town was like a carnival. Farmers from the outlying villages came and brought the machine-guns they had been hiding, and ammunition. From the other side of the river, in the Armenian quarter, we heard a few shots. Over there was already Russian territory. The Red Army Cavalry flooded the land, and in town a man suddenly appeared who had bushy eyebrows, a hooked nose, and deep-set eyes: Prince Mansur Mirza Kadjar. No one knew who he was and where he came from, only that his House was that of the Imperial Kadjars, and on his cap glistened the Silver Lion. He took the leadership in the manner born as one of Aga Mohammed's heirs. Russian battalions were concentrating towards Gandsha, and the town became crowded with refugees from Baku. They told of executed Ministers, of imprisoned Parliamentarians, and of corpses, weighted with stones, sunk into the deep Caspian Sea. 'The Mosque of Taza Pir is now a club, and when Seyd Mustafa came to pray at the wall the Russians beat him up. They bound him and put pork into his mouth. Later he managed to flee to Persia, to his uncle in Meshed. The Russians had murdered his father.' It was Arslan Aga who brought this news. He stood in front of me, looking at the weapons I was distributing.

'I want to fight too, Ali Khan.'

'You? You little ink-sprinkled piglet?'

'I'm no piglet, Ali Khan, I love my country, like anybody else. My father has fled to Tiflis. Give me a weapon.' His face was serious, his eyes flickered. I gave him weapons, and he marched in the columns I was leading for a sortie over the bridge. Russian soldiers held the streets on the other side. We crashed together in a man-to-man fight. I saw broad masks, and glittering triangular bayonets, and was gripped by a wild fury. '*Irali!*—Forward!' somebody cried, and we lowered our bayonets. Blood mingled with sweat. I raised the butt-end of my rifle, a shot grazed my shoulder. The Russian's skull burst under my blow. Grey brains poured into the dust. The dagger in my hand I stumbled over an enemy, and saw in falling Arslan Aga pushing his dagger into a Russian soldier's eye. . . .

From afar we heard the metal call of the trumpet. We were now lying behind a street corner, shooting blindly at the Armenian houses. During the night we crept back over the bridge, where Iljas Beg was sitting, festooned with cartridges, putting up machine-guns. We went into the mosque's court-yard, and by the light of the stars Iljas Beg told me how, once, when he was a boy he had nearly been drowned. He had been swimming in the sea, and had been gripped by a current. Then we ate soup and peaches. Arslan Aga was crouching in front of us, bleeding gaps in his teeth. During the night he crept across to me, trembling all over.

'I'm so afraid, Ali Khan, I'm such a coward.'

'Then put your weapons away and run across the meadows to the river Pula, and then to Georgia.'

'I can't, I love my country just as much as everybody else, even if I have the soul of a coward.' I was silent, and the new day dawned. Far away the guns blustered and near the minaret stood Iljas Beg with his field-glasses, next to the Prince of the Imperial House of the Kadjars. The trumpet sounded mournful and challenging, the flag was flying over the minaret, and some one started to sing the Song of the Realm of Turan. 'I have heard things,' said a man with dreaming eyes in a face dedicated to Death, 'a man has appeared in Persia by the name of Reza, he is leading many soldiers and chasing the enemy as a hunter chases the deer. Kemal is sitting in Ankara. He has amassed an army. We do not fight in vain. Twenty-five thousand men are marching to help us.'

'No,' I said, 'not twenty-five thousand men—two hundred and fifty million men marching, all the Muslims in the world. But whether they will come in time God only knows.' I went to the bridge, sat behind the machine-gun, and the bullets were gliding through my fingers as if they were rosary beads. Arslan Aga was sitting next to me, passing bullets to my neighbour. His face was pale, and he was smiling. There was a movement in the Russian lines, and my machine-gun was hammering away like mad. Over there the trumpet sounded for attack. Some-where from the Armenian lines came the notes of the Budjenny March. I looked down and saw the dry, cracked river bed. Russian soldiers were running across the square, knelt, took aim, fired, and their bullets grazed the bridge. I answered with wild firing. The Russians fell like puppets, but behind them new lines rose, running towards the bridge, falling into the dust of the river bank. There were thousands of them, and the thin bellowing of my lonely machine-gun sounded feebly on the Gandsha Bridge.

Arslan Aga cried out, high and plaintive, like a baby. I looked across to him. He was lying on the bridge, blood pouring from his mouth. I pressed the button of my machine-gun. A rain of fire fell on the Russians, and their trumpet sounded the attack again. My cap fell into the river, maybe it was shot away, maybe blown away by the wind in my face. I tore open my collar and coat. Arslan Aga's body was lying between me and the enemy. So a man could be a coward and yet die a hero's death for his country. Over there the trumpet sounded the retreat, the machine-gun fell silent, and I was sitting on the bridge covered in sweat, hungry and waiting for relief.

And now I'm sitting here in the shade of the mosque wall, eating soup. Over there, at the entrance of the mosque, Prince Mansur is standing, and Iljas Beg is bending over a map. In a couple of hours I will again be standing on the bridge. The Republic of Azerbeidshan has only a few more days to live. Enough. I will sleep till the trumpet calls me to the river again, where my ancestor Ibrahim Khan Shirvanshir laid down his life for the freedom of his people.

Ali Khan Shirvanshir fell at quarter past five on the bridge of Gandsha behind his machine-gun. His body fell into the dry river bed. I went down. He was pierced by eight bullets. In his pocket I found this book. God willing, I will take it to his wife. We buried him in the early morning, shortly before the Russians started the last attack. The life of our Republic has come to an end, as has the life of Ali Khan Shirvanshir.

Captain Iljas Beg, son of Seinal Aga, from the village of Biniyadi near Baku.